WITHDRAWN FROM
COLLECTION

SHARKMAN

STEVE ALTEN

TAYLOR TRADE PUBLISHING

LANHAM • BOULDER • NEW YORK • LONDON

For Mom

Published by Taylor Trade Publishing
An imprint of The Rowman & Littlefield Publishing Group, Inc.
4501 Forbes Boulevard, Suite 200, Lanham, Maryland 20706
www.rowman.com

16 Carlisle Street, London W1D 3BT, United Kingdom

Distributed by NATIONAL BOOK NETWORK

Copyright © 2014 by Alten Entertainment of Boca Raton, Inc.
"L.A. WOMAN," words and music by THE DOORS © 1971 (Renewed)
DOORS MUSIC CO. All Rights Reserved. Used by permission.

All rights reserved. No part of this book may be reproduced in any form or
by any electronic or mechanical means, including information storage and
retrieval systems, without written permission from the publisher, except by
a reviewer who may quote passages in a review.

British Library Cataloguing in Publication Information Available

Library of Congress Cataloging-in-Publication Data
Alten, Steve.
  Sharkman / Steve Alten.
    pages cm
  ISBN 978-1-63076-019-9 (cloth : alk. paper) — ISBN 978-1-63076-
020-5 (electronic)
  [1. Paralysis—Fiction. 2. Genetic engineering—Fiction. 3. Sharks—
Fiction. 4. Grandmothers—Fiction. 5. Korean Americans—Fiction.
6. Florida—Fiction.] I. Title.
  PZ7.A46343Sh 2014
  [Fic]—dc23

                                                    2014008955

⊗™ The paper used in this publication meets the minimum requirements
of American National Standard for Information Sciences—Permanence of
Paper for Printed Library Materials, ANSI/NISO Z39.48-1992.

Printed in the United States of America

Acknowledgments

It is with great pride and appreciation that I acknowledge those who contributed to the completion of *Sharkman*.

First and foremost, many thanks to Rick Rinehart; his assistant, Karie Simpson; assistant managing editor Janice Braunstein; and the great staff at Rowman & Littlefield. My heartfelt appreciation to my agent, Melissa McComas, CEO at Tsunami Worldwide Media. My gratitude to Rachel Eckstrom for her terrific story edits.

Special thanks to Batya Solomon and her son, Mordechai, along with Vikki Slaght and her students at Black River Falls High School and the Jackson County Public Library in Black River Falls, Wisconsin, for their input. Thanks as always to the tireless Barbara Becker for her work with the Adopt-An-Author program and to my webmaster, Doug McEntyre, at Millennium Technology Resources.

Last, to my wife, Kim, for all her support. And to my readers: thank you for your correspondence and contributions. Your comments are always a welcome treat, your input means so much, and you remain this author's greatest asset.

To personally contact the author or learn more about his novels, go to www.SteveAlten.com.

Sharkman is part of Adopt-An-Author, a free nationwide program for secondary school students and teachers. For more information, go to on www.AdoptAnAuthor.com.

Other novels by Steve Alten:

MEG: Origins (e-book only)
MEG: A Novel of Deep Terror
The Trench
MEG: Primal Waters
MEG: Hell's Aquarium
MEG: Night Stalkers (forthcoming)
Domain
Resurrection
Phobos: Mayan Fear
Goliath
The Loch
The Shell Game
Grim Reaper: End of Days
The Omega Project
Dog Training the American Male (written under the pen name L.A. KNIGHT)

1

Well, I took little downer 'bout an hour ago . . .
Took a look around, see which way the wind blow.
Where the little girls in their Hollywood bungalows.
Are you a lucky little lady in the City of Light—or just another lost angel . . .
City of Night, city of night, city of night, city of night.

—The Doors, "L.A. Woman"

The heavy staccato bass line of the Doors' "L.A. Woman" pulled me out of a wonderful dream.

In the dream I was playing basketball—a Korean version of Jeremy Lin. In the dream I was cat-quick, my quadriceps thickly coiled muscles that propelled me past defenders and above the rim for effortless two-handed reverse jams.

In the dream I was whole again.

Yearning to slip back into the dream, I leaned over to my right, slid my hand between the guardrails of my bed, and switched off the alarm clock's built-in CD player. With my favorite song silenced, I could hear my grandmother cooking breakfast in the next room. I knew she'd be in soon to check on my progress, tut-tutting my idleness in her broken English.

"Stop wallowing in the past, Kwan. Set your mind to moving forward. Always move forward. You must be like the shark. The shark must swim from the moment of its birth or it will drown."

Kwan Wilson . . . Sharkman.

This is the story of how I came to be.

Mornings are always toughest for me. An unwanted reality. Bare feet that form alien lumps beneath my sheet. Legs that have become flesh-wrapped anchors. An unseen butt forever prone to bed sores. A penis whose pleasures I will never fully know.

Paralysis is a life sentence I awaken to every day.

Just do, don't think . . .

Reaching to the crossbar above my bed, I gripped one of the metal handles, pulling myself into an upright position. My catheter is filled with urine, but thankfully there is no blood. My first month in the hospital there was blood. There was also pain and depression and tears. There were tubes running in my arms and one really annoying one in my left nostril that ran down the back of my throat into my stomach. Broken bones and I couldn't eat—but there were also visits from the queen.

The queen was a clear elixir they shot into my IV every four hours. Queen Dilaudid. Stronger than heroin, faster than a flowing vein, able to thwart pain in a single bound. Dilaudid is as smooth as butter and her sleep is seductive.

Sleep is necessary to heal. Back in the hospital I could fall asleep reaching for a cup of water and wake up a century later still holding it. I took deep catnaps and dreamt weird dreams, only to wake up two minutes later lost in a time warp.

Pain wakes you like a sledgehammer. So do nurses wanting blood at three a.m. and vitals at four a.m. and IV bag changes around the clock, each set to the Monty Python "machine that goes ping." What keeps your journey into madness locked away in the corral is pain medicine, and Dilaudid is queen.

For the first three weeks after the accident I found myself watching the clock, desperate to make it to my next syringe. Two milligrams every four hours was hitting me like a ton of bricks but deserting me forty-five minutes too soon, so my keepers and I settled into a nice three hour, one milligram groove and reality became optional again.

God, I miss the queen.

I don't miss the hospital. For months my lungs were filled with its scent; for weeks I wasn't allowed to eat or drink and that damn tube in my nose kept jabbing me in the throat until it became so loose I could snort it in and out. What I couldn't do is crap into my colostomy bag—a necessary prerequisite to eating and drinking after emergency colon surgery. Turns out the car accident that severed my spinal cord between my L4 and L5 vertebrae also tore a two-centimeter hole in my colon. That doesn't sound big, but it's big enough to allow wastes that are supposed to exit your butt to leak into your body—which can kill you. When a CAT scan revealed the tear, an emergency surgical team cut open my belly and removed the damaged section of my colon. Then they took the end closest to my esophagus and ran it out the left side of my stomach like a pink belly button. The pink belly button is called a stoma and it functions just like a butt-hole. My waste is collected in a colostomy bag—a plastic pouch that attaches to my skin. That may sound gross (and it is) but it beats wearing a big diaper and having to have your nurse or your grandmother change you like a baby.

As disgusting as these thoughts may be, they remind me how much worse my life was back in the hospital. Every morning when I wake up I tell myself that I need to be grateful, after all, I could be a quadriplegic, or brain damaged . . . or I could be dead.

Yep, I'm a lucky guy. Best to just forget about that vial of Oxycodone you have secretly stashed in your sock drawer. Forget about offing yourself, Kwan. Today is a beautiful day.

Except today sucked. See, today was to be my first day back in high school since the accident—a day I'd been dreading. New city, new school, no friends—that's scary enough. Now try doing it as a paraplegic.

Eight months had passed since my parents and I lived outside the naval base in San Diego where my father was stationed. Vice Admiral Douglas Wilson was forty-one when he married my mother, Mi Yung, who was only twenty. Mom raised me while Dad was at sea, which was most of the time. When he'd return home to his young bride, he'd treat her like a princess and me like one of his sailors, barking orders at me to clean my room and change my clothes, and why did I get a B in Algebra when I should have aspired to an A. In the military this is known as "dressing down" and it's supposed to build character.

The Admiral—as I called him—had visited me twice while I was in the hospital. On his first visit he scolded me for being irresponsible, telling me that my paralysis was the Lord's justice. On his last visit he berated me for attempting to undo the Lord's work by trying to kill myself. And that was the last time I saw my father.

After four months in the hospital and three more months in rehab, I was sent to live with my maternal grandmother, Sun Jung. Sun Jung lives in Delray Beach—a small town located just north of Boca Raton on the southeast coast of Florida. Sun Jung moved here thirteen years ago because it's warm all year round, which is good for her arthritis. I like Delray Beach because it's three thousand miles away from Admiral Asshole.

Stop holding onto your anger, Kwan. It is you who are the one who is suffering. Move forward.

Sitting up in bed, I lift my T-shirt to check my colostomy bag. There's a small half-dollar size smudge of brown inside—nothing worth cleaning. My big bowel movement of the day usually happens about twenty minutes after I eat breakfast so it's better to wait to change the bag. Besides, it's easier to deal with from my wheelchair.

It's easier to do most things from my wheelchair. I'm tall and gangly—I used to *stand* six feet four inches, and I weighed a buck eighty. Half of that is now dead weight. Try dragging a hundred and eighty pounds in and out of bed or a wheelchair using only your arms. Now try doing it without snapping a bone in legs that dangle below your waist like a stranger's extremities and you'll understand why—

"Kwan?"

My grandmother knocked and let herself in. If you're imagining an old frail Asian woman then you'd be wrong. Sun Jung was in her midfifties, but she looks ten years younger. Like my mother, she was born in South Korea—the democratic Korea, not the communist regime run by that Looney Toon Kim Jong Un. Sun Jung's been in the States since I turned seven—I'm seventeen, by the way—and she's become fully Americanized. Her hair is long and wavy and dyed auburn. She's not very tall, but she's strong and wiry from working out at the gym three times a week and her smile can light up a room. But she's old school conservative when it comes to respect and definitely not someone you'd want to piss off. She's a registered nurse, which is good for me, but she works twelve-hour shifts at the hospital so helping me to become an independent adult is number one on her priority list.

"Kwan, why aren't you dressed? The van is coming to drive you in forty minutes."

"I was just thinking about things."

"You're not thinking, you're wallowing. Stop wallowing in the mud like a worm. Sharks don't wallow, they just do. You want to be shark or worm?" Without waiting for an answer, she lowered the guardrail on the left side of my bed, pushed my wheelchair next to the bed frame, and tossed me my jeans. "I ironed your favorite shirt; it's hanging in the laundry room. Go eat while I get ready."

"I'm not hungry."

"Tut-tut. Big day, you need to eat."

I waited for her to leave before I grabbed the jeans and worked each pant leg over my bare feet, careful not to catch the little toes. Once I had the pants up to my knees, I slid the catheter out of my penis. Then I reached above my head for one of the crossbeam handles and pulled myself off the bed with my right hand while my left worked the loose-fitting jeans over my thighs and buttocks. Lying back down, I buttoned up, zipped the fly, and buckled the leather belt. Then I hoisted myself off the bed again before I gently lowered my legs and butt into the wheelchair.

I have two wheelchairs, both manual. This one is the standard model I get around in; the other I use strictly in the shower. One day I'd like to have a sports chair, or better yet an electric chair, but we can't afford it right now. My father could easily afford it, but that would circumvent God's punishment—a direct violation of the Admiral's code of conduct.

More about that later. Right now I need to empty my catheter bottle, eat, change my colostomy bag, brush my teeth, and finish dressing before the Medic-van arrives to take me to school.

Palm-pushing my tires forward, I guided the chair out of my bedroom and into the kitchen. My grandmother's home is a single-story, two-bedroom, two-bathroom dwelling with a fenced-in backyard that separates us from the Tri-Rail train tracks. The one-car garage is too narrow to hold her Ford pickup, so she uses it for storage and my exercise equipment.

For breakfast, Sun Jung had gone traditional, making me *gaeran tost-u*, which is an egg sandwich with brown sugar and cabbage. I discarded the cabbage because it makes my poop stink worse than usual. I ate the sandwich and the cut-up pear slices; then I watched TV while I waited for my colostomy bag to fill with sludge.

My grandmother was dressed in her nurse's attire by the time the first warm brown turds began twisting out of my stoma. "Kwan, I'm running late—can you manage yourself?"

"I guess so. Where's my backpack?"

"I left it by the front door. Your lunch is inside, along with a notebook. I put your cell phone inside the front pocket and twenty dollars in your wallet."

"What about the pepper spray?"

"No pepper spray."

"Sun Jung—"

"Kwan, you cannot bring pepper spray to high school; they won't allow it."

"I'll hide it on my chair." I gave her the puppy dog eyes.

"No pepper spray. Do you understand my English?"

"Yes, ma'am."

"Remind me later to call Dr. Chertok."

"Who's Dr. Chertok?"

"She's the psychiatrist the hospital referred. She wants to see you this week."

"Sun Jung, I don't want to see another shrink."

"When you tell your home nurse you are thinking about killing yourself, then legally you have to see a psychiatrist."

"Geez. It was an idle threat . . . a joke."

"Ha-ha, funny joke mister man. You want me to joke like this? Hey, Kwan, I hate everything today so I think I might drive off the interstate on the way home from work. Ha-ha."

"Fine. I'll see the shrink."

"No joking with this lady, Kwan. If she think you going to hurt yourself then you'll wake up in a psychiatric ward with crazy patients who eat their own boogers and talk to dead people. You understand my English?"

"Yes, ma'am."

She leaned over and patted me on the head. "I love you very much. You my favorite grandson."

"I'm your only grandson."

"Yes, but you still my favorite. Today begins a new journey. Make it special."

I have no doubt my grandmother loves me, but it's a conditional love. On the one hand, I remind her of her daughter, Mi Yung, who was the light of her life. On the other hand, I'm the reason her daughter isn't around anymore. See, the car accident that left me paralyzed also killed my mother—and it was entirely my fault.

And now you know why I keep that vial of Oxycodone stashed in my sock drawer, and now you know why I'm so angry.

I'm angry at myself.

It's seven thirty on a cool Monday morning in October. Cool in South Florida is any temperature below sixty-seven degrees. I'm waiting outside in my wheelchair for my driver to arrive to take me to school. My vintage Doors backpack is slung over my right shoulder, filled with stuff I'll need later, like a few spare colostomy bags and my catheter.

The backpack was a gift from my mother. Mom loved music, especially classic rock. She weaned me on the Beatles and the Stones, and took me to Green Day, Coldplay, and U2 concerts to seed me as a fan. She bought me a guitar when I was ten and taught me chords, but I gave it up for the keyboard as my musical tastes shifted to more electronic bands like Swedish House Mafia and Linkin Park. And then one day I rented *The Doors* movie and the music touched my soul.

For all you *Twilight* fangers who never saw the movie, the Doors were a sixties American rock band . . . only they had a different feel. Their lyrics were poetry set to music, and the best stuff was dark and deep and seemed to capture the way I felt about my life.

For the music is your special friend—dance on fire as it intends.
Music is your only friend—until the end . . .

The Doors' lead singer was Jim Morrison, a creative soul who lived on the edge and died at the age of twenty-seven from drugs. I bought the Doors' CDs and googled everything I could about the late, great Lizard King—only to discover that Jim Morrison and I were kindred spirits. Turns out Jim's father was also an overbearing rear admiral who liked to dress down his son, no doubt spawning songs like "The End" and its lyric, "Father . . . yes son, I want to kill you."

Rest in peace, *Mr. Mojo Risin'*.

The Medic-van turned into our cul-de-sac and parked in the driveway. The rear right panel door slid open and a gate lowered into position. The driver—a hairless dude named Bill Raby—said good morning while he locked my wheelchair onto the sled. Bill was in his forties, a happy guy who spoke like he was from Canada even though he's not, always adding the word *eh*.

"First day of school, *eh*?"

"Yeah."

"Good deal. Watch your hands, *eh*."

Bill raised the gate, closed the panel door, and we were off to my new high school. After a ten-minute ride past strip malls and gated communities we turned right at a welcome sign that read Seacrest High School—Home of the Eagles. The campus was much larger than my old school—a series of three-story white concrete buildings connected by catwalks. There was a cement courtyard and a football stadium . . . *and what am I doing here?*

I wanted to be home schooled. I've always been an A student. I could ace the California Exit Exam with my eyes closed—the equivalent of a high school diploma. I could score high enough on an SAT to get into most Ivy League schools.

My grandmother said no. "You very smart, Kwan, but you need friends, you need to socialize."

"Yeah, but—"

"Tut-tut. Even sharks need schools."

I'm not a shark; apparently I just became an eagle.

MORTON MANDAN PUBLIC LIBRARY

The van parked curbside and my worst nightmare began. It's 7:52 a.m. and there are students everywhere. Bill opened the side door and lowered the gate *and here I am, world—Mr. Cripple—*

And no one's looking.

Did it bother me that my arrival had gone unnoticed? Well . . . yeah! I mean, what's the point of being angry at the world if the world isn't paying attention?

Bill unfastened my chair. "Have a good day, *eh*. I'll pick you up right here at two."

"Okay . . . *eh*," I said sarcastically. Rolling ahead to a wheelchair-accessible section of curb, I searched for the administrative office. Two wrong turns and a second school bell and finally I located the entrance to the office—it's a heavy steel door that is not handicap friendly.

Ironic that the Doors fan hates doors. The truth is—I'm not good with them. The first time I had to push and roll my way inside a door I leaned too far forward and fell out of my chair. Now I push, hold and roll—by the inch it's a cinch, as Sun Jung says. Okay for getting inside. Getting out's a bitch.

Fortunately, most people will hold open a door for a guy in a wheelchair, which is what a girl wearing purple leggings and a white tunic does for me. I thank her and roll on through to an information desk that is higher than my head. It's like pulling up to a drive-in window on a tricycle.

"Excuse me? Hello?" Reaching up, I slapped the Formica countertop for service.

A woman—I'm guessing a secretary—leaned over and offered me a well-worn smile. "Well, good morning. I'll bet you're Kwan."

"Yes, ma'am."

"Come around this way. Our principal, Dr. Lockhart, is anxious to meet you."

Anxious to meet me? Was I a celebrity? The smiling secretary sure seemed excited.

Feeling slightly better about things, I wheeled around the barrier to where the secretary was waiting. She led me past a security guard and several student volunteers to a carpeted corridor.

The door to the principal's office was open. Inside were wood shelves and a matching workplace, a sofa, two chairs, and motivational sayings in frames. Seated behind his desk, talking on the phone was a black man in his late forties with short-cropped dark hair and a mustache. He was wearing a charcoal-gray sports jacket over a white dress shirt and a brown bow tie with gold polka dots which fostered an Ivy League aura. His reading glasses magnified kind eyes.

Seeing me, he quickly finished his phone call. "Kwan Wilson! Hey, man, we are so happy to have you here at Seacrest High. My name is Dr. Anthony Lockhart and I'm the principal."

No kidding. I'm paralyzed, not retarded. My eyes rolled involuntarily in my head. Okay, maybe not so involuntarily.

"Is something wrong?"

"To be honest—I don't want to be here."

"We call that 'first day jitters.' Everyone gets them."

"Not everyone's confined to a wheelchair."

"You don't seem that confined."

"Excuse me? Dude, I'm paralyzed."

"It's *Dr. Lockhart*, and what I meant is that you're not confined. After all, you made it to school. We had a quadriplegic student here a few years ago who obviously couldn't do much in a physical sense, and yet he enrolled in our IB—an International Baccalaureate program that provides a great stepping stone for advanced students like yourself. Doug graduated with honors and went on to Florida State."

"Good for Doug the quadriplegic. Good for Stephen Hawking and Christopher Reeve. Their successes don't make me feel any better."

Ahh, there's that anger talking. Only the principal doesn't seem to notice. Why was this guy so happy to see me?

I had a few thoughts and they were pissing me off.

"Kwan, you seem pretty angry. I realize you're still adjusting to major changes in your life—"

"Major changes? Did you ever play competitive sports, Dr. Lockhart?"

"As a matter of fact, I played football in college and ran track."

"I played basketball in high school. As a sophomore, I was the varsity's starting point guard. Averaged eighteen points a game, eight rebounds, and nine assists. One reporter called me the next Jeremy Lin, even though he's Chinese and I'm Korean. I was getting looks from Division I colleges—Stanford . . . UCLA. Best of all, I could shoot the three-ball. Steve Kerr made a living in the NBA off the three-ball. I had plans. I was working out hard back in San Diego, training with a Navy SEAL instructor. Then one day I was driving and . . ."

I was losing control, so I shut up and bit my lower lip and stared at the framed family photos on Dr. Lockhart's desk. He had a wife, a son, and three girls. They looked happy. Happy principal. Happy family.

I hated happy.

"Look, son, I can't begin to relate to what you must be going through, but I know what it feels like to lose your athletic dreams. Blew my Achilles out when I was a junior. Injuries happen. Age happens. Even professional athletes have to give up the game at some point and decide what they want to do with the rest of their lives. You're highly intelligent. You have options. Tell me—do you have any interest in sharks?"

Sharks? "Does this have something to do with my grandmother?"

"Why? Does she like sharks?"

"Never mind."

"Our school was selected to participate in a student internship program with a new facility in Miami—the Aquatic Neurological & Genetics Engineering Lab—ANGEL for short. They're harvesting stem cells from certain species of sharks in the hopes of developing cures for cancer and other diseases."

"Pass. I have no interest in swimming with sharks."

Dr. Lockhart smiled. "You misunderstood. Dr. Becker isn't looking for divers; she needs volunteers who possess data entry skills and tested high in the sciences."

"Pass."

"Before you pass, you should know that Dr. Becker is using these stem cells to repair spinal cords in rats. One day she hopes to use her protocol on humans."

"Do you know what I do all day? I surf the Internet. I read about every spinal cord study being conducted in every country . . . Korea, China, Israel, the EU. Stem cells are great and one day they may actually work. But for every one drug or treatment that works, a thousand fail. And the one that works—it takes twenty years and about $100 million to advance it from lab mice to gaining FDA approval. So you'll excuse me if traveling after school in a wheelchair to some fish lab in Miami just to enter data on a voluntary basis doesn't excite me. But hey, no worries. My 4.5 GPA and FCAT scores over the next two years should still help your school maintain its high academic status and prevent any losses in salary among you and your staff."

The principal stopped smiling.

"Was there anything else, Dr. Lockhart?"

"Mrs. Krantz has your class schedule. Have a good day."

Having "dressed down" the principal, I wheeled myself out of his office, experiencing the same rush of adrenaline and satisfaction the Admiral must have felt when he berated me back in the hospital.

3

My first period class was biology, in room 6107 . . . like that made any sense. By the time I located the right building and found the elevator to take me up to the second floor, I was already ten minutes late.

Arriving outside the classroom I faced a new challenge—the door opened outward on a seriously strong spring-loaded hinge—so strong that I couldn't open it wide enough to gain enough leverage before the damn thing would bang against my wheel and re-close.

After thirty seconds of this insanity a student held the door open from the inside.

The science teacher's name was Mr. Hock. He wasn't that old, but he seemed a bit grumpy. I'm guessing he was pissed off at me for interrupting his lecture.

"Class, this is Kwan Wilson—a transfer student from California. Kwan, I don't have a desk for you yet. Why don't you just park your chair by the wall for now and do your best to follow along."

"Yes, sir." I backed down the aisle between the first row of students and the wall nearest the door, stopping between the second and third desks. For a moment I debated internally about opening my backpack to retrieve a legal pad and pen, but feared the disturbance might further distract the teacher, who was already continuing his lesson.

"Last week we studied DNA; today we'll be looking at ways DNA can be genetically modified. Who can tell me one way a species can be genetically altered to create an entirely new species? Tara?"

A girl with Jamaican braids looked up from reading her text message. "Um, sorry. What was the question?"

"The question is—why are you texting in my class?"

"Sorry Mr. Hock. It's important. From my mom."

"Sure it is. Now put it away." Mr. Hock looked around the classroom. "I realize it's early, that your brains are still half asleep, so let's try this again. I'm looking for an example of one species genetically modified to create a new species. No one?"

I knew a dozen examples but remained silent.

"Anyone here own a dog?"

Hands shot up, giving the discussion a pulse.

"Who can name a breed of dog that was created by mating two different breeds?"

"Labradoodle," blurted out a guy seated in the front row. "That's a Labrador and a poodle."

"Good, Jason. Anyone else?"

"Pekepoo."

"Another poodle hybrid—good."

"Our Yorkshire terrier is part bichon. Does that count?"

"Absolutely. So we now know crossbreeding changes the genetic blueprint of an animal. Next question—why crossbreed a species?"

"To see what the puppies will look like?"

"Think a little deeper, Lance."

"To combine stuff you like in both kinds of dogs?"

"Very good, Susan. Can you give us an example? Here's a clue: try not to think like someone living in the twenty-first century. Imagine yourself a farmer living a thousand years ago. What traits might you want in your dog? Anyone? Just call it out—live dangerously."

"Protection?"

"Yes. And not just of the home. A sheepherder would want a species of dog capable of protecting his flock. What else?"

"Intelligence."

"Absolutely."

"Good with kids."

That one drew laughter.

Mr. Hock held up his hand for quiet. "Disposition is actually an important trait. Keep in mind that all dog breeds can be traced back to wolves. The ability to domesticate an animal was essential hundreds of years ago.

"So we all agree mating one breed of animal with another can improve the species. What about crossbreeding two completely different species—for instance, fruit trees. Cross-pollinate the seed and you change the fruit, right? Sometimes it happens naturally, like when the wind blows pollen from one tree to another. Or it can be deliberate, like when a fruit grower cross-pollinates an orange with a lemon.

"That leads us into today's lesson—GMOs. Who here has heard of genetically modified organisms?"

Nearly everyone raised their hand.

"Can anyone tell me how GMOs are engineered? Anya?"

I turned around—my senses assaulted by a mocha-skinned beauty seated in the last row. The silver wavy bindi she wore on her left arm like a jeweled tattoo revealed her Indian heritage, as did her high cheekbones and long jet-black hair—the latter westernized by two auburn strands. A tight chocolate-brown long-sleeved top and a white skirt revealed a body that would draw stares on any beach. But it was her eyes that poached my soul—bright blue eyes that glistened like the shallows of an azure sea. One could search all of India and never find eyes like hers, and when she spoke in a British accent I realized that she had probably been raised at some point in England.

Oh yeah . . . and she was smart.

". . . genetically modified organisms such as crop plants have been modified in the lab to increase their resistance to certain pesticides. Monsanto has used GMOs to monopolize the agriculture industry, creating seeds that are resistant to their own pesticide—Roundup. Back in India, our farmers were forced to buy GMO seeds from Monsanto. These seeds produced one crop and died, as opposed to healthy seeds which produced crops with seeds that could be harvested again and again. Monsanto genetically modified their seeds to be sterile and resist their own brand of pesticide, which gets into the food supply we consume on a daily basis, causing an increase in cancer and other diseases. Farmers have fallen into debt from trying to make a living growing Monsanto's genetically engineered Bt cotton. Over a quarter-million Indian farmers have committed suicide."

Beautiful and brilliant. And me? I was the human equivalent of Monsanto's GMO—a crop with a barren seed. And yet so smitten was I that I found myself raising my hand like a desperate frog hoping to plant a mental kiss on his princess.

"Anya's right. Roundup is a herbicide that contains glyphosates. Glyphosates have been shown to cause birth defects among animals and humans. Glyphosates are also responsible for wiping out bee colonies. Bees are important because they pollinate plants. Lose the bees and we're screwed."

I felt the class staring at me. They probably weren't expecting the gimp to have a brain.

The tall guy seated behind me to my left stood, pointing at my legs. "Look! He's peeing in his pants!"

I looked down. Sure enough, urine was flooding the front of my jeans, dripping onto the floor.

As a rule, I insert my catheter once every four hours. It had only been two and a half hours since I had woken up, but stress causes one to pee more frequently—and I was clearly stressed.

And helpless.

And humiliated.

And suddenly desperate to get out of there—the cell phones already starting to appear, their video apps threatening to turn one bad moment into a lifetime of grief.

I charged the exit, thankful the door opened outward. Ramming it open, I wheeled like a madman down the corridor—bypassing the elevator, hell-bent on flinging myself down the concrete stairwell and ending the torture.

Principal Lockhart appeared out of nowhere to block my attempt. "Whoa now, easy son! You're going way too fast—we have a speed limit, you know."

I was too angry to form words, so I just grunted, tears of frustration flowing past my cheeks.

He saw the tears; then he saw the front of my pants. "It's okay, I can fix this. There are laundry machines in the stadium. It'll be quicker if I push you."

Simple, quick, and logical.

Accepting his solution, I slumped in the chair and let him take over. We rode the elevator down one floor; then he pushed me across campus to the football stadium while he called a custodian on his walkie-talkie to let us into the equipment room.

There were two industrial-size washers and dryers that were used to wash the athletic teams' uniforms, along with open cardboard boxes stacked with clean towels. Feeling a bit uncomfortable, I stripped off my soiled jeans and boxers and handed them to the principal, who hand-washed them in a sink while I wrapped myself in a clean towel.

The seat cushion of my wheelchair is vinyl and easy to wipe clean—provided I'm not sitting in it. In order to vacate the chair I had to wrap my arms around Dr. Lockhart's neck and allow him to lift me up and place me in another chair—that was awkward. He wiped down the vinyl with a disinfectant, and then we waited while my clothing spun around in an industrial dryer.

"Heck of a first day," he finally said, flashing a disarming smile.

I nodded, feeling embarrassed about my behavior earlier in his office. "I'm sorry I disrespected you, Dr. Lockhart. The whole GPA thing . . . I've seen some schools fight over their top students just to keep federal funds."

"I'm sure that happens. At Seacrest, we're more concerned with educating all of our students."

"It would really be better for me if I homeschooled myself."

"First days are scary. You'll get through this, you'll see."

"You don't get it," I snapped, the anger returning. "I just peed in my first class. My urine is smelling up room 6107."

"It's already been cleaned, no worries."

"No worries? You can't hide from this—by now it's probably all over YouTube and Facebook."

"Along with a million other embarrassing moments—all of which makes us human. For now, just try to learn from it so it doesn't happen again. Doug used to wear his catheter around the clock. He ran the tube out the bottom of his pants to a catch bottle attached beneath his chair and never had a problem."

"That's not my point. I don't need to expose myself to this. I'm smart enough to ace my GED and get my diploma tomorrow if I wanted to without any of this bullshit."

"Is that how you want to spend the rest of your life—living in a cave? What about college? What about getting a good job after you earn your degree? Kwan, the longer you put off being part of the mainstream, the harder it'll be to come back. I know you're humiliated, but you're not the first person to go through something like this and you won't be the last. Every semester I have at least five incidences of students puking in class or girls unexpectedly starting their periods. Sure, it's embarrassing, but you go on."

He was right, and I knew it, but I had had enough for one day. "Okay, I'll stick it out. But please, Dr. Lockhart, at least give me a chance to fix my catheter before I try this again."

He thought for a moment. "All right. Skip the rest of your classes for today, we'll call it a mulligan and start fresh tomorrow." Reaching into his pants pocket, he fished out a business card. "My cell phone number's on the back—if you ever need me during the day just call."

"Thanks."

"Before you go, there's someone I want you to meet. She's a good person to know."

Thirty minutes later we were back inside the administration building. Principal Lockhart led me through the same carpeted corridor past his office, stopping at a door labeled Guidance Counselor: Grade 11.

The principal rapped his knuckles against the open door. "Rachel, you busy?"

"Not for you," said a short woman seated behind a desk littered with avocados. "Just doing some last-minute prepping for my horticulture club."

"This is Kwan Wilson. Kwan just transferred to Seacrest from a high school in San Diego, and he's had a challenging first day. Thought maybe you could spend a few minutes with him."

"That depends. Can I put him to work?"

"Absolutely. Kwan, this is Rachel Solomon." The principal squeezed my shoulders and then strode back down the corridor to his office, abandoning me in the hallway.

"This isn't a drive-thru window, Kwan. You in or out?"

I hesitated; then wheeled myself inside her office.

Rachel Solomon was in her early to midforties. Her skin was pale, her hair coffee-brown and shoulder-length, with bangs cut straight across her forehead just above her brow. She gazed at me through penetrating hazel eyes, the eyelids half-closed, appearing almost lazy. The effect was warm and disarming, yet seemed to say, *I know what you're thinking, Kwan, so don't try me.*

I knew those eyes. They were my mother's eyes—windows to a loving, empowering soul. They were eyes that would neither offer me pity nor any easy way out. Seeing them again, feeling their expressive gaze upon me gave me a familiar sense of comfort that I had not felt in nearly a year.

She smiled, as if she had been eavesdropping on my inner thoughts. *Did she know what I was thinking? Was the woman psychic?*

"You like avocado, Kwan?" Reaching into an open cardboard box, she removed a dark green avocado that was slightly larger than a softball.

"Yes. My grandmother buys them a lot."

"These aren't store-bought avocados, they come from our backyard. My husband and I have three trees at home—two Monroes and a Wilson. These are Wilsons. Wait, didn't Principal Lockhart say your last name was—"

"Wilson."

"Interesting." She handed me a sharp knife, placing the avocado before me on my side of her desk. "We'll save the meat inside, but we're after the seeds—I'm teaching my club how to grow an avocado tree from scratch. Cut the fruit slightly off-center so you don't damage the nut."

She demonstrated on another avocado, slicing it into two unequal halves, exposing the yellow meat and a brown, golf ball–sized seed. Using a spoon, she popped out the seed. After cleaning it off with a paper towel, she placed it in a freezer storage bag, then began scooping the yellow clay-like meat into a Tupperware bowl.

"Funny thing about my Wilson—in five years it grew twenty feet but didn't bear any fruit until we planted the two Monroes. Guess it was lonely."

"More likely, it just needed to cross-pollinate." Using the knife, I carefully sliced into my fruit. "Are all species of avocado named after dead presidents?"

"My grower had a Hardee, but he also had a row of Pinkertons, so I guess the answer's no. But let's talk about you. Today was your first day at Seacrest. Since you're not in class cross-pollinating, I'm guessing you experienced a few challenges."

"You could say that." Using the knife, I carefully plucked out the seed and placed it inside the storage bag with the others.

"Challenges are sometimes good. Of course, I'm not the one sitting in the wheelchair."

"I suppose you want to know how it happened."

"That's up to you. Here, take this spoon. Scoop the meat into this baggie; we don't want to waste it."

"It was a car accident."

"Were you hit by a car?"

"No, I was driving. I had just gotten my license."

She removed another avocado and placed it on my side of the desk. "This is still hard for you to talk about."

She was right. I never talked about the accident—at least never in detail. But those eyes—they seemed to draw it out of me.

"It happened on a Tuesday. I was driving—dropping my mother off at work so I could use her car after school to go to the mall. I was text messaging a friend—making plans. I took my eyes off the road for maybe five seconds when I heard my mother scream. I looked up in time to see a telephone pole, and then everything went blank."

"What happened to—"

"She died."

"I'm sorry."

"I woke up in the hospital. I was confused. Alone. For a while the doctors didn't know if I was going to make it. To be honest, I didn't care. My mother . . . she was more than just a mom. She was my best friend . . . taught me music . . . sports."

I had to stop, my voice cracking. Avoiding her eyes, I looked around her office, stalling to regain my composure.

"You said you were alone . . . what about your father?"

The subject of my father sobered my emotions. "My father's an admiral in the navy. He wasn't around much, which was actually a good thing. He came to visit me a day after the accident. He made sure I knew my goofing off had killed my mother. He told me my paralysis was God's way of punishing me for screwing up. I found out later his priority in coming to the hospital was to sign a Do Not Resuscitate order."

Mrs. Solomon placed the avocado she was working with on her desk. "I guess that makes us kindred souls."

"Why? You hated your father, too?"

"Couldn't stand him . . . such an angry man. He was a workaholic so he was hardly ever around, and when he was around he drank vodka and got angry. I was the second youngest of five siblings, and for some reason my father targeted me for his physical and verbal abuse.

"When I was fifteen, he and I got into a huge fight and everything just welled up inside of me . . . the anger and resentment, the years of feeling abandoned. I shouted at him, 'I wish you'd drop dead.' And he did."

"Wait . . . for real?"

"It happened three months later, out of the blue. He literally dropped dead of a massive heart attack. Words can be powerful things."

"How did that make you feel?"

"Probably the same way you felt when you found out your mother had died. Racked with guilt. Depressed. Angry. For years there wasn't a day that passed where I didn't beat myself up. My guilt eventually sent me on a spiritual journey. I read every book I could find concerning life after death. I met with rabbis and came away with more questions. I researched Buddhism and Christianity; I saw a shrink . . . I studied Kabbalah and read the Zohar. It was only then that I began to understand there are no coincidences: that the chaos in our lives—the accidents and bad luck—happen because we don't know the rules of the game. I realized that constantly beating myself up about my father's death had turned me into a victim."

"I'm not a victim, Mrs. Solomon. I admit that I'm responsible for my mother's death. It was my fault . . . I screwed up bad. How do I live with all the guilt? How do I go on?"

"You begin by first taking responsibility for your actions."

I pounded my fist against the armrest of my chair, the woman pissing me off. "Didn't you hear what I just said? I just said—"

"What I heard was a confession, not a course of action that will allow you to experience happiness in your life."

"Who said anything about wanting to be happy? I killed my mother. I don't deserve a speck of happiness."

"Spoken like a true victim. Trust me—you're looking at someone who chose to remain a victim for twenty years. My parents, too. These were people who survived the Holocaust; they saw things no child should ever witness. My father couldn't get past it; as a result he died an angry, bitter man. It's your choice, Kwan. If you want to honor your mother by spending the next seventy years wallowing in your own misery—go for it. Or you can make her proud by doing something meaningful with your life. Remember, within you lies the force of giving, sharing, loving, caring, and being generous to others. No matter what you've done, there's good still inside you, Kwan Wilson, after all every soul is pure. What you clothe it in while you live out this lifetime is ultimately up to you. Find happiness through the act of sharing. Help other people . . . that's how you'll earn your redemption. Okay?"

I didn't know whether to agree or disagree, so I just nodded.

And then this woman whom I had just met did something my own father refused to allow himself to do—something Sun Jung had managed to avoid doing since the day I had accidentally killed her daughter.

Rachel Solomon walked around her desk . . . and hugged me.

Overwhelmed with guilt, I had marooned myself on an island of shame and refused to be rescued. To suddenly, unexpectedly feel the warm embrace of another human being . . . to know someone else cared about me unconditionally . . . it was like being freed from a life sentence in prison.

On that first day of high school, God sent me a stranger's kindness to remind me that he still loved me.

And oh my, how the dam did burst—a dam of emotions I had no idea even existed. Wrapping my arms around Mrs. Solomon's neck, I wept a river of tears, clinging to her like a drowning child clings to a life preserver.

5

I left Rachel Solomon's office just after one o'clock, eating avocado from a paper cup. I felt lighter, like a weight had been lifted, but emotionally I was spent. I still had half an hour until school let out, so I found my way to the cafeteria to grab something more substantial to eat.

Café Seacrest was set up like a food court you'd find in a shopping mall. I wheeled past Beyond Burgers and Asian Experience, checked out the menu at Mangia Mangia, and finally settled on a turkey sandwich and Coke from the Seacrest Gourmet Deli. I found an empty table near an exit and attacked the food.

"You a fan?"

I turned. Standing behind me was a guy my age, with uncombed long dark brown hair and a thin, prominent nose set on a narrow face. He was lanky and thin, and he was pointing to my backpack.

Raising my defenses, I lashed out. "Yeah, I'm a fan. So what? You probably wouldn't know good music if you fell over it."

"Dude, I don't even know what that means."

"It means you'd have to be a musician to appreciate a group like the Doors."

"I am a musician. Robby Krieger . . . the guy was a genius on the Gibson."

"You play guitar?"

"When I'm not being pissed on by cripples. Sorry, I know you had a rough day." Pulling out a chair he sat beside me, propping his retro Converse on the table. "Jesse Gordon. So? You paralyzed or hurt?"

"Paralyzed."

"That must suck. You were in my biology class this morning until you took off like a bat out of hell."

"It was an accident."

"Ley sure got a big laugh out of it."

"Who's Ley?"

"Stephen Ley, the dumb jock asshole who was sitting behind you. Real dick. Basketball star. Hates Jews, Blacks, Browns, and I'm guessing Asians, too." A security guard walked by, prompting Jesse to lower his feet. "You play?"

"Basketball?"

"Basketball? Dude, how can you play basketball without any legs? Music. I play in a garage band. We do a lot of sixties stuff, that's why I was curious about the Doors. Can you sing? Our singer sucks. He's like a lounge singer, plus he can't remember the words or when to come in. He's like musically retarded."

"I can sing a little, but I'm better on harmonica."

"You play harp? Excellent. Give me your number. We're trying to set up a practice at my house on Saturday around three."

"Saturday? Yeah . . . I just need to see about a ride. Text me your address."

We programmed each other's numbers in our cell phones as the school bell rang, ending seventh period. I tossed the rest of my sandwich in a trash can and followed Jesse out the café exit to the pickup area.

And then I saw her. She was standing by the curb next to an Asian girl, the two of them texting.

"Jesse, who is that?" My voice trailed off, growing hoarse.

"The hot Indian girl? Anya something. Her dad's some big-shot professor at FAU."

"She's beautiful."

"Not my type. Smart chicks think too much. You should go talk to her."

"Me? No."

"Go on. You're a brainiac. Plus you're a harmonica player in an up-and-coming rock band. Plus I hear she's into gimps."

"Really?"

"No, man, I'm just messing with your head. But go on, what have you got to lose . . . your virginity? Sorry. Seriously though, how's that work? Is there any way to prop it up?"

Ignoring the sex comment, I unlocked the brake on my chair. "Call you later about Saturday."

I wheeled away from Jesse and down the sidewalk toward Anya, my mind racing. *Anya was obviously part Indian. What did I know about India . . .*

I braked, smiling stupidly. "So . . . how about that Taj Mahal?"

She looked up from texting.

Her Asian girlfriend gave me an *oh no, you didn't just say that* look.

"Is that all you know about India—what you learned from watching *Slumdog Millionaire*? Do you even know what region the Taj Mahal is located?"

"The Northern Province."

Her eyebrows rose. "Congratulations. That makes you smarter than ninety percent of the students in this school. Anya Patel. And I'm only part Indian. My mother is from London. This is my friend, Li-ling Chang."

"Let me guess . . . Beijing?"

"America," she sneered. "Born in North Miami, Mr. South Korean know-it-all."

"I'm only half Korean."

"Yeah? Which half? The half that works?"

"Li-ling's just kidding. Sarcasm is her second language."

"She seems pretty fluent."

They turned as a white passenger van pulled over to the curb. A royal blue logo was painted on the side door panel: ANGEL.

Anya held out her hand. "Nice to meet you, Kwan Wilson."

"You remembered my name?"

"She also remembered you pissed in your pants," said Li-ling, "so don't get too excited."

I watched the two girls climb into the back of the van—Anya offering me a wave that sent my heart fluttering.

Rachel Solomon had challenged me to find happiness. Well, being around Anya Patel made me happy. She was smart and gorgeous and had an air about her that made me feel more alive inside . . . like life was worth living.

Was there a future with Anya? Who could tell? We were both smart and science oriented . . . maybe we'd both get into the same university . . . major in the same field. And sex wasn't necessarily out of the picture. Even if I couldn't feel them, I had gotten spontaneous erections on occasion, and my body was still producing little Kwan juniors, so children weren't out of the question either . . .

Stop!

I had spoken to the most beautiful girl in the world for three whole minutes and in my mind's eye I was already marrying her. *Ass-wipe . . . at least give her a chance to get to know you before you start picking out baby names . . .*

And then I had an idea!

Retrieving my cell phone, I called the principal. "Dr. Lockhart, it's Kwan. Sir, I changed my mind; I'd really love to be involved in that shark stem cell research program."

"Fantastic. I'll call Dr. Becker this afternoon and get back with you tomorrow."

And so ended my first day back in the real world—an exhausting, emotional day that had begun eight months earlier when a momentary lapse in judgment had cast me down a path I could never have imagined.

A path that was even now intersecting with yet another life-and-death moment taking place below the sea, nine hundred nautical miles to the east . . .

The Atlantic Ocean, seventy-two miles northeast of Puerto Rico

The steel beast was as long as a football field and weighed six thousand tons. It had been moving at a steady thirty knots over the last twelve hours—a top speed usually reserved only for its younger siblings.

The US Navy had inactivated the USS *Philadelphia* (SSN-690) on June 10, 2010, after thirty-three years of exceptional service, decommissioning the Los Angeles Class attack sub a short time later.

How was it then that she was racing west across the Atlantic Ocean?

Captain Matthew Cubit dwelled on this very thought for at least the hundredth time as he coughed into his handkerchief. For a long moment he stared at the Rorschach pattern of blood staining the linen before he continued his inventory of the crew.

Pale, sweaty faces. Feverish eyes. Brave men who would never leave their posts, yet not a man among them who didn't regret their decision to accept the covert mission and the raise in pay grade that came with it.

The two-month Black Ops mission to the Persian Gulf had gone according to plan, culminating in the successful midnight extraction of six private militia commandos off the coast of Iran aboard a motorized raft. There had been a harrowing game of cat and mouse with an Iranian cutter, but in the end the *Philadelphia* had made it through the Strait of Hormuz and out of harm's way to begin its twenty-three-day journey back to the United States.

A week out from their rendezvous site, the Chief of the Boat fell ill. Soon other enlisted men began reporting to sickbay, all signs pointing to radiation sickness.

The nuclear reactor had checked out. That left the mysterious object stowed in the crate in the torpedo room as the suspected cause—the contents of which were being protected around the clock by the six well-armed militia men.

Rather than risk a confrontation, the captain had sent a transmission to Admiral Wilson that the *Philadelphia* would arrive a full day ahead of schedule.

In the interim, the COB had died.

"Captain, we've arrived at the designated coordinates. Sir?"

Cubit wiped sweat from his forehead. "All stop. Dive Officer, take us to periscope depth."

"Aye, sir. One hundred feet . . . eighty feet . . . sixty feet—all stop."

Moving to the periscope, the Officer of the Deck pressed his eyes to the rubber housing, giving the horizon three quick sweeps. "No close contacts, skipper."

Captain Cubit reached for the internal microphone. "Radio, Conn. Anything on the VLF?"

"Conn, Radio, transmission coming in now, sir."

"On my way. OOD, you have the Conn."

"Aye, sir, I have the Conn."

The naval commander made his way aft down tight passageways, registering the silent stares of his crew as he approached the communications shack.

The radio officer handed his captain the message transmitted over the Very Low Frequency bandwidth, watching Cubit's face as he read the message. From the skipper's dour expression, he could tell this was clearly not the information his commanding officer was expecting.

Commander Roy Katzen arrived, the second-in-command clearly agitated. "Two more dead, another dozen too ill to report for duty. Is that the destroyer's coordinates?"

Cubit handed his XO the message. "Admiral Wilson didn't dispatch a destroyer. We're to rendezvous with a Canadian trawler in thirty-six hours."

Katzen shook his head. "In thirty-six hours we could all be dead. We need to make port in Puerto Rico and get this entire crew to a hospital."

"The admiral's aware of the situation."

"With all due respect, sir, Wilson's way out of bounds on this one. This mission should have been red-flagged the moment he chose to refit the *Philadelphia* instead of using an active boat and a Navy SEAL team. I don't know what's in that crate, but I didn't spend fifteen years in the navy so I could end up in a cancer ward."

"Agreed. Assemble an armed detail and meet me in the torpedo room in five minutes."

"Aye, sir!"

Located in the lower level of the forward compartment, the torpedo room housed the equipment used to quickly lift and load torpedoes into the sub's four forward tubes. Deck-mounted racks held stacks of Mk48 ADCAP torpedoes and Tomahawk cruise missiles. Sealed shelves contained an assortment of mines.

For the last twenty-two days, the torpedo room had been commandeered by the six members of Black Widow, an international private assault force. The men were on six-hour shifts guarding a four-by-three-foot crate adorned with Arabic letters and a nuclear radiation symbol—the mission's prized bounty.

While the Black Widows were equipped with lead-lined commando suits and iodine pills, the *Philadelphia*'s crewmen remained exposed to radiation. To protect his men, Cubit had ordered the torpedo room sealed for the duration of the voyage, but radiation was still seeping through the sub.

Five minutes after rising to periscope depth, a six-man detail entered the chamber in fire-retardant suits to complete a scheduled systems check. Two techs worked together to perform a diagnostics test on the loader, both men anxious to vacate the toxic area.

"I'm telling you, Artie, my balls are aching."

"Maybe you ought to give the *Penthouse* magazines a rest."

"I'm talkin' about cancer. Whatever's in that crate is giving off heat." The technician purposely raised his voice, "And these hired jack-offs pretending to be SEALs know it."

One of the "hired jack-offs" had been pushed too far. The Scottish commando—a man named Lars—unsheathed his knife as he slowly circled the two crewmen. "Tell ye what, lad. How 'bout I give the short and curlies a bit of a trim, then feed 'em to ye."

The other submariners quickly closed ranks behind their threatened crewmen while the other members of Black Widow fingered the triggers of their assault weapons.

Captain Cubit entered the torpedo room moments later, quickly sizing things up. "Back off, mister. And sheathe that weapon."

Lars turned to a Syrian named Mahdi, the militia's squad leader. The freedom fighter approached Cubit. "It has been a long mission, friend. We're all on the same team—let us finish this as professionals."

"I don't know what team you're on, *friend*, but the men on my team are pissing blood. There's a salvage ship due to arrive in thirty-six hours. Grab a few life rafts, rations, and whatever's in that container—you and your men are vacating this boat now."

Mahdi smiled. "Admiral Wilson is in charge; we only take orders from him."

Commander Katzen entered the chamber, accompanied by eight armed crewmen—a Mexican standoff.

Cubit stepped between the warring parties. "Lower your weapons; there's already been enough loss of life on this mission. Mahdi?"

The Syrian commando nodded to his men.

Cubit removed his cap, wiping sweat with his free hand. "You Black Widow boys are tough, I'll give you that. Wilson must have paid your team a king's ransom to infiltrate Iran's heavy water reactor to obtain that uranium."

Mahdi grinned. "More than you and your entire crew will see in a lifetime, captain."

"Good for you. Payable on delivery, I imagine."

"The only way to ensure the mission's success."

Cubit smiled, his hand casually removing a metal object hidden in the brim of his cap. "If I were you, next time I'd ask for an advance."

Mahdi's expression went blank as a bloody third eye suddenly materialized above the bridge of his nose—a charred hole in Cubit's cap revealing the presence of his hidden pistol.

The corpse collapsed as Commander Katzen's men wounded and disarmed the private militia before they could get off a shot.

Lars was lying on his chest, bleeding badly from a belly wound. As two crewmen rolled him over, he pulled the pin on the grenade he had removed from his belt and tossed it across the deck with his last dying breath.

Captain Cubit's eyes followed the grenade as it skipped between his XO's feet, rolled beneath a steel rack of torpedoes . . . and settled by the starboard hull.

"Oh dear Lord—"

Wa-Boom!

The explosion rained a lethal dose of hot shrapnel upon the shocked crewmen a microsecond before the blast tore a hole in the ship, unleashing the sea.

The wounded beast swallowed the Atlantic, its steel plates groaning as it sunk to the bottom of the ocean.

7

I woke up the next morning to find a gray-haired woman in a yellow-flowered dress searching through my dresser drawers.

"Hey, sunshine . . . can I help you?"

The gray-haired woman turned briefly to make eye contact then continued emptying my drawers. "I'm Dr. Beverly Chertok, your new mental health counselor."

"I didn't know shrinks were allowed to just come in and search through your stuff."

"When a patient tells his home nurse he's thinking about killing himself, you do what you have to do."

"It was a joke."

"Is this a joke, too?" She held up the bottle of Oxycodone.

"My doctor prescribed them after I fell and bruised my ribs. I need them for pain."

"Did you need them for pain when you OD'd back in San Diego?"

"Different time, different place. I'm not suicidal, Dr. Chertok."

"How would you feel if I prescribed an antidepressant?"

"You mean one of those serotonin neurotransmitter inhibitors that can cause suicidal thoughts as a side effect? No, thanks. But if you want to write me a script for medical marijuana, my grandmother has a great brownie recipe."

She smiled, defrosting her cold introduction. "How was your first day of school?"

"I survived. Now do you think you could leave so I can get dressed?"

"Sure, as soon as the nurse checks you for bed sores. I'm going to confiscate the Oxycodone, just to be on the safe side." She opened my bedroom door and instructed the home nurse who had ratted me out to come in and do her duty.

"Good luck in school, Mr. Wilson. I'll be back to check on you in a few weeks."

Sun Jung entered my bedroom after the nurse had left. "Oxycodone, huh?"

"It was for my ribs."

"You lying, Kwan—I can see it in your eyes. Don't ever lie to me again. You understand my English?"

"I understand. I also understand why you look at me sometimes with shark eyes."

"What you mean . . . shark eyes?"

"Sharks have eyes that are cold and uncaring. Do you ever regret taking me in, Sun Jung? Do you ever wish I was living someplace else . . . that you were on your own without having to take care of the grandson who killed your daughter? Answer *my* question, Sun Jung, and don't lie—do you hate me sometimes?"

Her eyes teared up. "I don't hate you, Kwan."

"It's okay if you do. Sometimes I hate myself."

"I don't hate you."

"But you can't bring yourself to hug me?"

For an awkward moment she just stared at the wall, her silence a clear reply to my question.

"Get dressed, Kwan. The van will be here soon."

And that's how my second day of school began.

Bill Raby picked me up at seven thirty. We arrived at Seacrest High ten minutes later. While I waited for Bill to set the lift in place, I saw Anya climb out of a silver 2014 E-Class Mercedes-Benz. The driver was Anya's father—a slender Indian man with short jet-black hair and a kind face.

Last night, I had googled Florida Atlantic University's staff directory. Tanish Patel was a professor of economics. Before taking a teaching position at FAU, Dr. Patel had worked for the World Bank and the Council of Foreign Relations—a think tank whose members read like a who's who of former world leaders, bankers, and corporations.

Anya's old man was the academic version of the Admiral—except he had a heart.

I wheeled over to Principal Lockhart, who was greeting students as they entered from the school parking lot.

"Good morning, Kwan. I spoke with Dr. Becker, the director of the aquatic research center in Miami. She's willing to bring you in as a volunteer."

"Awesome."

The internship's every Monday and Wednesday from three to eight o'clock in the evening and every other Saturday from ten a.m. to four in the afternoon." He reached into his sports jacket pocket and removed a thick white envelope. "This is a standard release all student interns have to sign; parents and guardians, too. Bring it with you tomorrow afternoon. One thing—Dr. Becker said you'd have to arrange your own transportation to the facility."

My pulse quickened with the bad news. "Why do I need my own transportation? Why can't I just ride down with Anya and Li-ling?"

"The lab's van isn't wheelchair accessible."

"I can manage. If the driver can help me up—"

"Kwan, the center's not insured to transport you. Is there any way your service can drive you?"

"I guess it's up to the insurance company. I can ask my grandmother to make a few calls."

"Do that and let me know." He paused to listen as the school bell sounded. "Better get to your homeroom, you don't want to be marked late."

My homeroom was on the first floor, the classroom packed with forty-two students whose last names began with W thru Z. I settled into a tight parking spot and texted Sun Jung, who called the insurance company.

I left early to get to my first period science class. I was already parked along the outside row when Anya entered. She looked amazing in her black tunic and faded jeans. She offered me a wave and a smile. I waved back, pretending not to notice Stephen Ley, who was pulling on the corners of his eyes as he cracked a joke with his friends—imitating me peeing in my pants.

Jesse Gordon came in late, earning Mr. Hock's wrath.

Second period English.

Third period history.

Fourth period econ. Jesse Gordon stopped me outside of class to remind me about band practice on Saturday at his house. He said he'd text me a song list, *and did I like Elvis Costello?*

I told him I did.

I received my grandmother's text by fifth period lunch—the insurance company had denied her request.

I sat alone, feeling dejected, the insurance company's decision sending my plan to get to know Anya spiraling into the toilet. I wondered if my confrontation with Sun Jung earlier this morning had affected her attitude with the insurance company representative. *Funny how they'd pay a shrink to see me if I threatened to off myself, but if I needed transportation to do something positive with my life . . . hey, wait!*

It took me ten minutes to track down Beverly Chertok's office number, another five to get her on the phone to plead my case.

By seventh period history, my psychiatrist had texted me back with good news—she had received approval from the insurance company, convincing the rep that the trips to Miami were a necessary part of her recommended therapy.

Sometimes when you look back on stuff in your life you realize that it was dumb luck which kept you progressing down a certain path. Miss a three-point shot during tryouts and you could get cut from the team; sink the same shot and your dreams get to live another day. A million random moments, a million chance meetings—a million possible different outcomes.

Or maybe, as Rachel Solomon would say, all roads still lead to one destiny.

The call from my driver came with the final bell. One of Bill's autistic riders had suffered a seizure and had fallen from his wheelchair, striking his head on a steel guardrail. Bill was en route to the hospital—"I'll only be about an hour late, eh?"

My reply was cut off by the first cold, heavy droplets of rain. Within thirty seconds the deluge was in full force, chasing me back inside the high school.

Being confined to a wheelchair limits one's options. Like it or not, I was stranded until my driver arrived. The only question now was where to wait—the cafeteria or gym?

Ah . . . sweet destiny, always pretending to be random.

Lured by the sound of bouncing basketballs, I found my way to the gym—my heart pounding like it used to do just before practice.

Warming up at both ends of the court were the fifteen members of Seacrest's men's varsity. Six wore their reversible jerseys in white, the rest in green. They were clowning around and a few were slap-fighting, led by their six-foot-seven-inch cocaptain and starting power forward—Stephen Ley.

I had never met head coach Bradford Flaig, but he seemed like he was in a foul mood as he wheeled a cart holding a television and DVD player across the sideline to the home bleachers. I was surprised when he gestured me over, handing me the plug end of an extension cord.

"You my new manager?"

"No, sir."

"Well . . . make yourself useful anyway. See if you can find an electrical outlet."

Wheeling down the sideline, I quickly located the removable disk covering the floor outlet that was used to power the game clock.

I plugged in the cord and returned to Coach Flaig, who had powered up the unit and was advancing the game footage using a remote. "You're Kwan, right?"

"Yes, sir."

"You look like you have some size to you. Did you play any ball before . . . you know."

"I was our starting point guard. I was second team all-conference last year as a sophomore."

"We could have used you." He gestured to the screen. "Our first scrimmage. Got our asses kicked. Want to sit in on the film session?"

"Sure."

Coach Flaig blew his whistle. "All right, ladies, balls in the rack and have a seat."

I rolled backward, parking to one side of the stands as fifteen bodies stormed up the bleachers like a herd of buffalo.

"Yo, Coach, why's he here?"

It was Ley, and the douche bag was pointing at me.

"I invited Kwan to sit in on practice. That okay with you, superstar?"

Ley ignored the coach's sarcasm. "Sure, Coach. Just don't piss him off."

The team cracked up, guys pounding knuckles and slapping palms. The jock world lives by the law of the jungle—the strong always picking on the weak. Back in San Diego, I had fought my way from being locker room prey to earning a place at the table, and there was nothing better than being one of the predators—one of the guys.

There was nothing worse than being the team meal and Stephen Ley clearly had a boner for me.

"All right, knock it off. We open against West Boca in two weeks; play the way you played Saturday against Seminole Ridge and we'll be lucky to finish the season at .500."

Coach Flaig started the DVD. "Defense. We opened in man-to-man, hoping to put pressure on their guards. They must have run this same high screen and roll twenty times, and twenty times our guards were late contesting their three. Stephen, that's your man setting the pick. What's missing here?"

"Looks like Jerome, Coach. Yo, 'Rome, I told you all game, you got to fight your way around the screen. Same for Michael Jay and Rusty. You guys got lit up."

"Shut up, Ley."

"Stephen's right. Seminole's backcourt scored forty-one points—including seven treys. Who can tell me why?"

Heads dropped, except for Stephen Ley's—the "emperor" proud in his royal clothes—only I could see that he was naked.

"Ley didn't hedge the screener," I heard myself saying.

Heads turned. *Was the crippled antelope really challenging the lion?*

"Explain it to him, Kwan," Coach Flaig barked.

I rolled out from the shadows of the bleachers, my heart pounding as I pointed to the frozen image of the screen and roll. "The defender guarding the guy setting the screen has to hedge . . . he has to jump out on the opposite side of the pick, forcing the ball handler to go wide. That buys the defending guard an extra second or two to fight through the screen, catch his man, and defend the shot."

"Owned," yelled Jerome. "Yo, Ley, why you making us look so bad?"

"And you never called out the picks," chimed in Rusty.

"Shut up, scrub." He turned to me, his eyes full of venom. "Who the fu—"

Coach Flaig blew his whistle, cutting him off. "We win as a team, we lose as a team, and we play help defense as a team. Everybody has to talk. Bigs have to hedge. Guards have to fight over the screen. Get it now, because we're gonna drill the screen and roll all afternoon until you do. Everyone on the baseline for suicides."

Groans and moans as the team stomped down the bleachers, a few sneakers kicking at my chair.

Coach Flaig smiled at me. "I'm still looking for a team manager. You up for it?"

"No, thanks, Coach. I already volunteered for another program."

I rolled out of the gym as the whistle blew, sending the team sprinting from the end line to the foul line and back, to half court and back . . . to the opposite foul line and back—and finally from end line to end line and back.

Suicides. Pounding hearts and burning lungs and quads drenched in lactic acid.

I hated suicides—all basketball players do, yet I would have traded my right arm to be able to run them again.

Wednesday. I woke up, excited to begin my internship with Anya at the facility in Miami.

First, I had to survive the wrath of Stephen Ley.

The basketball star was pissed off, and he was letting everyone know it on Facebook and Twitter. Heading to first period, I could feel the stares and hear the whispers from the other students—herds of strangers, pointing at the "dead man rolling."

High school's like that. Students move in groups. There's protection among your own kind, a feeling that you belong. Doors open, you get invited to parties . . . what counts is you're not one of the losers who stay at home on Saturday nights, you're not the slowest camper—the one who gets eaten by the bear.

Back in San Diego I had been a jock, at the top of the pecking order. Here in Delray Beach, I was the Asian freak in the wheelchair—a cripple's version of *The Scarlet Letter*.

I hated that book.

Ley struck right before first period biology, assaulting me outside the classroom with a shaken can of soda, taking photos of my stained pants with his iPhone to create a new album of embarrassing photos. Anya stepped in to defend me—only making it worse.

"Why do you have to pick on Kwan, Stephen? What did he ever do to you?"

"For your information, *Anya*, his gook relatives killed my uncle's wife's brother in Vietnam. What's it to you anyway? Unless you like him. You do! Hey guys, Anya has a new boyfriend—Kwan the Cripple."

"Stop it!"

"Go on, Anya, give your boyfriend a lap dance." He pushed Anya onto my Coke-drenched lap, her sudden weight displacement nearly tossing me sideways.

"He's not my boyfriend, now stop it. Ugh, you stained my skirt, you asshole!"

Mr. Hock stepped out into the hallway. "Anya? What's going on out here?"

Ley grinned. "It's Kwan, Mr. Hock. He got excited over Anya sitting in his lap and had an accident."

The rest of the class laughed. Anya stormed off to clean her skirt in the bathroom—and suddenly I didn't give a damn about the internship or school . . . or life.

Bill Raby was waiting for me curbside when the seventh period bell mercifully ended my day. A small crowd of Ley disciples recorded my chair being loaded aboard the van. I didn't even bother to turn away from their cell phones, having already disappeared.

"Miami, eh?"

"Just take me home, Bill."

"Can't do that. Work order says I have to take you to Miami and pick you up at eight."

"Take me home, I don't feel well."

"If you don't feel well then I'm supposed to take you to the doctor."

"Listen, asshole, I don't want to see the doctor, I just want to go home and lie down."

"I could lay you down on the gurney."

"Are you hard of hearing or just stupid? I just want to go home."

Forty-five minutes later we arrived in Miami.

* * *

The Aquatic Neurological & Genetics Engineering Lab—ANGEL for short—was located on Virginia Key, which is a small island situated in Biscayne Bay that harbors the Miami Sea Aquarium. I would learn that the sea aquarium leased their unused land to the genetics lab and shared its water purification plant, which fed both facilities' salt water tanks.

Bill had to cross over the Rickenbacker Causeway twice before he found the lab's unmarked dirt road entrance. He cursed the entire bumpy half mile before we reached a steel gate securing a twenty-foot-high perimeter fence capped with barbed wire. A security camera was mounted atop a light pole, a two-way speaker attached to a post.

"Hey kid, where they got you working—Folsom prison?"

"Dude, just roll down your window and press the intercom."

Bill shrugged and complied. "Afternoon, *eh*. I'm delivering Kwan Wilson, your new intern."

After an annoying minute the gate buzzed, then swung slowly inward on its hinges.

Bill drove onto a recently tarred two-lane road which curved to the right around a privacy shrub that concealed the facility from the causeway. "Nice view, *eh* . . . for a dump."

He was right. Spoiling the sparkling turquoise-blue horizon that was Biscayne Bay was a two-story rectangular brown brick building that looked like it had been built back in the 1950s. To the left of the structure were four double-wide trailers, their rusted steel bottoms resting on cinder blocks. The back end of the trailers lined up along a weed-infested stretch of fencing that separated the lab from the aquarium's water treatment plant before cutting west across a barren stretch of beach, enclosing the six-acre facility.

Making his way down a cement sidewalk that separated the building from the trailers was a stocky man in his early thirties. He had short brown curls for hair, a high forehead, and pale skin that probably burned easily in the sun. He was at least four inches shy of six feet, but he had thick wrists to go along with a barrel chest and looked like he played football.

Make that rugby. The accent was Australian, his vocabulary heavy in "strine"—Aussie slang.

"G' Day. Name's Joe Botchin, I'm the head duffer around here, and the unofficial lord of the manor." He poked his ten gallon head inside Bill's window to have a look at me. "So you're the new Jackaroo. Not sure we're fully wheelchair accessible, but we'll make do. You got here ahead of the two Sheilas, but no worries, I'll give you the five quid tour. Well, come on then, Shark Bait, let's get going."

Bill opened the panel door and lowered me to the asphalt. We agreed that I'd be picked up at eight; then I followed Joe down the cracked sidewalk.

"How hurt are you, Wilson?"

"I'm paralyzed from the waist down."

"The old fella, too?"

"Excuse me?"

"Kwan junior. Your thingo. Can you crack a fat or no?"

I gritted my teeth. *Why did people always want to know about my penis?* "No, dude. I can't 'crack a fat' if that's what I think it means."

"Don't get cranky, Shark Bait. I'm only asking because we've had some success with repairing rat spinal cords using the stemmies. We're not there yet, mind you, but we're doing cutting-edge stuff here."

My adrenaline started pumping. "What exactly are you doing?"

"Best I let the geniuses explain that. But I'll show you the beauties makin' it all possible."

The path led behind the building to a pavilion overlooking a circular concrete canal that was situated twenty feet below the ground. The channel was wide enough to accommodate a pickup truck and was a tenth of a mile around, and it was filled three-quarters high with seawater.

I pressed my wheelchair sideways against the five-foot-high guardrail and peered below at the olive-green water. Swimming lazily just below the surface were sharks. Lots of them.

"What kind of sharks are they?"

"By last count, we've got thirteen different species. That Sourpuss, she's a lemon. Devo's a thresher, you can tell by his tail."

"Devo?"

"As in 'whip it—whip it good.' It's an old song—never mind. Anyway, that dorsal there belongs to our mako; that one with the bite mark is a blue, and the critters camped out in groups along the bottom are nursies."

"Wow, what's this big one swimming along the surface?"

"That's Maxie. She's a tiger. Twelve and a half feet from her snout to the tip of her upper lobe. Big fish, but she's a pussycat compared to Taurus. Here he comes, zigging back and forth like he owns the place. Taurus is a bull shark—eight feet and six hundred pounds I'm guessing. He was patrolling the shallows along Miami Beach when my boys netted him. Put up quite a fight. Taurus is scheduled for this afternoon's get. Been watching him all day, workin' out how I'm gonna get him into the paddock."

"What's that?"

"The paddock? Follow me." Joe led me around to the area of the canal closest to the building where a secondary channel ran from the main pen into the ugly brick building. "The paddock loops into the main tank. My job is to herd our volunteer through the gate without lettin' anyone else inside. Last month one of the dogfish squeezed into the paddock with Maxie and Maxie didn't take well to it—meanin' she bit her tail off and ate what was left. Doc Becker was as cross as a cut snake, but what was I supposed to do? Rover darted in underneath Maxie—ain't nuthing to be done about it, right? Besides, we already tested Rover's stemmies, which was as useless as your . . . well, never mind. Anyway, that's the paddock."

"Any great whites?"

"Whites? Nah. Pen's too small. Besides, the whites tend to die in captivity. Taurus is mean enough. Lots of testosterone in the bulls. Hopefully, that's a good thing."

"It hasn't worked out too well for you."

We turned as Li-ling entered the pavilion area, followed by Anya.

Joe greeted her with his own rendition of the Troggs' "Wild Thing." "Li-ling . . . you make my heart sing. You please my ding-a-ling—"

"You can please your own ding-a-ling."

"Ah, come on, my little Asian delight. You love me. Admit it."

"Mr. Botchin!"

"Crikey . . ."

Emerging from the back of the building was a short woman in her midfifties, her strawberry-blonde hair wrapped in a tight bun. She wore a white lab coat and a nasty look on her petite face, and I had no doubt she was in charge.

"Dr. Becker . . . I was just—"

"I'm well aware of what you were just doing. Let me remind you that my interns are not here to entertain you in any capacity, is that clear?"

"Yes, ma'am."

"Where is Mr. Roig?"

"I sent him to fetch a hunk of tuna for our friend. Are you ready for him?"

"I was ready for him ten minutes ago. Li-ling and Anya, I need you in the lab." She turned to face me. "You're Kwan?"

"Yes, ma'am."

"Do you have a signed release form for me?"

"Yes, ma'am." I reached inside the Doors backpack and located the six-page legal form, handing it to her.

She methodically checked to make sure each page had been initialed, then pocketed the release. "We'll talk later. For now, keep an eye on 'Wrangler Joe' here, then join us in the lab." She held the steel security door open for Anya and Li-ling, allowing it to slam shut behind her.

Joe wiped sweat beads from his heavy brow. "That was Dr. Barbara Becker, the boss lady."

"Is she always this angry?"

"Only when the Jackaroos from the Pentagon crawl up her freckle. We don't talk about it, but the military's taken a keen interest in our work of late."

"Why would they care about a shark stem cell program?"

"You don't really get what these stemmies do, do you? Imagine a billion microscopic cells injected into your blood stream, programmed by nature to fix everything that ain't working. Shark stem cells have a special gift—they have these little doovalackys in them that hate cancer. A stem cell sees a cancer cell and it gives it a gobful. Blasts the bloody cancer into scar tissue—splat."

"I still don't get—"

"Nuclear war, Shark Bait. Let's suppose Iran develops the bomb and they give it to Hamas or Hezbollah or one of them other terrorist groups who delivers a suitcase nuke into Israel. The Israelis launch a counterstrike . . . who knows what will happen. But it'll be bad. Purple Rain bad."

"The radioactive fallout will cause widespread cancer, only—"

"Only the doc's working on a potential serum that not only cures the Big C, it boosts the immune system so you never get it in the first place. Just because you nuke Iran doesn't mean all that oil has to go to waste."

"I get it. The Pentagon wants to inoculate our soldiers just in case we have to nuke Iran."

"Or use the technology to barter for a peace treaty in the aftermath . . . at least that's what the doc's trying to convince herself of every time she accepts one of those six-figure Black Ops deposits that keep the lights on."

"What lights? This place is a dump."

"Sure it is." Joe turned and waved at an approaching golf cart. "About bloody time."

The driver, a Hispanic dude a few years older than me skidded into a parking place by the edge of the canal. "Sorry. Sea aquarium left me with the frozen chum. I had to warm it. Who's this?"

"Johnny Roig, say hello to Wilson Kahn."

"Actually, it's Kwan Wilson."

"That's what I said." Joe popped open a fifty-gallon ice chest strapped to the back of the golf cart, then used a steel hook to pull out the severed head of a tuna, which still must have weighed a good thirty pounds. The Australian expertly threaded a nylon rope through the fish's mouth, then held up the dripping mess and took a whiff. "Smells like a Sheila I once dated back in high school. Come to think of it, it kind of looks like her, too. Johnny boy, get your reach pole and man the paddock gate. Juan, park yourself over there and yell out when you see Taurus swimming toward us. Big brown fin with a—"

"It's Kwan . . . ah, never mind." I rolled a quarter of the way around the canal and positioned my wheelchair so I could see the surface without the afternoon sun's blinding reflection on the water.

Twenty paces behind me, Joe lowered the fish head into the canal, bobbing it a few times between passing dorsal fins. The scent set off dinner bells, the olive waters frothing.

I never saw the bull shark's dorsal fin, only the pale underside of its blunt snout as it rose from below to snatch the bloody offering—nearly dragging Joe over the rail, the Aussie having wrapped the nylon rope around his forearm.

"Damn it, Kwan, I told you to warn me!"

"I didn't see him. And technically you told Juan."

John Roig smiled. "*Sí, Señor.* I thought you were talking to me."

"Shut up and open the bloody gate. Crippled kid, grab a hunk of bait from the ice chest and toss it in the paddock. And don't miss!"

Two quick rolls and I was back at the golf cart. Opening the bait container, I shoved my right hand into the icy, bloody goop and grabbed a slippery, slimy hunk of tuna ass and tail. Holding it away from me, I wheeled with my opposite hand, then tossed the bait into the paddock waters.

The severed fish landed five feet from the open gate, prompting Taurus to release Joe's bait and swim after it. John Roig quickly shut the gate—mission accomplished.

Joe pulled in the remains of the chewed up fish head. Using his hunting knife, he cut the nylon rope free and tossed the mangled remains back into the canal. "Nice throw, Kwan. Sorry about the cripple thing. Taurus damn near snapped my bloody arm off."

"Forget it. Is there a bathroom where I can wash this chum off my hand?"

"Come on, you can soak it in the piranha tank." The Aussie slapped me across the back of my shoulder and led me inside.

9

Okay, so I was wrong.

The interior of the genetics lab was like one of those old urban manufacturing plants that gets gutted and turned into luxury condominiums. Only in this case, the condo was an ultramodern, high-tech facility featuring walk-in freezers and power generators, and a massive chamber the size of Seacrest High's gym.

The paddock fed inside this section of the facility where it emptied into a thirty-foot-in-diameter cylindrical aquarium. The depths of this immense pool actually resided one floor below on the basement level; from my vantage all I could see was the open top of the aquarium poking four feet above the first floor decking.

Taurus had been trapped in a medical pool—a sort of shark pit stop that separated the paddock from the main tank. The big bull shark was pissed off, rolling and slapping inside this four-foot-deep tub, which was rapidly filling with a milky substance—apparently a sedative.

Within thirty seconds, the predator had been subdued.

By now, Joe Botchin and John Roig were dressed in thick waterproof rubber overalls and matching boots. Wasting no time, they climbed into the medical pool with the sedated shark, securing a canvas harness around its girth, Taurus's pectoral fins protruding through the sleeves. Activating a winch, they rolled the shark onto its back, exposing its slick white belly. Joe positioned a hose inside the sleeping shark's jaws, which passed seawater through the creature's mouth and out its gills—intubating the fish, allowing it to breathe . . . pretty sick.

Enter Dr. Becker, assisted by Anya and Li-ling. All three women were dressed in white lab coats and were wearing rubber gloves. Anya was pushing a medical cart on wheels.

Dr. Becker spent several minutes taking the shark's vitals. When she was done, Li-ling wheeled over a portable ultrasound machine. Gripping the handle of the transducer probe, Dr. Becker rolled the device over the shark's belly, the internal organs appearing on a twenty-inch monitor.

"What I'm doing, Mr. Wilson, is marking the precise location of the shark's liver. The liver is our target—we're going to inject the organ with a drug that, over the next week, will cause Taurus's liver to increase its white cell production tenfold. At the end of the week, we'll siphon out these excess white cells, which contain the shark's stem cells. The stem cells will be injected into our test subjects."

"Rats," Joe whispered.

Using a black marker, Dr. Becker circled a small area on the shark's belly, directing Li-ling to swab the spot with an antibiotic. Dr. Becker nodded to Anya, who handed her a ten-inch-long hypodermic needle connected to an IV syringe. Carefully, she pressed it down into Taurus's exposed belly, then slowly injected the clear elixir into the sleeping bull shark's liver.

Her work done, Dr. Becker turned the job over to the shark wranglers, who flipped Taurus right-side up. After they climbed out of the medical pool, Joe switched the hose from sedative to pure seawater. Within minutes Taurus was conscious again, slashing his head back and forth, whipping his tail.

Using a remote control, John opened the hatch separating the paddock from the main tank, releasing the agitated bull shark into its temporary home.

Joe, John, and Li-ling walked down a spiral stairwell to the lower level while Dr. Becker, Anya, and I took the freight elevator.

"Anya, I want you to show Kwan around, then take him to the Alpha lab and ask Dr. Kamrowski to teach him how to catalog the TS subjects."

"Yes, ma'am."

The elevator doors opened, revealing the lower level.

"Very cool."

The chamber was dark, save for the turquoise glow coming from the immense aquarium. Within these shimmering crystal clear waters swam Taurus, the cylindrical shape of the tank magnifying the size and majesty of the predator, which glided effortlessly through the water like a gray demon, its head on a swivel, its mouth slack-jawed and open, its beady eyes taking in everything.

If a bull shark was a human athlete, it would be a wrestler—either that or a fullback. The shark was stocky; its body short and thickly muscled from its blunt rounded snout to its bloated midsection which was topped by a triangular dorsal fin. The pectoral fins were big and active along either side of its body and the caudal fin reminded me more of a triangular boomerang than a sickle, with the upper lobe longer than the lower. For the most part the tail remained pretty rigid, but every once in a while it would flick the water with a powerful thrust, accelerating Taurus on its counter-clockwise revolutions around the tank.

As I sat in my wheelchair watching the six hundred pound fish circle, I experienced a sense of envy. The shark was epic—a master of its physical domain, the product of millions of years of evolution. It seemed to move through the water at will; a shiver of muscle sent it gliding through liquid crystal, the slightest rotation of its pectoral fins and it turned. It never worried about swag or impressing girls or whether a building or sidewalk was handicap accessible; all it did was eat and impregnate females and it never stuck around to raise the kids.

Sort of like the Admiral.

I could have sat in my wheelchair and stared at that bad boy all day—only Anya had her orders to train me.

"Are you ready, Kwan? The tour starts here in the observation hall. The observation tank is equipped with sensors, so we can monitor the subject's vitals. The drug we gave Taurus will cause some agitation and cartilage pain, so he'll receive meds tonight with his dinner. Everything we feed our sharks has been fortified with vitamins, nutrients, and fats that are designed to maintain optimal health. Sharks must be here a minimum of thirty days before they can be used as a subject."

"Do you get *their* written consent? Sorry."

Her eyes glowed turquoise in the reflected light. "I wouldn't joke around if I were you. If Dr. Becker thinks you're a goof you'll be kicked out of her program just like your friend, Jesse."

"My bad."

"And the teen slang—never use it around Becker or Dr. Kamrowski. They hate it."

She led me out of the observation chamber and through a basement corridor, the hallway white and antiseptic looking. We passed several small offices before coming to a steel and reinforced glass door labeled BSL3-A.

"Kwan, this is the real serious stuff, so no joking around, okay? All of our animal labs are Bio-Safety Level Three environments. Four is tops, used for stuff like Ebola, so three is pretty safe. Don't worry, we're not working with viruses or toxic substances, but we do work with rats that have the potential to escape the facility. There are four labs which rotate between night and day settings. The walls inside are three-feet-thick cinder block—even if a rat were to escape there's no place for it to go. You have to enter the lab through an airlock with self-closing doors. Once the outer door is secured we'll be able to enter the lab. The lab uses negative airflow to contain airborne agents."

"Why all these precautions if you're not using toxic substances?"

"Rats have fleas. Fleas can escape. We don't want a flea that has bitten a treated rat to leave the lab—negative airflow prevents that from happening. So do our plastic cages. And our waste policies. All waste *must* be decontaminated before it's incinerated—especially dead animals."

"Do I have to wear one of those spaceman suits?"

"No. That kind of stuff is only worn by lab techs who are in contact with the rats. Ready to go inside?"

"I guess so."

She pulled open the outer door, which hissed from the air pressure differential. I followed her inside a small room which separated the corridor from the lab. When the door behind us clicked shut, Anya pushed open the interior door. She held it for me and I rolled my wheelchair inside the lab.

The room was rectangular, about forty-feet long and half as wide. Along the wall to my right were three workstations with aluminum tables, microscopes, and a sink powered by a foot pedal. Above the basin were shelves stocked with test tubes and beakers and petri dishes. The closest work area was occupied by a woman in her thirties. She wore a blue lab coat and was peering into the lens of a microscope, her back to us.

Anya led me to the opposite wall where metal shelves held three foot-long clear plastic containers. Inside each container was a white rat.

"See these hoods on top of the cages? They're used to ventilate the rat's habitat. Each unit has piles of wood chips that the rat uses as a nest and a water bottle designed with a sipper feeder tube. The green stuff is rodent chow. None of these rats have been treated yet. They're being acclimated and prepped for the stem cell injections we'll be extracting from Taurus."

"I hate rats," I said, a bit too loud.

The woman in the blue lab coat looked up from her microscope. "Anya, bring your friend over here please."

Anya shot me a harsh look then led me over to the first work station.

Dr. Nadja Margareta Kamrowski was half German, half Polish. She had dark brown hair cut very short and gray-hazel eyes—only the left eye was off, in a perpetual squint. Anya told me later it was caused by a birth defect.

"Dr. Kamrowski, this is Kwan Wilson, our new intern."

"Do you know why we use rats in medical experiments, Mr. Wilson? We use them because their genetic, biological, and behavior characteristics closely resemble those of humans. We use them because diseases and conditions that affect humans can be replicated in mice and rats. We use white rats because they are genetically consistent—meaning an experiment conducted on a white rat in Miami can be easily replicated in Munich using the same species. We inject these creatures with experimental drugs that alter their DNA. We expose our rats to high doses of radiation to give them cancer so we can try to cure them. We're severing their spinal cords to cause paralysis in an attempt to repair the damage. This is only a Phase I protocol, meaning we're still learning. Do you know how many rats suffer and die during a Phase I protocol, Mr. Wilson? The answer, so far, is all of them. These rats are our soldiers in the medical field, so if I were you I'd reevaluate your position on these noble creatures. Thanks to their sacrifice we're on the verge of a major breakthrough."

"Sorry. But how can you claim to be close to a major break-through if the patients keep dying?"

"Come with me and I'll show you."

She led us out the two exit doors and back into the main corridor to the next lab, labeled BSL3-B. We entered the anteroom, which was lit only by a purple interior light. The lab on the other side of the door appeared to be dark.

"Rats are nocturnal," Dr. Kamrowski explained. "The labs are kept on rotating light shifts to simulate day and night. We handle the subjects in the light when they're more docile. But it's in the dark where we see the full effects of the drug. Stage 1 is the initial phase of the injection where the subject's biology begins assimilating the shark stem cells. Stage 2 is the miracle—the bursting of cancer cells . . . the healing of the spinal cord. Wherever the damage exists, the stem cells seek it out and aggressively affect repairs. Stage 3 is the side effects. Anya, you've never seen a Stage 3 response, have you?"

"No, ma'am."

"Stage 3 occurs when the stem cells attempt to correct what they construe as deviations in the human genome. Weak spots are targeted and genetically altered. Before we go in, let me remind each of you that you've signed releases which prohibit the disclosure of anything you're about to see. If you feel you cannot abide by that agreement, then wait outside in the corridor."

Anya nodded. "I want to see."

"Me, too."

Dr. Kamrowski reached into a cardboard box on a shelf and removed three pairs of night vision glasses. "Put these on and follow me."

The night glasses illuminated the darkness into an olive-green world. I watched in fascination as Kamrowski pushed open the lab door—unleashing a burst of air and the tortured squeals of rodents. The sound was unnerving—had Anya not been by my side squeezing my hand I would have surely spun around and retreated. I prayed she could not hear the trickling gurgle of my catheter bottle filling—my bladder's response ruining our first moment of physical contact.

Dr. Kamrowski led us to the first row of rat habitats, their tags labeled in green glow pen as Stage 1, dated two days ago. The white rats' eyes glowed luminescent-gray as they lay on their sides in obvious distress, panting heavily. A few habitats were labeled Hodgkin's lymphoma; other rows included various tumor-based cancers. The last row was for those rats suffering from induced paralysis—their spinal cords severed at a point that impaired their hind quarters.

Now I understood what Nadja Kamrowski meant when she called these miserable creatures noble. They had been bred to be sacrificed, and the thought of that brought a lump to my throat.

After a few minutes we made our way to the Stage 2 habitats—each cage containing an invigorated, healthy white rat. Coming to a cage labeled Paralysis, I found myself mesmerized, my heart pounding with adrenaline at the sight of a rodent who had regained the use of its hind legs—jubilant at its own renewed sense of freedom.

The terrifying sounds coming from the next set of habitats were almost too unnerving to investigate.

"Oh . . . God." Anya's nails dug into my palm as our eyes darted over the first series of cages. Every rat had shed its fur, giving it a gruesome baseline appearance. From there, the shark stem cells had unleashed liberties upon its hosts' DNA that seemed to have been spawned from the sociopathic mind of Josef Mengele, the monster of Auschwitz who performed live experiments on Jewish children.

Bulging eyes. Gill slits along either side of the neck. Thickened scale-like skin and mutilated tails that had been metastasizing into freakish caudal fins. The tortured rodents were bashing their rapidly evolving carcasses against the interior of the habitats in powerful spasms. There was blood in several cages, and a few of the rodents had actually succeeded in cracking the plastic. One rat—possessing hideous fangs, had bitten through the hose of its water bottle, flooding the cage. Now it lay in two inches of water, gasping painful breaths.

We told Dr. Kamrowski we had seen enough.

She led us to the final series of habitats—Stage 4 . . . death.

Cage after cage held the evidence of a miracle gone awry—dead rodents, tortured by their evolving deformities until death had mercifully granted them a reprieve.

I heard Anya ask, "How did they die?"

"They suffocated," replied Dr. Kamrowski. "After a day or so, cartilage forms in the esophagus, obstructing breathing. We'll perform autopsies before we dispose of their remains. I realize this is shocking to see, but this is how we find cures for diseases. If we can overcome the cross-species rejection, then . . . well, there's hope."

Hope . . .

I stared at the deformed creatures, recalling a poem my mother had often recited to me as a child: *"Hope is the thing with feathers . . . that perches in the soul. And sings the tune without the words, and never stops at all."*

Emily Dickinson had called hope a "thing with feathers."

My hope had gills.

While I was wasting Dickinson on dozens of dead rats, rodents of a different ilk were circling their "cheese" nine hundred nautical miles to the southeast.

To the casual observer, the presence of the 165-foot fishing trawler, *Malchut*, in the deep waters off Puerto Rico probably seemed natural—the vessel dragging its nets, encircling a school of fish.

A closer inspection of the Canadian-registered ship would have revealed a different story.

Although the trawler was equipped to fish commercially, the deck space between the net drum and bridge was designed to accommodate a helicopter. The fish holds had been converted into a weapons bay, with mounts for two .50 caliber machine guns hidden within the base of the trawl gantry.

The biggest difference between the *Malchut* and a standard fishing trawler was located underwater. Fastened beneath the keel like a twelve-foot remora was a gondola-shaped device that housed a multibeam echo sounder (MBES)—a sophisticated sonar array equipped with the latest in underwater imaging.

Over the last four hours the *Malchut* had been slowly circling the same patch of sea, allowing the MBES array to develop detailed images of the USS *Philadelphia*. The sunken Los Angeles Class attack sub was resting 220 feet beneath the Atlantic, its hull balancing precariously on a rocky precipice above the 28,000-foot-deep Puerto Rico Trench.

Along with the five crewmen who operated the bridge, engine room, and galley, there were with two Americans on board the fishing vessel—both former Navy SEALs trained to locate and salvage sunken ships, along with nine Arab mercenaries. The latter were members of the Al-Nusra Front, a private militia that fought with the Syrian People's Coalition against the oppressive regime of President Bashar Assad. Al-Nusra has been blacklisted by the Obama administration as a terrorist organization—a fact that only made the renegade militia more attractive to the CIA and other black ops groups.

The commandos received their orders from the only woman on board.

Sabeen Tayfour was the lone surviving child of Adad Tayfour, a former Syrian general who resigned from President Assad's forces to join the people's revolution. Only nineteen years old, the raven-haired beauty with coal-black eyes had already borne witness to several lifetimes of cruelty. She had lost her mother and younger siblings when Assad's forces fired Scud missiles upon her city, and for six brutal weeks she had been held captive while guards tortured and violated her. Sweet Sabeen, who had once aspired to a career in dance, no longer existed. The woman known to her commandos as Onyx was a cold-blooded killer. The leader of the Black Widow brigade operated under a simple directive—revenge.

Cameron Reeves was out on deck, pretending to check his diving gear while his eyes behind the dark sunglasses focused on the athletic Arab woman bench pressing her weight in the blue neoprene two-piece. Two members of the Muslim Brotherhood watched the American commando suspiciously, but Reeves didn't care. Muslim or not, a woman doesn't wear skin-tight fabrics to work out in public unless she wanted to be watched, and the former Navy SEAL was only happy to oblige.

Reeves's dive partner, David Watkins, was a linebacker-sized Californian who refused to function on land without his San Francisco 49ers hat, which he always wore backward. The two Americans turned in unison as they heard the helicopter's pounding rotors approaching from the northwest.

Three minutes later, the Sikorsky S-434 light chopper landed on deck.

The man who climbed out of the cockpit was my father. Admiral Douglas Wilson was dressed in civilian attire, the sleeves of his embroidered Hawaiian Tommy Bahama shirt flapping beneath the slowing rotors.

Watkins greeted his black ops employer. "Your downed lady's in two hundred and twenty feet of water, with her ass-end hanging over the edge of the Puerto Rico Trench. If she goes, you'll need a DSRV to reach her."

"Why the hell are we having this conversation? Go down and get me what I want."

"Money first, Admiral," Reeves said, entering the conversation. "And you can save the bad dog bit for the enlisted men."

Admiral Wilson reached inside the four-passenger helicopter and retrieved an aluminum suitcase from beneath the copilot's seat. "One million dollars—half a million apiece for doing a job the navy trained you to do for free."

Watkins took the suitcase and passed it back to Reeves. "What do we do about the woman? She's insisting on making the dive."

Onyx stepped forward. "I can speak for myself."

The admiral's eyes widened behind his mirrored sunglasses. "Sabeen, so nice to see you again."

"You will address me only as Onyx. I will make the dive with your team."

Watkins looked up from counting the shrink-wrapped fifty-thousand-dollar stacks of money. "You're too young; it's way too dangerous."

"I'm old enough to kill."

"Onyx—"

"Admiral, my cousin Mahdi was aboard the submarine. My father has instructed me to recite the *Salat al-Janazah* among our dead. The prayer is a collective obligation among Muslims. If no one fulfills it, then all Muslims will be held accountable."

Admiral Wilson pulled Watkins aside. "Let her dive. She can pray over her dead while you and Reeves load the package into the flotation harness . . . or she can join them if she screws up."

The difference between a recreational dive and a technical dive is depth. Depth determines the mixtures of gases one will use to breathe and the number of decompression stops on the way up to prevent nitrogen narcosis. The preferred mix for dives exceeding 185 feet is Heliox, which is helium and oxygen. Unlike nitrogen, helium does not have an intoxicating effect, but its thermal conductivity is six times greater than that of nitrogen, causing the diver to lose body heat rapidly. Because helium dissolves quickly, divers must decompress more often during their ascent or risk the formation of nitrogen bubbles in their blood, a dangerous condition known as the bends.

Cameron Reeves joined David Watkins on the dive platform mounted along the trawler's stern. Both commandos were wearing dry suits, with their main Nitrox tanks on their back and their two Heliox cylinders strapped in place along their flanks. In addition, Watkins carried a backpack containing a harness attached to an inflatable bladder.

Reeves looked up as Onyx climbed down the aluminum ladder to join them. Kneeling on the swaying platform, she carefully worked one bare foot at a time into each flipper, the muscles of her legs and buttocks flexing beneath her wetsuit.

The former Navy SEAL stared at her painted red toenails. "I didn't know Muslim women went in for that."

"How many Muslim women do you know?"

"Point taken. However, you really should be wearing a dry suit and rubber boots; it'll be cold down there."

"I prefer to feel the water; it is easier to swim. You have done this before?"

"Deep salvage dives? A few. The key is to keep your focus and watch your time. It'll take us about seven to ten minutes to reach the sub. That leaves us fifteen minutes to locate the package and inflate the harness. Do your praying and wait for us outside the torpedo room, and we'll surface together. Remember, we decompress at a hundred and fifty feet, then every thirty feet, just to be safe."

She winked—then stepped off the platform and plummeted feetfirst into the sea.

"Hey, wait!" Reeves turned to Watkins, who was testing his regulator.

"Let her go, buddy. One way or the other, that crazy bitch'll get you killed."

Reeves nodded. *She's reckless . . . like a wild stallion. Is she really interested, or is she just playing me?* Shoving the regulator into his mouth he checked the air flow, then stepped to the edge of the platform and jumped into the sea.

Watkins joined him in the water, the two divers floating along the surface while they checked their equipment. After several minutes they deflated their buoyancy control vests and descended together through a frenzy of air bubbles, falling rapidly into the deep blue underworld.

The pressure squeezed Sabeen's ears, forcing her to slow. Pinching her nose, she filled her cheeks with air and popped open her ear canals, relieving the ache. The American commando was right—only halfway down and the cold was already seeping through her wetsuit.

She had been through far worse.

Sabeen continued her descent, the royal blue waters deepening into shades of gray until the bottom came into view and she saw it—a long, dark, log-shaped beast, a third of its girth poised over a crevasse so deep and vast it sent a shiver through her spine.

Orienting her approach so that the submarine appeared as it did on the sonar images, Sabeen quickly located the weapons bay and the blast that had most likely sunk the warship.

Sixty-seven meters . . .

Sabeen had never dived this deep before. She could feel the weight of the sea pressing in on her skull and face mask and felt herself trembling. Locating the fifteen-foot-wide blast hole, she switched on her underwater light and entered the dark, hollow chamber.

Time, depth, and current had swept away the evidence of a crime scene. Her eyes caught movement and she turned, her light catching the golden-brown flank of a shark. Eight feet long, with a prominent first dorsal fin, the sandbar shark swam in jagged, dizzying circles around the female diver until Sabeen realized there was more than one creature present.

Perhaps a dozen sharks moved through the flooded torpedo room, each one circling a rectangular crate—the crate her men had given their lives to transport halfway around the world. Sabeen quickly realized what was attracting the sharks—the water was warmer—she was no longer shivering. *It's the radiation . . .*

Then she saw Mahdi.

Her cousin's face was bloated and gray, his eyes open in death. The commando's upper right quadriceps had been eaten clear down to his femur, only it was not a shark that had killed him—it was the bullet hole in his forehead, clogged from the inside with fragments of his brain.

The sight of the gruesome corpse would have sent most divers fleeing. Sabeen simply pushed her dead cousin aside, refocusing the beam of her light on the racks of platter mines.

Cameron Reeves was first to reach the damaged hull. Switching on his light, he swam into the cavernous opening—twisting sideways at the last moment to avoid being rammed by a torpedo-shaped mass that suddenly appeared out of the darkness. A slap of the shark's powerful tail struck the Heliox tank hanging along Reeves's left hip.

Watkins pulled him away from the hole, signaling him to wait. Unzipping a pocket on his dry suit, the commando removed several underwater flares, passing one to Reeves. The two divers popped off the caps and tossed the sizzling pink sticks into the flooded chamber. Within seconds they witnessed a shark exodus, the agitated predators streaming out of the hole and past the men into open water.

Satisfied, Watkins led Reeves inside an interior space that now listed at a thirty-degree angle. Racks of torpedoes were tilted sideways, control panels covered in sand.

In less than three minutes they managed to locate the crate with the warnings written in Arabic and Farsi and swim it out of the downed attack sub, laying it on a stretch of rocky bottom.

The woman joined them. She watched the two men as they laid out a canvas harness attached to a deflated underwater balloon. She pointed to the sharks, which were circling the periphery.

Reeves gave her a reassuring wink, then proceeded to inflate the open-ended parachute-like balloon with a pony bottle of compressed air.

Sabeen remained behind the two men for protection as first the balloon, then the crate began rising off the bottom.

That's when the Black Widow struck.

Poised behind David Watkins's back, she cut the air hose of his regulator with her dive knife. As air bubbles streamed out of the severed hose, she reached for Cameron Reeves and yanked the mask off the startled commando's face. Releasing it, she scissor-kicked herself away from the bottom and inflated her dive vest, quickly distancing herself from the two distressed divers.

The former Navy SEALs never panicked. Engaging a buddy system, Reeves shared his regulator with Watkins, who became his eyes, locating the discarded mask. Refitting it to his face, Reeves quickly cleared his eyepiece, then—arm in arm—he and Watkins began their ascent, anxious to gut and drown the voluptuous Syrian assassin.

Wa-Boom!

A deafening roar of thunder rolled into multiple explosions—the platter mines detonating at staggered intervals around the hull of the downed attack sub. Before they could react, the two divers were swept up in a current and tossed across the coral-strewn bottom like tumbleweed.

Cameron Reeves was barely conscious when another sound reached him—the sound created by six thousand tons of shifting steel, the sub's keel crushing him in a burst of warm white light.

* * *

From her vantage seventy feet above the action, Sabeen looked down upon a sandstorm of rolling black thunder. Her heart pounded with adrenaline as she watched the bow of the USS *Philadelphia* rise away from the bottom on a sixty-degree vertical plane before sliding stern-first into the dark depths of the Puerto Rico Trench.

Seconds later, a current of shrapnel hit her like a swarm of stinging wasps, her ears assaulted by metal striking metal as her air tanks were struck like hail on an aluminum rooftop. Abandoning her decompression, she kicked for a safer vantage, only to realize the balloon she had been rising with was now moving the other way—its inflated bladder torn, the trailing crate sinking fast.

The rectangular object and its bubble-trailing tethered buoyancy device hit bottom, bounced twice, and—as Sabeen watched in horror—was inhaled within the vortex created by the plummeting Los Angeles Class attack sub, following it into the 28,000-foot abyss.

11

The ride home from the lab that first night was an exhausting one—mentally, physically, and emotionally. I had pressing questions for Dr. Becker . . . *Why weren't human stem cells as effective as shark stem cells at restoring damaged spinal cords? Was there a way to counteract the side effects by reducing the dosage? Was it possible that a human subject would fare better than a rat?*

The answers to these questions and dozens more would have to wait. Upon concluding my "sneak peek at the future of stem cell therapies" lecture and tour, Dr. Kamrowski had put me to work entering gobbledygook subject data into a computer. Four hours of tedious work . . . with no chance of face time with her majesty, Dr. Barbara Becker.

Still, using the lab's computer did offer me access to the boss's personal files.

I'm not a hacker by trade, but yeah, I know how to do it—thanks to Clark Newsom. Clark was my best friend back in San Diego. His parents owned a cybersecurity company and Clark often tested his parents' clients' firewalls, getting cash bonuses for hacking their sites or identifying honey pots—traps designed to detect someone illegally accessing a system. That knowledge became especially useful when we decided to hack into the navy's site to access the Admiral's private e-mails. We shut down after reading a series of encrypted messages from my father about some top secret deal called Operation Strawman.

Dr. Becker's firewall was more of a Strawman than a real security system—designed to intimidate, but with little substance. By the time my driver, Bill, had us heading north on Interstate 95, I was already accessing her files on my iPad, perusing a list of links.

Background of protocol.
Granulocyte counts (listed by shark species).
Subject results.
Genetic mutations.

I clicked on *Genetic mutations*, which brought me to a page of links corresponding to every rat used in the study. I randomly selected Rat TS-19 . . . the TS an abbreviation for tiger shark.

Appearing on my screen were two images of a double helix. One twisting spiral ladder was the rat's DNA *before* the stem cell injections; the other was the rat's DNA *after* it had received an injection of the tiger shark elixir. In both the *before* and *after* double helixes of DNA, green, yellow, and red specks appeared along the twisting strand like lights on a Christmas tree.

A quick search of Becker's notes identified the green points as the rat's normal functioning genes. The yellow spots were noncoding DNA—insignificant to the animal's genetic code. The green and yellow DNA in the subject's before and after helixes were identical.

The differences were rooted in the red spots—the rat's transposons. According to Dr. Becker's notes, transposons are parasitic DNA—a hand-me-down that was left over from the earlier phases of mammalian evolution. Found in both rodent and human genes, parasitic DNA disrupts normal gene function and is what causes cells to mutate into diseases like cancer.

Rat TS-19 had been purposely stricken with cancer to test the tiger shark stem cells. The good news was that the stem cells had gone after the rat's transposons, destroying the cancer cells. The bad news was that, instead of forming scar tissue, the transposons had adopted the traits of its dominant benefactor—the tiger shark

DNA. These mutated cells were spreading rapidly among TS-19's genetic command center, and the green specks which represented the rodent's normal functioning genes were too few in number to fight off the invading force.

In plain English—the stem cells had killed the cancer but had mutated the host into a species that was half-rat and half-shark . . . essentially killing it.

Hope is a double-edged sword—it can save you and it can cut you to the quick. For the next two days my mind was severely screwed up; by Friday I was officially depressed. Jesse Gordon texted me a reminder about Saturday's band practice, but even that barely raised my pulse.

Leave it to Stephen Ley to resuscitate me.

With no appetite, I headed for the gym during my lunch period, hoping to break my lethargy by shooting hoops. Coach Flaig wasn't around, but his office door was open, so I borrowed a basketball from his rack and wheeled myself out onto the hardwood court.

As I mentioned earlier, my wheelchair isn't made for sports. Lacking leverage and a harness, I nearly heaved myself out of my seat on the first shot—an air ball from the lower block—about a three-foot bank shot. My next dozen shots were bricks—until I gradually began compensating by holding the armrest with my left hand and shooting one-handed with my right. Within fifteen minutes I had worked up a sweat and was consistently making shots from as far back as the foul line.

I started to feel better. A few times I actually smiled.

And then Stephen Ley entered the gym with his entourage.

"Kwan-san! Shooting some hoops, buddy? Let me help you." Ley grabbed the rebound from my miss and gently tossed it to me as if I were a three-year-old.

I knew better; I should have left. But there were students watching . . . a few had their cell phones out. So I shot . . . *swish.*

Ley grabbed the rebound. "Nice shot, buddy." He walked the ball over to me and offered a low-five—pulling his hand away as I reached out and whiffed.

Palming the ball, he teased me with the offering, performing for his pals.

"Twenty bucks . . . you and me, Ley. Ten foul shots each."

It was a bold move, but in my mind a win-win. By challenging Ley I stopped the teasing. If he accepted the bet, the worst thing that could happen is that I lost a foul shooting contest to the best basketball player in school.

Oohs and *ahhs* from the entourage, which had been growing steadily into a crowd, forced Ley into accepting my terms.

Ley smirked. "Where's your money, honey?"

Reaching into my backpack, I pulled out the twenty. "Put up or shut up, bitch."

More *oohs* and *ahhs*.

Now Ley couldn't back down. Removing his wallet, he fingered two tens and dropped the bills on the court. "Shoot." Ley slapped the ball dead onto the wood floor, forcing me to bend over to pick it up.

My first shot missed badly.

He made his shot . . . and the next five. After seven shots, Ley was up six to four when I started feeling it and he started acting like an asshole, shooting behind his back.

I hit my tenth shot to tie it at seven.

He had the last shot . . . and missed.

"Sudden death," I said, rolling after his rebound.

Behind my back, he was instructing the crowd.

Returning to the foul line, I set myself. Now my ego was pushing me . . . *now I wanted to win!* I took a calming breath and shot—only to see Ley smack the ball into the bleachers, the students laughing.

Ley had regained control. I should have left. I should have done a million other things. Instead I retrieved the ball like a dummy, intent on winning the battle of egos.

"You afraid, Ley? Afraid of losing to a cripple?"

"Shut up and shoot."

Setting myself, I went through my preshot ritual and launched the winning basket—which the asshole blocked again.

I felt my heart pounding in my chest like a bass drum; I felt my blood pressure rising. Maybe it was the fact that I was being denied an opportunity to compete, maybe it was Ley just being a jerk, humiliating me yet again in front of my peers—but I lost it. Lowering my head, I rolled as hard as I could for him, aiming for his shins—and missed him as he easily stepped out of harm's way.

Tears of frustration in my eyes, I went after him again—nearly tipping over on one wheel as he performed his bull-fighting act to the cheering crowd.

Kwan the bull. Stubborn and snorting snot and tears, I charged again and kept after him.

The act quickly turned from comedy to pitiful. Embarrassed, the students filed out.

I was spent. Breathing heavily, I bent over to catch my breath.

Ley picked up his cash and tossed it at me. "You win." He turned and walked away.

This time I didn't miss.

The foot-holders of my chair struck the basketball star full-force in the back of his calves and he fell onto his knees, screaming in pain. Rolling onto his back, he kicked my left wheel and suddenly I was airborne.

And then I hit my head.

It must have sounded bad because Ley panicked. He righted my chair. Then he grabbed me from behind, picked me up by my armpits and dragged me backward onto the seat.

Ever handle a drunk? A paraplegic with a concussion is ten times worse. It took Ley several tries before he figured out how to wedge my shoes onto the foot-holders so I wouldn't slide. He swore again as my pants flooded with urine—my catheter having pulled out in the fall.

He shoved the basketball in my wet lap and fled the scene.

"Kwan? Are you all right?"

It was Anya—the last person in the world I wanted to see. Still woozy, I tried to wheel myself away.

"Where are you going, let me help you. Oh my . . . Kwan, your pants—"

"I know!" My face must have been bright red with embarrassment and purple with rage *and what the hell should I do first?* I couldn't think, my mind lost in a fog—*urine was dripping down my seat onto the floor!* It was splattering everywhere, and I had no control.

I became an animal. I grunted and cried and babbled something incoherent as my mind crawled back inside my mother's womb.

It was dark when I woke up.

I t's scary waking up in the hospital. It's like being zapped from one moment to the next. You don't dream. You don't register the passage of time. You just open your eyes and your throat is as dry as a desert day and there are tubes sticking out of your arms.

Basically, I was toast.

A female voice was calling me *Mr. Wilson*—which made the whole thing seem even creepier.

"Can you hear me, Mr. Wilson?"

"Throat . . . dry."

"Here's some water, just sip it. The doctor will be by to see you. Do you remember hitting your head?"

"No . . . yes."

"Your girlfriend called an ambulance. You have a concussion and a few bruises we'll need to keep an eye on. We called your grandmother—she'll be here soon."

"How long . . . do I have . . . to stay here?"

"That's up to the doctor."

"Tell . . . me!"

"At least three days."

They kept me in the hospital eleven days. Eleven days of IV bags. Eleven days of being woken up eight times a night. Four roommates, three who snored, two visitors, and no Dilaudid, just enough antibiotics to cure all the gonorrhea in Las Vegas.

Every morning after breakfast the orderly came for me. He'd wheel me across the hall and past the nurse's station to the elevator; then we'd ride down three floors to the hyperbaric chambers.

A hyperbaric chamber is an enclosed pressurized cylinder where you breathe in pure oxygen. Pure oxygen helps heal the brain, decreases swelling, and fights off infection.

What it doesn't help is the claustrophobia induced by being locked up for four hours at a time in an enclosed pressurized cylinder.

Eleven days. Ten sessions. Four hours a session.

Forty hours of oxygen therapy—nearly two complete days stuck in an isolation tube with nothing but my Doors CDs and my rancid, ugly, self-loathing thoughts . . . a deadly combination.

This is the end . . . beautiful friend. This is the end—my only friend, the end.

Anya came to visit me on day seven. It was her visit that set my "elaborate plans" into motion . . .

"You're looking better," Anya lied. "When will they release you?"

"I don't know."

"You seem depressed. Don't be depressed. Things will get better."

"Whatever."

"Stephen Ley was suspended on Wednesday. Principal Lockhart saw the Facebook photos taken in the gym."

"It doesn't matter," I said, looking away. "I'm not going back to school."

"What do you mean? Kwan, you have to come back. If you're not at Seacrest, you can't intern at the stem cell lab."

"Big deal. Why do you care anyway?"

The moment I said the words, I regretted it. I liked Anya . . . hell, I loved her. Okay, the whole college relationship leads to marriage deal—that was YOLO fantasy camp. . . *You Only Live Once so What-the-F?* But Anya was also my friend (counting Jesse, one of only two) and I had just told her she could bail on the cripple.

Maybe it was her British-Indian upbringing or just her strong character . . . but she didn't leave.

"Kwan . . . I thought we were friends."

"Are we friends, or do you just feel sorry for me?"

"Kwan, I like you. You're real. Most Americans are con artists—what we used to call *jinelz* back in London. As in, *I don't trust 'im, 'e's a jinelz.*"

Her cockney slang made me smile.

She sat on the edge of my bed, her closeness causing my flesh to tingle. "Back in August, the first week I was here, a girl who lived in our neighborhood invited me to a party. Stephen Ley was there; he put something in my drink to get me *chenzed.*"

"*Chenzed?*"

"Drunk. Did you ever?"

"Ever what?"

"Try to sleep with a girl by getting her *chenzed.*"

"No."

"See? That's why I like you, Kwan, you have morals. When I lived in New Delhi, I couldn't walk the streets or ride the train without some guy rubbing his hand or his groin all over me. In London and here in America it's all about partying; in India the women are openly abused. I'm glad my father brought us to the States—I wanted to be able to do something positive with my life . . . something to help other people. That's why I'm interning at the lab. A good person like you deserves to walk again."

"Do you even know how I injured my spine?"

"To be honest, I was waiting for the right time to ask. Why don't you tell me now?"

So I told her. Everything. From texting and killing my mom to being disowned by the Admiral, to my attempted suicide back in the hospital . . . everything.

When I was done, she hesitated, contemplating her response. "Becker had a breakthrough last week."

"What kind of a breakthrough?"

"I'm not supposed to say. I'll tell if you promise not to breathe a word of this to anyone—especially Li-ling."

"I won't tell. Now tell me."

"We started injecting the rats with Taurus's stem cells last Monday—with one change. Dr. Becker had me set up a separate experimental group of rats. We gave these rats a daily two milligram injection of mouse growth hormone."

"Mice have growth hormones?"

"Everything has growth hormones. We used mice GH because it's ninety-five percent compatible with rat physiology and shares sixty-five percent of the same proteins found in human growth hormone. Anyway, it's been a week since the two subject groups received their bull shark stem cell shots. The control group has already regressed into Phases 3 and 4—the mutation and death stages. But the rats that received growth hormone shots haven't shown any ill effects—no mutations whatsoever."

"Anya, what about the rats that were paralyzed?"

"They're crawling on all fours again."

I sat up in bed, my pulse numbers racing on the cardiac monitor.

"Kwan, it's early—there may still be side effects. Dr. Becker has to test the GH doses, perform full physiological tests on the—"

"But it worked! Does Becker know why it worked?"

"She thinks the growth hormone caused an intergenic suppression."

"In English?"

"The growth hormone diverted the shark mutation by causing a second mutation somewhere else within the rat's genome . . . they call that an intergenic suppression. The second mutation released a protein inhibitor which suppressed the shark mutations, protecting the rat's DNA."

"How soon?"

"You mean for human trials. I knew you'd ask me that. Don't ask me that. And don't ask Becker because you're not supposed to know. No one's supposed to know. But if you came back to the lab, then you'd eventually find out. You'd have the inside track. In a few years, when the medical profession allows Dr. Becker to begin human trials—"

"I can be first in line." I closed my eyes, my thoughts racing. *Why are you telling me this, Anya? Is it to give me hope, or is it something else? Are you saying that there's a place for me beside you—but only if I was whole again?*

"You're right, Anya. I need to get back to school . . . I need to be putting in time at the lab. Thank you for trusting me with this. I promise it'll stay our little secret."

After she left, I formulated a plan. There was no way I was going to wait two or three or four more years . . . I wanted to walk now! I wanted to play ball again . . . play in college and the pros . . . above all, I wanted Anya.

To complete my mission, I needed the bull shark stem cells and human growth hormone.

My first call was to the principal. "Dr. Lockhart, it's Kwan. Sir, I hope to get out of the hospital soon, and I'd like to square things with Stephen Ley."

"No need to worry, son. Mr. Ley has been suspended."

"Yes, sir, I heard. But what happened was partly my fault. If it's okay with you, I'd like to propose a truce—if you'd get him to agree to my terms."

The suspended star of Seacrest High's varsity basketball team entered my hospital room a day later carrying a grudge. Maybe it was my imagination, but when he saw the IV bag and tubes, I thought I felt the Grinch's heart soften.

"Lockhart said he'd remove the suspension from my record if I came to visit you. So? I'm here. I suppose you want an apology?"

"What I want is a favor. I need you to score me some human growth hormone. It has to be the natural stuff, not the synthetic crap. You know . . . the injections."

Ley shook his head in disbelief. "HGH? First, I don't do HGH. How am I supposed to get it? B—that stuff's expensive—a month's worth of injections runs about three grand. And three— even if I liked you I wouldn't do it. If I got caught, no college recruiter would touch me."

"Fair enough. Now here's why you *are* going to do this. A—because you owe me for putting me in here. B—because if Lockhart doesn't remove your suspension then you'll be labeled a bad risk by college recruiters, so bye-bye scholarship offers, hello junior college. C—because if you know what it costs, you probably know someone who uses it, maybe a relative or a doctor. And D—because I'm going to pay you well to get it for me."

I handed him a debit card. "There's five thousand and change in that account, all that's left from my inheritance. Go to any ATM and withdraw what you need—my pin number is one-nine-five-nine. Bring me a month's worth of injections and you can keep what's left over. But you'd better bring the real stuff, because if you try to screw me I'll know, which means I'll file assault charges and we'll see which college coach wants to recruit your ass then . . . *buddy*."

I held out my hand for him to shake. He ignored it, took my debit card and left.

13

I awoke the next morning to a visitor—a familiar-looking man seated in a chair at the foot of my bed. He was in his early fifties—slender and just short of six feet tall, his hair jet-black and kept neat, his skin mocha-brown. His dark eyes smiled warmly at me from behind wire-rimmed glasses.

"Good morning, Mr. Wilson. I hope I am not disturbing you."

"Do I know you?"

"My name is Tanish Patel. I am a professor of economics currently teaching at Florida Atlantic University. My daughter, Anya, suggested I pay you a visit."

I sat up in bed. "Professor Patel, it's so nice to meet you."

"The honor is mine. May I call you Kwan?"

"Please."

"Anya told me what happened to you in school. My eldest, Rudy . . . as an adolescent, he possessed a temper that often led him into confrontations which ended badly."

"Sounds like me."

"Yes." The professor flashed a smile, his lower lip quivering for a revealing moment. "Anya also tells me you are quite brilliant. Do you play chess?"

"These days, only against the computer."

"Is that a reflection of your skill level, or the void in your social life brought about by your recent paralysis?"

"Both, I suppose."

"Then perhaps you and I might play sometime. I doubt I'd offer you much of a match, but it might be fun. They say one can only learn the game by exposing oneself to better players."

"I suspect you're far better than you let on."

"I suspect the same of you." He smiled, this time uninhibited. "I suppose that leaves both of us suspicious of one another, an interesting beginning to what I hope will be a lasting friendship."

"I hope so, too."

"Then please forgive me if this comes across as intrusive, but Anya may have mentioned in passing that you and your father suffer from a strained relationship. Rudy and I, too, lacked the common ground Anya's academic interests provide. I realize, of course, the circumstances are completely different . . . my only purpose in bringing this up is simply to offer my services to you—not as a surrogate father, but as a friend. If you ever require my assistance in any capacity—free of judgment or conditions, it would honor me if you called."

He reached into his shirt pocket and handed me a business card.

The emotion welled up in my throat. "Thank you."

Stephen Ley stopped by a few hours after Anya's father left—my drug mule coming through like a champ, delivering four hypodermic needles of natural human growth hormone directly to my hospital room. Ley claimed the stuff had cost him every penny in my bank account, but I knew he was lying. Having accessed his Facebook page, I was quite aware that Ley's older brother, Ronnie, was a physician's assistant at a wellness clinic in Boca and could get whatever supplies he needed. The brothers had made a nice profit off of me, but I didn't care. As long as Ley didn't bring me Restylane, I was in business.

After he left, I drew the privacy curtain around my hospital bed and injected the first dosage of the clear elixir right into my IV, hiding the remaining three needles in between the double lining of my Doors backpack. If anything bad were to happen, at least I was in the hospital.

I waited two days. Experiencing no ill side effects from the first shot, I gave myself a second injection. I was released from the hospital Tuesday afternoon, my cells now saturated with HGH.

I returned to school Wednesday morning. Principal Lockhart greeted me at the student drop-off zone with a warm smile and handshake and confirmed that I'd be going to the ANGEL lab after school. He told me Rachel Solomon was asking about me and I promised I'd stop by before the week was over.

With HGH flowing through my body, the school counselor with the penetrating eyes and mother's intuition was the last person I wanted to see.

Anya came over to talk to me before first period started and told me I looked much better. Li-ling was her usual self, telling me I needed to eat more, that I had lost too much weight. She suggested that I stop at the local kennel for a snack—a crack about Koreans eating dogs (something I've never done). Stephen Ley ignored me, as did most of the other students . . . gotta love high school.

I didn't. All I cared about was avoiding Rachel Solomon, making it through the day, and getting to the lab.

There was a brief moment of joy when I cut seventh period and met Jesse Gordon in the music room. The two of us jammed for almost an hour—me on my harmonica, him on his acoustic guitar. I impressed him with "Midnight Rambler" by the Rolling Stones, then we did Neil Young's "Heart of Gold" and finished with the Doors' "Roadhouse Blues."

When the bell rang, he escorted me outside where my van was waiting. "Dude, I'll set up another band practice, just promise me— no more hospital stays. We got the makings of a great band. You were actually smiling when we jammed. I've never seen you smile before."

Jesse was right. Playing music seemed to lighten my soul.

Maybe Anya would see me differently as a musician? But how could I play for her without seeming like a dickwad?

An idea popped into my head. Bill arrived and I challenged him to beat the ANGEL van to Miami. My plan was to be casually playing harmonica to the sharks when Anya arrived—that way it'd seem more natural.

Bill came through and we arrived at the lab ahead of the girls. Things were loose—Dr. Becker was away on business in Washington, DC, so I waited for Anya at the shark canal, serenading the circling predators on my harp as I awaited my audience.

Anya and Li-ling arrived while I was playing "Isn't She Lovely." It was meant to be a romantic offering—only Li-ling ruined the moment by snatching the harmonica from my lips midverse.

"Shut up with that squawk box, I already have a headache."

Li-ling was assigned to work with Dr. Kamrowski in one of the two labs on a nocturnal schedule, while Anya worked in the two daylight labs changing out rat feed bowls and refilling water bulbs.

I was given a stack of files and told to enter the data.

I selected an empty computer station adjacent to the observation room. Before me glowed the luminescent-blue aquarium. The tank was empty, Taurus having been returned to the shark canal days earlier. I knew the bull shark's harvested stem cells—or whatever was left of them—would be held in cold storage in one of the four labs' walk-in refrigerators.

Timing was everything. I needed to grab as many IV bags as I could stow in my backpack without getting caught.

The staff broke for dinner at six fifteen. I told them I wasn't hungry and continued to work until seven. With no one around, I hacked into the lab's security system, bringing up the facility's video monitors on my laptop. Sixteen black-and-white rectangular images appeared across my screen, each box a live feed taken from somewhere inside the ANGEL facility. I zoomed in on Anya in Lab A, then confirmed Dr. Kamrowski and Li-ling were still working in the darkened confines of BSL3-D. The Aussie was in his trailer—probably watching porn; the rest of the staff were gone for the day.

It was time.

Leaving the observation room, I headed for BSL3-C, one of the two labs on a daylight schedule. Entering through the anteroom, I waited for the door to seal, then entered the lab.

The rats were asleep. Rolling quietly past their cages, I approached the walk-in refrigerator at the end of the room. Gripping the handle, I yanked open the aluminum door and pushed myself inside.

The temperature was set at a chilly forty-two degrees Fahrenheit. Wooden shelves held open file boxes of sealed plastic pouches, each stem cell sample coded by species and date.

It took me a few minutes to locate Taurus's samples—only nine of them left. I grabbed three pouches. Then I heard the anteroom door open.

A moment later, I rolled out to find Anya pushing a cart holding rodent feed and a twenty gallon container of water. She looked up, startled, as I exited the refrigerator.

"Kwan, what are you doing inside the walk-in? The coolers are off-limits to interns."

"Sorry. No one told me."

"What were you doing in there?"

"Getting my dinner." I unzipped my backpack, retrieving a turkey sub wrapped in plastic and a can of soda. I opened it wide so she could see my school binder and laptop, along with the vinyl bottom of the backpack—the three pouches of stem cells hidden beneath the false interior liner.

"You're lucky Dr. Becker didn't catch you. There's a refrigerator in the staff kitchen, from now on use that."

"I will. Uh, where exactly is the staff kitchen?"

"Exit the lab, turn left, and go to the end of the corridor."

"Thanks." I wheeled past her, sweat beads dripping down my face, despite the cold.

"Hey, Kwan . . . I enjoyed listening to you play. Maybe you could play for me again sometime when Li-ling's not around."

"That would be great. I'm playing in Jesse Gordon's band; maybe you could come to our next Saturday jam session?"

"Okay."

Leaving her to feed the rats, I exited through the anteroom into the corridor, the door sealing shut behind me. I rolled down the empty hallway toward the kitchen, detouring into the men's bathroom.

Pushing my way inside a handicap stall, I pulled out my laptop and checked the security cameras in BSL3-C. Anya was inside the refrigerator, looking around for anything that appeared out of place.

Accessing the stored video, I replayed the time line from where I had entered the walk-in, erasing the minute and thirty-four seconds which showed me rooting through the stem cell inventory. With that section deleted, it now appeared as if I had rolled in and removed my sandwich and soda from a shelf—something I had done before leaving the walk-in. Hopefully, no one would notice the missing minute and a half of video.

Shutting down the laptop, I washed my hands and exited the bathroom. I ate my dinner in the staff kitchen, worked another twenty minutes mindlessly entering data, then took the elevator up to the main floor. I exited past the unmanned security desk and wheeled out to the circular drive where Bill was smoking a cigarette beside the van.

It took fifty minutes to drive back to my grandmother's house. She was already in bed by the time I keyed in. I waited another ten minutes just to be sure, then set to work.

Sun Jung kept a second refrigerator in the garage. Before leaving for school, I had left a small Tupperware bowl of lettuce in the veggie compartment. Opening it now, I removed a handful of salad and hid two of the three stem cell pouches inside the plastic container, burying them beneath lettuce. Then I replaced the bowl and went to my bedroom, locking the door.

Inside my closet, hidden in the pocket of my varsity letterman jacket was a half-full IV bag of saline still attached to an intravenous needle. I had removed it from my arm during the last day of my hospital stay between staff shifts, informing the incoming nurse that I had finished my last bag an hour earlier and no longer needed fluids as I was leaving the next morning. She never bothered to check.

Using one of the empty HGH syringes, I methodically drained needle after needle of the shark stem cells, injecting them into the bag of saline. When I was through, I hid the evidence in the false lining of my Doors backpack. Then I set my CD alarm clock to awaken me an hour earlier than usual.

I pulled myself out of my wheelchair and undressed, my upper body shaking with adrenaline. I rigged the IV bag of saline and stem cells to my bed's overhead bar; then, using an alcohol pad, I sterilized the IV needle and the flesh along my left forearm.

I had spent eleven days in the hospital. The first twenty-four hours were almost unbearable. I was depressed, emotional, and trapped. Trapped in a body that anchored me to a wheelchair. Trapped in a house with a relative who was more caretaker than grandmother.

As the days passed, my thoughts turned to a place I had not visited since the accident . . . suicide. If there was an afterlife, then I welcomed it. If there was a price to pay for taking the easy road out, then I'd do my time in hell . . . anything had to be better than this.

On the seventh day Anya had come to see me, offering me a third option—an option of salvation. If the stem cell therapy worked, I would no longer be held a prisoner to my paralysis. If the HGH failed to prevent the mutation, a few hours of suffering and I'd be dead.

Either way, I'd be free.

I opened and closed my fist, causing my veins to become more pronounced. My heart raced as I slid the needle into the largest blood vessel in my forearm. Reaching up, I adjusted the drip, registering the cool sensation of a foreign fluid entering my bloodstream.

I tossed my T-shirt over the support bar, covering the IV bag just in case Sun Jung entered unannounced. Then I laid my head back on my pillow, anxious to see what card fate would deal me next.

ate had dealt my father a card from the bottom of the deck—
the bottom being the deepest part of the Atlantic Ocean—a
monstrous 497-mile-long gorge which marked the border between
the North American and Caribbean sea plates.

Accessing the crate in several hundred feet of water had been
a moderate challenge; retrieving the same object five miles beneath
the surface was something altogether different. Water pressure
increases at a rate of 14.7 pounds-per-square-inch for every thirty-
three feet of descent—a unit of measure defined as an atmosphere.
Unlike fish, mammals and submarines have air cavities, rendering
them vulnerable to the effects of water pressure. A scuba diver
equipped with the right combination of gases can descend to three
hundred feet—beyond that, the pressure squeezing inward on his
lungs and nasal cavity would be lethal.

Water pressure constricts equally around an air cavity. A diver
enclosed in a JIM suit can venture as deep as 1,968 feet, while attack
subs like the USS *Philadelphia* could barely descend beyond half
that depth due to the oblong configuration of their hulls. The *Alvin*
submersible, designed to explore the deep, is essentially a bathy-
scaphe—a round hull surrounded by a motorized chassis. While the
Alvin can reach depths of 13,000 feet or more, a vessel lacking an air

cavity, like the remotely operated tethered vehicle *Jason*, can descend even farther to 19,600 feet.

The Puerto Rico Trench plunged to a depth of 28,373 feet, exerting more than 12,600 pounds-per-square-inch of water pressure. The five-mile mark had only been achieved by a handful of piloted vessels, the last being movie producer James Cameron's *Deep Sea Challenger*, which had reached the bottom of the Mariana Trench—the deepest location on the planet—seven miles below the surface of the western Pacific.

My father was running a black ops mission—he was in no position to commission a privately owned sub, let alone one belonging to a public figure. His only option was to procure *Nereus*, a remotely operated hybrid untethered vehicle, developed by the Woods Hole Oceanographic Institute to explore the planet's deep-sea trenches.

While an elixir of shark stem cells were seeping through my body, my father was en route to Washington, DC, aboard a private jet, owned and operated by Mr. Nicholas Byron, an oil executive with British Petroleum. The Admiral needed Byron to act as his front man in order to rent the *Nereus* without drawing attention to Operation Strawman. Byron would contact Woods Hole, claiming his company had located a deep water drill site and required the use of a deep-sea underwater vessel to map out the ocean floor. For his role as an intermediary, the oil exec would receive half a million dollars in cash—half the sum Sabeen Tayfour had saved the Admiral when the teenager had murdered the two salvage divers.

My father considered the American commandos loose ends. While he needed their skills to locate the *Philadelphia* and salvage the missing package, he feared the former Navy SEALs might talk once they learned the identity of the downed submarine. Sabeen's orders had been simple—kill the divers after they had recovered the package, then send the ship's remains to the bottom of the trench.

The Syrian freedom fighter's failure to retrieve the Iranian crate had jeopardized the entire mission, forcing my father to make other arrangements. As far as the Admiral was concerned, Sabeen owed him. The intoxicating beauty would have to make it up to him when he returned to the ship.

The private jet touched down in Washington at 7:25 a.m. Two hours later, Nicholas Byron had secured the delivery and rental of one of Woods Hole's two operational *Nereus* subs. One problem—the next available vessel was being used in Guam and would not be free for at least two weeks.

Admiral Wilson was not a happy camper.

Having dealt with one "fire," my father left the private jet, exited the hangar, and climbed in the back of an awaiting limousine to deal with the next challenge at hand.

Barbara Becker had flown to DC to procure far more than half a million dollars in funding. After years of intensive research, the ANGEL director believed she had finally resolved the genetics version of a perpetually mutating Rubik's cube. Before she committed to entering the next phase of her cancer protocol—human trials—she needed capital.

Admiral Wilson stared down the sharp-tongued academic seated across from him in the back of his limo. "You're asking for a lot of money, Barbara."

Dr. Becker removed a three-page report from her briefcase and handed it to my father. "Genetics is expensive, Douglas. Preparing thousands of doses of an anticancer vaccine—assuming we now have it, is an even more expensive process."

The Admiral glanced at her report. "I need to know how effective this vaccine will be on a surviving populace caught in a nuclear gray zone. How quickly can these stem cells neutralize lethal doses of radiation?"

"That's the reason we're using sharks, Doug. Their stem cells mobilize and mutate faster than any other donor subject we've tested. You need that when dealing with the survivors of a nuclear explosion."

"I need a timetable."

"How many doses of vaccine are we talking about?"

"Upwards of half a million."

Dr. Becker swallowed hard. *Was the Admiral planning an invasion?* "That's a lot of vaccine. Even with an expanded staff—eighteen months at best. That's assuming you can ram the study through the Institutional Review Board."

"Forget the IRB. We don't need their approval on this one."

Jesus, what have I gotten myself into? "Admiral, with all due respect, I can't begin human clinical trials for a cancer cure without IRB approval."

"The Defense Department overrides the Review Board. I need vaccines ready inside of thirty days."

Becker smiled. "Thirty days? Douglas, this isn't Tylenol we're mass-producing. It's an immune system booster using live shark stem cells—stem cells generated by *real* sharks. I'd need to hire local fishermen to net at least fifty more bull sharks—where do I put them? I'd need new tanks . . . filtration systems. I'd have to hire six more marine biologists just to administer the white cell stimulant."

"Barbara—"

"Plus I'd need cold storage units and a dozen new apheresis machines—the list is endless."

The Admiral gripped her arm. "We're not bombing another country. Intel intercepted messages about a possible nuclear attack on US soil—a suitcase nuke, packing roughly fifteen kilotons. About the yield of Hiroshima."

The blood drained from Dr. Becker's face. "On American soil? Where?"

"A major city, that's all we know. That and the fact that the uranium was produced from an Iranian nuclear reactor."

"Sons of bitches."

"Thirty days, Barbara. Every vial of vaccine saves a life."

"Don't put this on me, Admiral. You knew 9/11 was coming and you let that happen. Why don't you and the rest of the assholes in the Pentagon do your jobs this time around and save them all?"

The limo stopped, the driver having arrived at Dr. Becker's hotel.

"We're doing our best, Dr. Becker. You do yours. Generate as much of the vaccine as you can. The funds will be wired into your account later this afternoon."

"Yeah, well you can triple that figure and call it an early Christmas present. Maybe I'll even add your son on full-time; we could use his brain."

My father reached out and grabbed her by the arm, pulling her back inside the limo. "What about my son?"

"Kwan was selected as an intern; we have him doing data entry. You didn't know?"

"We don't speak."

"Well, maybe you should. He's a smart kid. One day that vaccine you're funding may just help him to walk again."

"No! Nothing for Kwan. No vaccine . . . no internship."

"Why the hell not?"

"For starters, he's not to be trusted. Check your firewall—he's probably already hacked into your computer files."

"Come on, Admiral—"

"This is nonnegotiable, Barbara. I know my son. I want him off the project."

15

"*You know the day destroys the night—night divides the day. Tried to run—tried to hide . . . Break on through to the other side.*"

I reached over to the CD alarm clock and shut Jim Morrison off midverse. My bedroom was dark, save for the glow of my cell phone mounted on its charger. Reaching up, I removed my T-shirt from the bedframe's support bar, exposing the IV bag.

Empty! The shark stem cells were in me . . . but did I feel any different?

I tried to move my legs . . . nothing.

Again and again I tried to find a hint of improvement . . . a hip roll . . . a toe wiggle. Sweat broke out over my body as I turned the event into a full-blown workout in bed—and still there wasn't a pulse of movement.

It's only been five hours, asshole. Did you expect to leap out of bed doing the Macarena? Hide the evidence and continue with the second dose tonight.

I undid the empty IV bag from the crossbar, then slid the needle out of my vein, drawing blood. Using my T-shirt, I applied pressure to the wounded vessel, which I knew would bruise over the next few days.

That was a potential problem.

Making a mental note to wear long-sleeved shirts, I hid the IV bag and needle inside the false bottom of my Doors backpack, reset my alarm for six o'clock, and went back to sleep.

I made it through to fifth period lunch. There were still no physical changes to my lower body. Wheeling over to an empty table, I started to eat when I saw Principal Lockhart enter the cafeteria. He looked around, saw me, and walked swiftly toward me with purpose in his step.

"Kwan. I just got off the phone with Dr. Becker—did something happen at the lab?"

My heart rate jumped. "At the lab? Why? What did she say?"

"She said something came up and she had to cancel your internship."

I felt lightheaded . . . scared. *Should I confess? Would they arrest me?*

"Kwan, are you okay?"

"I really liked it there. I just wanted to help . . . you know—to find a cure. Did she say why she was kicking me out?"

"She couldn't talk. She was in a rush to catch a flight out of DC."

She must've met with the feds. The FBI will probably be waiting at your door. You gotta get those two stem cell pouches and inject them before they do a search and seizure.

"Sir, I'm not feeling well."

"You look a little pale."

"I think I need to go home and rest."

"I'll call your grandmother—"

"No, it's okay. She's on a twelve-hour shift. I'll call my driver; it'll be fine."

Bill picked me up in front of the school half an hour later. On the way home, I asked him to stop at a pharmacy—that I needed a bottle of saline solution to cleanse a wound.

The "genius" exited Walgreens with my change and a bottle of hydrogen peroxide.

"Bill, I need saline, it comes in a pint bottle. This stuff is too harsh."

He got the order right two trips later.

There were no squad cars at the house, no federal marshals or members of the SWAT team. I keyed in and waited another twenty minutes for the big drug bust but no one came.

Decision time. I had two pouches of stem cells, a vial of HGH, and enough saline to fill an IV bag. I could mix everything into one big, juicy, dangerous cocktail, or feed it into my system every few days.

Asshole, you don't have a few days. By tonight, Becker and a dozen deputies will be slapping on the cuffs while they search the house. You either inject it now or dump it in the toilet and burn the pouches—otherwise, come morning, you'll be pleading your case in front of a judge.

Paranoia is a tough foxhole from which to assess your options. Fortunately, I had already considered all of mine back in the hospital.

It was four thirty in the afternoon by the time I had prepared the IV bag, burned the empty stem cell pouches on my grandmother's outdoor grill, and sterilized the needle for insertion into a fresh vein.

My hand shook as I pierced my skin. I watched my blood curl up the IV line—coaxing the clear elixir to open up and flood it back inside my vein. And then I grew scared.

Maybe I should wait a week? Given my cells a chance to acclimate. I still hadn't started the flow—it wasn't too late. Was there a place in the refrigerator I could stow the IV bag?

Despite all the indignities of paralysis . . . despite drowning in a sea of guilt over my mother's death, I realized I didn't want to die.

Lying in bed with the needle in my vein, I thought about my mother. *Would she approve of the risks I was about to take?* I remembered a lecture she had given me when I was eight or nine years old . . . a lecture about right and wrong after she caught me stealing a candy bar from a convenience store shelf.

"Kwan, all of us have voices in our head. One voice is your conscience . . . it's a voice that tells us we are about to do something wrong. Then

there's another voice—a louder, more confident voice—a voice that tells
you exactly what you want to hear instead of what you need to hear. It's
a voice that knows you intimately—it knows which buttons to push and
what words to say to get you to do something bad."

"But how do I know the difference?"

She tapped me on the chest. "Your heart knows."

What was my heart telling me now?

It was telling me that my coming to Seacrest High . . . meeting
Anya . . . interning at the lab as well as every event that led me to be
lying in bed with this elixir poised to enter my vein—none of it was
a coincidence . . . it was fate.

Rachel Solomon had told me I could only cleanse my soul by
helping others. Well, wasn't this helping others? By proving Becker's
serum worked, I would be accelerating a medical breakthrough that
could change the lives of millions of suffering human beings.

Kwan Wilson . . . hero.

Reaching up, I opened the IV bag and adjusted the drip drip
drip. Then I turned on my CD player and closed my eyes.

"Break on through to the other side. Break on through to the other
side . . ."

I was floating, drifting in an island of muted, painless calm—while
below the paramedics worked on my body, which appeared broken
and cumbersome . . . and lifeless. Sun Jung was shaking her head,
clucking like an animated chicken, and Dr. Beverly Chertok—the
one who had found me—was giving a statement to a police officer
in another room.

I had forgotten the shrink was coming to see me.

None of this bothered me in the least as I floated past the circling red and blue lights, beyond the night into the day—only not
day, just light . . . warm and loving like a mother's embrace—which
is exactly what it was.

My mother's soul was cradling me, washing away all the hurt,
all the pain, all the toxins and mud and chains that bound me to life
like a lead casing. Time did not exist. Ego had been flushed with

my passing as I bathed in a sea of love . . . break on through to the other side.

You cannot stay, Kwan. You have to go back.

Mother, why?

It's not your time.

Am I still being punished?

The Creator does not punish. I left because it was my time.

I don't want to go. I don't want to leave you.

We were never separated. Every soul remains bound through eternity . . . every act intended to help us reach fulfillment.

And then she let me go . . . and I fell back into my prison cell.

Comatose, I somehow remember hearing Sun Jung confront the Colombian doctor as if he had been reading from the wrong medical chart. "My grandson's been lying in a coma for four days, and now you're telling me his legs are working? What the hell you talking about?"

Dr. Xavier Prettelt attempted to calm my grandmother, who kept smacking my still-detached body—her words piercing my consciousness which remained semilost in the ether. "I didn't say his legs were working, Sun Jung. What I said was that his leg muscles are receiving nerve impulses, and that's what's causing the severe spasms in his lower extremities. I've had two neurologists examine him and both specialists concurred with that diagnosis. There's simply no precedent for this—then again, we still have no clue what was in that empty IV bag that caused his white cell count to rocket so high. We've managed to drop his fever, but until your grandson regains consciousness his condition remains a mystery."

It was pain that forced me awake. Imagine a thousand needles stabbing bone-deep in your feet, legs, and butt while your skin itched and burned so badly that it felt like you had stepped in a nest of fire ants. I cried out in my delirium, only there was a tube down my throat which muffled the sound. When I reached up to rip the damn thing out, I discovered my wrists were bound to the rails of the bed.

I don't remember any of this, or what happened next. I only know now because the doctor showed me the evidence of my violent awakening, hours later, after my soul had fully returned to my body.

"You bit clear through the intubation tube." Dr. Prettelt handed me the ten-inch-long plastic tube that had been inserted into my trachea to help me breathe. Sure enough, the last two inches had been crushed and punctured, as if by a steak knife. "I don't know how you did that—it looks like something my German shepherd does to his Frisbee. I also don't know how you managed to snap the leather wrist straps from your bedrail."

"Guess they were loose." I shot him a cocky half grin as I flopped my legs beneath the bedsheets. Waking up to find my lower limbs dancing was like waking up on Christmas morning with the Admiral stationed overseas. Then the pain hit. It felt as if my lower body had been frozen for eight months and was experiencing a slow, painful thaw. Fortunately the queen arrived to ease my agony, allowing me to figure out if I could move my legs myself. Unfortunately the muscles were too weak, but after a few hours of practice I found I could roll my feet and slightly bend my knees—the movement like a supersized epic orgasm.

"I'm starving, Doc. When can I get some real food?"

"I ordered lunch. Are you still in pain?"

"It's tolerable." I glanced to the IV bag on my right where my old pal, Dilaudid, was dripping its warm blanket into my veins.

Sun Jung squeezed my wrist, her eyes rimmed red with exhaustion. "What was in the IV bag, Kwan? The other IV bag."

"Like I told the doc, saline and HGH. At least the guy who sold it to me said it was HGH. Is that what healed my spinal cord?"

"We don't know what caused your spinal cord to heal," Dr. Prettelt replied. "Before we christen this a miracle, we need to assess the extent of the repair, whether it's permanent, or if your leg muscles will ever regain enough strength to allow you to walk again."

"Why would you give yourself an IV?" my grandmother asked for the third time, growing more annoyed.

STEVE ALTEN   95

"I told you, the guy who sold me the HGH said it would work better as a drip."

"Why you buying HGH? Since when are you allowed to self-medicate?"

"I wanted to get stronger. I'm sorry, Sun Jung, what I did was stupid. But if by some miracle it helped heal my spinal cord . . . ?"

Lunch arrived—three pieces of greasy baked chicken, french fries, and chocolate cake for dessert. I was so hungry I asked for a second helping of everything.

After lunch, Dr. Prettelt removed my catheter and gave me a urine bottle—a trial run to see if I had regained control of my bladder . . . and more important, my little fella. I could squeeze the muscles constricting my groin, but the area still felt numb.

Later that afternoon a physical therapist by the name of Gary Blackwell came by to see me. With me lying on my back, Gary manipulated my legs while I attempted to offer resistance. The pain was excruciating—it felt as if someone were lashing my lower back with a whip, and it took all of my willpower just to hold my trembling legs up to his chest.

I endured the torture for an hour. After twenty minutes of ice packs on my spine, I was taken downstairs for three hours of isolation in my old oxygen bunker. That was followed by dinner and another visit from the therapist, who massaged my cramping leg muscles, which were twitching and throbbing so badly that I wondered if I had made a huge mistake.

What if I never regain control? What if my legs become so annoying that I'm forced to have them amputated just for a moment's peace?

A shot of Queen Dilaudid put me out until three fifteen in the morning.

When I awoke, everything felt different.

The first thing I noticed was that I could feel my penis and the fullness of my bladder, which I joyfully relieved into the urine bottle. After I peed, I realized the pain in my legs was gone. Pulling away the sheet, I stared at my bare feet and wiggled my toes. Encouraged, I brought my right leg up to my chest, held it, then lowered it to the bed—a movement I was unable to complete hours earlier without my therapist's help. Adrenaline coursed through my body as I repeated the exercise with my left leg, alternating three sets of fifty reps.

My limbs were responding, but they needed more.

Quietly, I dropped the rail of my bed, then rolled my legs to the side and positioned my bare feet to the cold tile floor. Gripping the rail with one hand, my IV stand with the other, I shifted my weight onto my wobbling legs . . . and stood—then cried out as I tumbled sideways onto the mattress, tearing the IV from my hand.

The old man sleeping in the next bed over continued snoring through the disturbance.

It took me several minutes to stop my torn vein from bleeding. At some point, I looked toward my roommate and spotted the old man's walker.

Using the furniture as crutches, I made my way over to the four-legged aluminum device and stood once more, this time allowing the walker to bear most of my weight and balance. One step followed the next, until I was standing/leaning outside my room in the empty corridor.

I turned left to bypass the nurses' station and continued placing one foot after the other as I leaned on the walker, gradually allowing my legs to bear more and more weight. Each baby step was a tutorial for my brain as I relearned how to shift my weight and balance. I'd count twelve steps and pause, then attempt to stand as long as I could on both feet.

I was back in training, lost in the world of reps and sets . . . in essence, I was *me* again! The fact that I had brought myself to this place by facing my fears stoked my ego even more.

After about an hour, my quaking legs began to regain some coordination. With coordination came muscle memory, and with muscle memory came strength through repetition.

Repetition? Using that walker, I made my way from the west wing to the east and back again six times. I must have trekked two miles before I returned to my room just before the seven a.m. shift change. Climbing back into bed, I rang for the day nurse, who redid my IV and gave me a shot for the pain. By now, my muscles were quivering as if I had run a marathon.

I slept through breakfast. When I awoke, my therapist was standing over me, along with Dr. Prettelt, the nurse, Sun Jung, and three other physicians—everyone staring at my legs.

"What's wrong?" I sat up, my heart racing.

Sun Jung shook her head. "What did you do to yourself? Your legs . . . they no longer scrawny—you understand my English?"

I looked down. Somehow in the span of four hours my quads, hamstrings, and calf muscles had literally doubled in size.

"Lower the rail on my bed, I want to stand!"

The nurse complied. Swinging my legs around to the side, I stood on leg muscles as secure and balanced as the Rock of Gibraltar.

Gripping my IV bag, I walked across the room to the corridor. And then I jogged past the nurses' station and sprinted back, leaving my grandmother giggling and the medical staff dumbfounded.

Dr. Prettelt ordered more blood work, along with a battery of neurological tests.

"No," I said, handing the nurse my IV bag. "No more tests. No more drugs. No more hospital stays. Sun Jung, tell them to get my discharge papers ready, I'm going home."

The pain seized me then, as if someone had plunged a hunting knife into my internal organs. I collapsed to my knees, crying out in agony.

I was placed on a gurney and given a shot of Dilaudid, then rushed inside a CAT scan chamber where an arc attached to an X-ray machine passed over my outstretched body.

Sun Jung squeezed my hand as Dr. Prettelt gave me the news.

"It's bad. For some reason your stoma closed. Waste has been backing up into your intestine. We're prepping you for emergency surgery. If we can we'll try to reattach your colon."

A dozen thoughts rambled through my mind as nurses rushed into the room to obtain signatures and attach blood pressure cuffs and EKG electrodes, while an anesthesiologist checked my jaw and teeth. *Had the HGH injections failed? Were my internal organs changing?*

Was I turning into a bull shark?

At some point he injected a liquid into my IV. The queen took over and *blah, blah, blah, blah* . . .

17

The infusion of shark stem cells into my bloodstream had set my immune system into overdrive. Anything considered a threat was annihilated; any abnormal function attracted my genetically enhanced stem cells like engineering bees to a leaking dam of honey.

That's what happened with my colon. My jacked-up stem cells interpreted my stoma as a tear and sealed it up. Fortunately, my surgeon was able to reconnect my colon—an unexpected happy ending to an emergency that nearly killed me. Four hours after being wheeled into the operating room I woke up, groggy, medicated, and no longer needing a colostomy bag. In every physical sense, I had been granted a "do-over."

What I didn't know was that the aggressive concoction of stem cells and HGH that had healed my spinal cord was far from satisfied with the original genetic design of its host.

Take my previously mentioned ability to heal. Reversing a colostomy leaves a deep wound in place of the stoma—a hole which usually takes two to three months to close. To my surgeon's amazement, the hole in my belly filled in sixteen hours! This wasn't just a record; this was impossible—at least for humans.

Don't even go there, I told myself. After all, sharks don't heal like this either. But clearly something was happening to me that was more than a bit unnerving. And it was attracting lots of attention.

The hospital administrator came to visit me a day after my surgery, accompanied by a cute thirtyish brunette in a sexy business skirt. Annie Moir owned a public relations firm in Boca Raton; the hospital had hired her to issue a press release about the "local paraplegic whose spinal cord had been healed at Bethesda Memorial Hospital." Annie needed permission to use my name, since I was technically a minor.

"I don't know, Annie. I sort of figured I would keep this on the down low."

"Kwan, a week ago you were bound to a wheelchair; two days ago you were doing wind sprints up and down the hall. Trust me, the word's out. The hospital's already fielding hundreds of interview requests, including producers at *60 Minutes, The Today Show*, and *David Letterman*. You need someone to control the media circus, sweetie. Hire me to be your manager."

Normally my ego would be supersized, but after all that had happened, I felt wiped out. "Sorry, Annie, but Sun Jung's already struggling to support us on her limited income. I seriously doubt she could afford you."

Annie smiled. "Kwan, sweetie, you don't pay a manager. A manager works on commission. Standard in the entertainment industry is fifteen percent."

"Wait . . . are you saying I can make money from this?"

"Are you kidding? Kwan, you're a walking miracle. Who wouldn't want to eat the breakfast cereal you eat; wear the track shoes you wear? Sweetie, if you're not a millionaire in six months, go ahead and fire me, because I didn't do my job."

Millionaire? Screw the emo shit . . . You only live once!

I smiled from ear to ear. "Do it. Make me rich and famous."

Turns out Annie already had a plan. The hospital would discharge me on Tuesday—the best day of the week for media exposure. We'd do a press conference in the hospital cafeteria with all my doctors and the administrator present to answer questions. Then we'd fly to New York to do either *Today* or *Good Morning America* on Wednesday, then *Letterman* that evening. I would be bigger than Psy—another Korean phenom, only better since I was half-

Caucasian and a hundred percent American, making me far more endorsement friendly than "Mr. Gangnam Style."

Kwan Wilson: Celebrity millionaire.

"Annie, what about school?"

"You'll be tutored. Better yet, why not just take your GED test now. Use this next year to help your family and—"

"No. The money sounds great, but I want to go back to Seacrest High. I want to play basketball for the varsity, earn a college scholarship."

"Sweetie, last week you couldn't walk, now you want to play for the school team? I mean, it's a great story, but maybe you need to let your body get a bit stronger first—the last thing we need is another emergency surgery . . . oh my, what are you doing?"

She backed away as I continued pressing my palms against the aluminum rails of my bed until the support screws popped and the metal bent in half.

"I feel pretty strong right now."

Annie's eyes lit up. "Outrageous. You have got to do that for *60 Minutes*."

And so it went—my body growing stronger every day, my ego keeping pace. Three days after surgery, I was pumping iron with a private trainer in the hospital's weight room, my muscles responding as if they were engorged with steroids. The hospital administrator moved me to a private room where teams of specialists could examine me by day while allowing me to rest at night. Of course, I really didn't need to be there, but Annie insisted I remain a patient until Tuesday morning's big press conference. She also decided it was better I return to school the following day—that way she could use the announcement to set up endorsement meetings in New York the following week when I was scheduled to do the *Today Show* and *Letterman*. "Trust me, sweetie, by next week, the name Kwan Wilson will be trending at the top of the A list."

Annie wanted Principal Lockhart to schedule a special assembly on Wednesday for my triumphant return to high school, but I shut that idea down in a hurry. It was more important that I remain a regular guy at Seacrest High—part of the student body.

Kwan Wilson: Regular Guy . . . *yeah, right.*

That inner voice of mine was blowing so much smoke up my ass it must have been seeping out of my colostomy scar.

The Tuesday morning press conference in the hospital cafeteria was mind-blowing. There must have been fifty news vans in the parking lot with several hundred reporters crowded around a makeshift dais. The hospital administrator gave a brief synopsis of what had transpired, purposely skipping any details about the IV bag and HGH injections, sticking to the agreed upon statement, "We're still analyzing blood and tissue samples in the hopes that we can replicate this miracle and provide it to other paraplegic and quadriplegic patients around the world."

Dr. Prettelt was next. He spoke in medical jargon about what had happened over the last week, gave a shout out to my grandmother, "a valued member of our nursing staff," then he introduced yours truly to the world.

I stepped to the dais and read from a prepared statement, which included a brief mention that my injury had occurred while I was driving my mother to work and that she had died with me at the wheel. "No miracle can ever bring her back, but I know she played a part in my healing." Then I jogged in place and performed a dozen jumping jacks before turning the proceedings over to Annie, who introduced herself, explained that a foundation would be set up in my name "to fund the medical means by which we hoped to spread this miracle to others." She thanked everyone for coming as I was ushered out of the room by my keepers, all of us refusing to answer the reporters' questions and their demands for more information.

Sun Jung and I arrived home twenty minutes later. There were already four news vans staked out by the curb. By dinner that number increased tenfold. The story was spreading around the Internet faster than Annie could track it; the video of the press conference surpassing ten million hits.

The circus had indeed come to town and I was its ringmaster, enclosed in a new kind of paralysis.

I was up before the sun bled the night gray, my head too full of thoughts to sleep. Today would be another milestone, one I faced with excitement and dread. Excitement because Anya would be seeing me for the first time as a fully functioning man (if you're wondering if I was functioning fully down below, the answer is yes—although it took a few tries before I could get the "pump" fully primed). I was also excited to have received a phone message from Coach Flaig, inviting me to scrimmage with the varsity.

So what was I afraid of? How about everything. When I decided to risk my life by injecting shark stem cells into my body, my only desire was to be able to walk again or end my misery—nothing about being the google center of the world. Admittedly, the thought of being a celebrity was stroking my ego, but things had quickly gotten out of control. Strangers were blowing up my cell phone with crazy messages, I couldn't step outside my grandmother's home without being bull-rushed, and a few religious zealots were claiming I was the anti-Christ.

To Sun Jung, I was her long-lost grandson returned from the dead. Maybe it was all the attention or the lure of money—maybe it was just me no longer being a burden. Either way, I seemed to have found my way back into my grandmother's heart.

And what about Anya's heart? Now that I was no longer the nonthreatening Asian guy bound to a wheelchair, how would she feel about me? Was I "hook-up potential"? Was there an attraction? Looming over any chance of a relationship was a pending trust issue. Anya wasn't stupid; by now she had to know I had stolen the stem cell pouches when she caught me in the lab refrigerator. *Would she be angry at me?* Who was I kidding; I had lied to her.

And what about Dr. Becker? Would she come forward, claiming credit for my miracle or simply have me locked away? The press conference had most likely saved my ass against the latter, but I knew at some point I'd have to answer for my actions.

While all this was happening, I was fighting to adapt physically and mentally to my body's continuing metamorphosis. It had been almost a year since I had last stood, taken a step, or dressed myself without performing gymnastic maneuvers. Even a seemingly natural act like taking a dump in the toilet felt completely alien to me after having used a colostomy bag for so long. It had taken months of therapy to adjust after the car accident. Now everything was happening so fast; it was disorienting.

Add to that my still-evolving musculature. Paralysis had caused my legs and butt to atrophy—now the shark stem cells seemed to be targeting these weak areas, directing the human growth hormone that was saturating my cells to increase the strength, size, and density of these damaged muscle groups. With each passing day, I was looking more and more like a professional bodybuilder. The problem was that I hadn't worn my new physique long enough to develop any coordination—a necessary skill in shooting a basketball. Having been invited to a tryout with the varsity, I was scared shitless my shots would either fly over the backboard or dent the rim. The last thing I needed was to be putting up cinderblocks during my first team practice—in front of an army of cameras, no less.

There was only one solution: I needed to practice—away from the media.

Keeping the lights off, I fished out a pair of shorts and a T-shirt from a drawer and dressed. It was a surreal feeling to wiggle my toes as I pulled on my socks—but how great was it lacing up my high-tops again—even better than spanking the monkey!

Searching my closet, I found a basketball; only it needed air. Quietly, I left my room and made my way through the hall to the pitch-dark kitchen, feeling my way along the wall to the door leading out to the garage, where I knew I would find the air pump.

Touching the door, I froze. There was someone in the garage—three people! They weren't speaking or uttering a sound, and yet I knew they were in there, in fact I was certain they were sleeping.

How did I know this?

Palms pressed to the door, I could *feel* their beating hearts! Not hear . . . *feel!* Somehow I felt their pulses in my neck and wrists, and in the femoral artery running up into my groin. It was like they were in my blood, beating like three independent timpani drums. Two thudded heavier than the third, who I surmised was female. Of the two men, one heartbeat was strong and slow, the other rapid and irregular, and for some peculiar reason (hell, the entire episode was beyond peculiar) I found myself drawn to Mr. Irregular Pulse like a lion to a wounded wildebeest.

And now something else was happening—I could see! My eyes were adjusting to the darkness, only not in a normal way; this was more like a soldier donning a pair of night vision goggles. Within this gradual illumination of violets and purples, the kitchen sink, stove, and refrigerator appeared to materialize out of the dark ether.

All of these changes were really cool and I probably could have remained there until daybreak, absorbed in this bizarre, adaptive predator dichotomy of the senses, only what I really wanted to do was to find out if I could still play basketball. So very quietly I unbolted the garage door and pushed it open.

A gust of air offered a brief resistance. The lock on the garage window had been pried open, allowing one of the more aggressive news crews access into our home. The two men whose heartbeats were registering within my own bloodstream were asleep on the floor, their equipment defining them as a cameraman and sound man. The woman was blonde and pretty, and she was asleep in a lounge chair—her pulse causing her carotid artery to flutter.

And suddenly there were so many options . . . all disturbingly violent.

I could have ripped that artery out with my teeth and bled her to death. I could have bashed in Mr. Irregular Pulse's skull with his camera, then strangled the sound man with his cords.

How do I describe these bizarre thoughts? In retrospect, they felt more like a physical temptation than a voice in my head—predatory instincts, bordering on lust.

Instead of entertaining these thoughts, I simply swatted them aside. Locating the air pump, I stealthily slipped out the open garage window.

The night was tinged with tobacco smoke and urine, the pungent remains of take-out, and the festering odor of human sweat. My nostrils flared at the potpourri; my suddenly adept sense of smell guiding me around a maze of sleeping bodies and idling vehicles until I was beyond the paparazzi, moving at a pace I couldn't begin to fathom.

The park was closed—*good*. I vaulted the eight-foot fence and found my way to the two asphalt basketball courts. I added air to the ball, dribbled my way to one of the four foul lines, then set myself and hoisted a no-arc shot that thudded off the backboard without coming close to the rim.

I spit in disgust. The basketball player I had left on the San Diego hardwood was gone, replaced by a muscle-bound bricklayer.

Suck it up and go back to basics . . .

When I was twelve, I attended a summer basketball camp visited by Hall of Fame basketball coach Herb Magee, the legendary "Shot Doctor" who piled up wins by the hundreds at Philadelphia University. Coach Magee taught us how to develop "a feel" by shooting two feet from the front of the rim with one hand.

"Snap your wrist and follow through, Kwan, and you'll create backspin on the ball. Make sure you point your second and third fingers at the target. Don't take a step back until you feel the ball entering the hoop. Good! Step back and we add your guide hand. Step back some more and bend your knees, generating power from your legs. Back away another

step and we add a jump. Shoulders square, shooting elbow at ninety degrees. Miss two in a row and take a step in."

It was frustrating; my muscles were tight, refusing to cooperate. But I wouldn't give up, and after about twenty minutes I found a rhythm. By the time the sun came up, I was shooting jump shots from the elbow—the corners of the foul line.

I switched to layups off the dribble and reverted back into Dorkenstein. Again, I had to break things down into simple movements until my brain tapped into my muscle memory and uploaded the information to my new lower body. Twenty minutes later I had my footwork down and was doing reverse layups.

It was getting late—maybe seven o'clock, leaving me little time to shower and change. But before I could leave the court I needed to know one last thing . . . how strong were these new legs of mine?

Leaving the ball by the foul line, I took a running start and jumped for the front of the rim—and smashed into it with my elbows!

I landed from the fifty-three-inch vertical jump, dazed and giddy. Dunking had never been a part of my game. My high school coach who was Jewish used to tease me by saying, "The only thing more grounded than a Jew was a Korean." On my best day I could barely grab the rim with both hands.

But this? This was ridiculous.

Grabbing the ball, I dribbled toward the basket and leaped, easily dunking with two hands. Circling the arc, I drove and elevated again, laying down a vicious one-handed tomahawk. That was followed by a two-handed reverse, a nasty left-handed windmill, and a cock-the-hammer, in-your-face rim rattler. I didn't care about the time. I didn't care about Anya or Dr. Becker or school or appearing on *Letterman* or even being rich and famous. This was heaven, every flush an orgasm, every move as smooth as butter and I couldn't wait to dunk on Stephen Ley in today's scrimmage. With any luck, it would find its way onto *SportsCenter.*

Gonna make you my bitch . . .

Drenched in sweat, I finished my workout with an off-the-backboard, Blake Griffin jaw-breaker, thunder-maker, molar-loosening throw down that ended with a yell into the heavens—probably more Michael Jackson than *Rambo II*.

Grabbing the air pump, I set off for home.

Even with the police escort, I was late to school and had to report to the office. Principal Lockhart saw me at the front desk filling out a late slip and his jaw dropped. Seriously—the dude's chin was just hanging over his bow tie. Rachel Solomon came over and gave me a tearful thirty-second hug.

By the time she pulled away, there were a dozen students aiming iPhones at us.

"Sorry I'm late, Dr. Lockhart. Do I need a note to get into Mr. Hock's class?"

"Mr. Hock? No . . . but I need to see you in my office—damn, you filled out. You're not on steroids, are you?"

"No, sir."

"Because that stuff'll screw you up. You heard of roid rage, right?"

Roid rage? What the hell was he yabbering about? So what if I had contemplated chewing on a woman's carotid artery? I wasn't on steroids.

He led me to his office door, which was closed. "Go on in, I'll be there in a minute."

I entered, the door pulled shut behind me.

Oh, hell . . .

Seated behind Principal Lockhart's desk was Dr. Becker.

19

Are you insane?"

I sat down, readying myself for her lecture. "Lost in a Roman wilderness of pain . . . and all the children are insane."

"Excuse me?"

"It's a line from a Doors' song, about the big sleep, you know—suicide. Maybe I was insane. All I know is that I couldn't handle things anymore; I was either going to walk again or die trying. I'm sorry for stealing the stem cells, but they worked and I'll forever be indebted. Anyway, the good news is I proved the treatment is safe for humans. You could come with me on *The Today Show*. Think of all the money I could help you raise."

"Sit down and shut up." She walked around the desk, a medical bag in her hand. "Listen carefully," she said, preparing a syringe to draw blood, "you're not going on *The Today Show*; you're not going to say anything. When those reporters ask you about your internship at ANGEL, and eventually they will, you'll tell them it was a data entry position, but you left after two days because the trips to Miami were too hard on you. When they ask you about the nature of our work, you'll say you have no idea. Make a fist."

I clenched my left hand, allowing her to swab my forearm with rubbing alcohol. "I don't understand. If I tell everyone that it was your stem cells that repaired my . . . ouch!"

She stuck me with a needle, filling the first of a dozen plastic vials with my blood. "You're still not getting this, are you, Mr. Wilson? Besides being extraordinarily dangerous, what you did can't possibly be repeated. It lacked methodology, oversight, quantified doses, proper testing, and data collection—in short, it was worthless. You also violated FDA and IRB testing protocols, jeopardizing years of hard work and research, and very possibly the hopes of tens of thousands of people suffering from spinal injuries—not to mention millions of cancer patients. All because you were too impatient to wait until we officially began human trials. It was a selfish act that may very well result in your own death."

"What do you mean? I feel fine."

"Sure you do. You went from being a paraplegic to a world-class athlete in a week . . . and this is fine? Whatever concoction of chemicals you injected into your bloodstream has caused your DNA to destabilize and mutate."

"Mutate?" My heart started beating rapidly. "You mean, like those rats with the gills?"

"I don't want to say until I analyze your blood. But you clearly overdosed on the stem cells. What else did you take?"

"Human growth hormone. Three injections. I was also in a hyperbaric chamber prior to the first pouch. Doc, please—"

"Keep your head, control your thoughts. Stress can alter your pH, rendering you more acidic. Mutations prefer an acidic environment. We'll start you on an IV as soon as we get back to the lab, something that will raise your alkalinity."

"I'm not going to the lab. I have to go to class. I'm trying out for the basketball team."

"Out of the question. Your father would have my head on a stake."

"My father? What's he got to do with this?"

Dr. Becker hesitated. "Your father assists us with procuring funds. I happened to mention to him that you were interning at the lab—"

"And he canceled the gig."

"It was for safety reasons. He was afraid you might be tempted to try something dangerous, and he was right."

I shook with rage. "My father doesn't give a damn about me. I haven't seen or spoken to him since I was in the hospital." Tears welled in my eyes, blurring my vision. "And just so we're clear, the only reason the Admiral canceled my internship was because he was afraid your treatment might actually work, undoing my penance for killing my mom."

Dr. Becker looked at me strangely. I don't know what I was expecting . . . compassion, empathy—maybe a tissue. What I wasn't expecting was for this short, wiry scientist to suddenly grab a fistful of my hair from the back of my head in order to draw me nearer so she could stare directly into my eyes, the tips of our noses maybe an inch away.

"What . . . are you doing?"

"Your eyes . . . they just changed." Still gripping my hair, she dragged me over to the desk and grabbed the lamp with her free hand, shining it in my face. "I can't tell if your pupils hyperdilated or your irises just turned black. Now I can't tell anything; they're reflecting so much light I can't see them. How's your vision?"

"Everything's sort of green."

Releasing my hair, she reached around to my right eye with her thumb and index finger, intent on prying the lid open wider.

What happened next happened so fast that I never processed it. One second, Dr. Becker was reaching out to examine my eye—the next, she was lying on the floor behind the principal's desk, her strawberry-blonde hair splayed across her face.

"Doc, are you okay?" She winced as I picked her up and carried her to Lockhart's sofa. "What happened?"

"You don't know?"

"No."

"Your right eye disappeared; it rolled completely back into your skull a millisecond before you clubbed me across the chest with your forearm."

I stared at my arm, the syringe still dangling from my vein, dripping blood everywhere.

She connected an empty vial to the line, then looked into my eyes again. "It's gone. Your pupils are brown again. That's incredible."

"I don't understand. What just happened?"

"You were crying. The saltwater served as a catalyst, causing the cells in your eyes to react."

"React how?"

"I don't know. It may have been nothing. Let me analyze your blood and—"

"React like a shark? Is that what you mean?"

"Kwan, listen to me: Human DNA is composed of approximately twenty-four thousand genes. Of these, only eighteen genes have been found to be unique among humans. Eighteen out of twenty-four thousand. The rest are shared with other species or consist of old genes we picked up on the evolutionary trail. These older genes are what feed mutations. In addition, there are long stretches of noncoding or junk DNA that don't seem to contribute to the production of proteins, yet may play an essential role in our genetic workings.

"Injecting stem cells from another species into the human genome is a double-edged sword. The good news is that shark stem cells aggressively attack mutating cancer cells and rapidly effect repairs to other nonmutating cells. The bad news is, the shark stem cells seek out weakness in the genome and convert these old genes into something resembling its own kind. The challenge, therefore, is to allow the stem cells to kill the mutating cancer cells, or in your case to heal your severed spinal cord, while making sure we prevent the stem cells from altering the genetic recipe that makes us human. In essence, you introduced a schizophrenic onto the DNA bus—one that has the ability to convert the other passengers to his particular set of character traits. As long as he allows the human genes to drive the bus, we don't care who else is on board."

"What happened to my eyes?"

"Have you ever seen a chameleon's skin change color after it's been placed on a leaf? For a brief second, your tears elicited a similar change, only it happened even faster—sort of like flipping a light switch. The fact that your eyes reverted back to normal so quickly is a good sign; it means the switch prefers to remain in its natural human Up position. In terms of our metaphor, you hit a speed bump but you're still driving the bus. What I need to do is to analyze your DNA and introduce protein inhibitors into your bloodstream that will keep these mutating shark stem cells away from the eighteen key human genes."

She finished filling the last vial with my blood, retracted the needle, and applied a Band-Aid to my punctured vein. Maybe it was the ease at which I had launched her across the room, or maybe she just realized I was flying too high above the celebrity radar to control, but Dr. Becker suddenly had a change of heart.

"Tell you what, Kwan, why don't you go back to class while I run the tests. I'll prepare an IV, then have Anya deliver it to you tonight at your home. That way you can still try out for the basketball team."

"Thank you."

I entered Mr. Hock's science class thirty minutes late—to a round of applause. Embarrassed, I found an empty seat and took out my notebook as iPhones snapped my photo and the girl sitting next to me with the long, dark curled locks of hair squeezed my right quad.

"Ew, nice. I'm Shaniqua."

"Kwan." I glanced to my left to see Anya staring at me with those penetrating bright blue eyes.

Mr. Hock banged on his desk for quiet. "Wheelchair or no wheelchair, Mr. Wilson, you seem to have a knack for disrupting my class. We're on page two-thirty-one, review question six. Mike Tvrdik?"

"Yes?"

"Answer the question."

"Which question?"

"God help me . . . Page two-thirty-one, review question six."

Stephen Ley nudged my leg, passing me a note. The chicken scratch indicated Ley's brother wanted me to tell the world that I had bought my "miracle HGH" from the medical practice where he worked. In exchange for the endorsement I'd receive a month's worth of human growth hormone.

The bell rang, ending class. I hurried outside to wait for Anya, only to be swarmed by a growing crowd of students.

"Anya—wait!" I pushed through the wall of bodies, my legs pumping hard to keep up with her. "I missed you."

"Shut up."

"Are you mad at me?"

"Did those muscles make you stupid?"

"Please don't be mad."

"You think I don't know what you did? I trusted you, Kwan. I trusted you with a secret and you burned me." She walked faster, forging her way through a river of students rushing to get to their second period class.

In two strides I was ahead of her, cutting her off. "Anya, wait."

"Kwan, leave me alone."

"Fine, but you need to know something. Back in the hospital, you saved my life. I know you don't trust me, but trust me—I'd be dead right now if it wasn't for you. You gave me a reason to live, Anya, and I love you for that. I'm serious."

It was a ballsy play, but I meant every word of it. Anya's blue eyes glistened with tears and she would have kissed me right there had a hundred iPhones not been pointing at us. Instead, she leaned in and whispered in my ear, "Fifth period. Meet me backstage in the auditorium."

She pushed through the crowd and was gone.

Time slows when you're watching the clock, when you're counting the minutes until that next great epic moment. Anya had become my addiction, and with all addictions there are times when you're in seventh heaven and times when everything just hurts. You're either high or low, but you're always thinking about that next great epic moment, forsaking everything else.

When fourth period ended, I was the first person out the door. Descending the stairwell two steps at a time, I managed to avoid the convergence of zombies rushing up from the first floor, making it out to the courtyard before the first "Kwan!" registered in my brain. Avoiding teachers and students, I ducked into the auditorium and reveled in its privacy.

And then I heard the guitar riff.

I followed the sound, which led me backstage to the music room. Seated on the floor, his guitar resting on his lap was Jesse Gordon.

It had been two weeks ago since we had jammed together; two weeks since I had injected myself with predatory stem cells and ended up back in the hospital.

I approached Jesse, who never looked up from playing. It was an old Stones song we had tried together but had stopped because he needed to learn the chords.

While I was learning to walk again, he had learned the song.

Recognizing the second verse, I sang, "... *gonna find my way to heaven 'cause I did my time in hell—wasn't looking too good but I was feeling real well.*"

We sang the chorus together in a wailing harmony that would have made Keith Richards proud. "*After all is said and done, I gotta move—I had my fun. Better walk before they make me run.*"

He stopped playing. "Your voice sounds sick. More confident."

"Better lung capacity. Sorry I missed the last practice."

"You promised to stay out of the hospital."

"Two weeks in bed to walk again . . . I'll take it."

"Have you seen Ley's Facebook page? He claims his brother cured you with HGH."

"You believe that?"

"I'm smarter than a fifth grader, Kwan. I know it wasn't the HGH, but it was something with a serious kick, which means you can bet your ass everyone's gonna want it. Which means you won't be singing with us anytime soon."

"Why not?"

"Dude, I worked at ANGEL last summer. I didn't have the kind of access you probably had, but I spent many a long afternoon getting high with the shark wranglers. Do you know who funds Becker's lab? It's DARPA, as in the Defense Advanced Research Projects Agency. You seriously think the psychopaths at the DoD are gonna allow you to go on *Letterman*? And I know Anya has you whipped, but did you ever google her old man?"

"Yeah? So what?"

"So what? Dude, the guy worked at the CFR and is a member of the Trilateral Commission. Patel's New World Order."

"Right. And he's teaching at FAU to do what? Take over Boca? I met Professor Patel, he happens to be a nice guy. So tuck your conspiracy theory string away."

"Fine, make me out to be the *frenemy*. But at least take my advice as a fellow musician. Walk now before they make you run. Disappear before they disappear you."

Was I disturbed by Jesse Gordon's warning? Not really. Jesse had a rep for being paranoid, and Professor Patel was a million miles from being a New World Order fanatic.

My father, on the other hand . . .

Anya was waiting for me backstage. After making sure we were the only ones around, she led me down a short corridor to a dressing room. Dragging me inside, she locked the door.

Before I could say a word, she hugged me. It started off like an "I missed you" hug that melted into a slow dance embrace.

How good did it feel to be standing and hugging this beautiful girl?

Better than a two-hand jam.

We rocked together, our legs entwined, and it was as if time no longer existed. At some point she looked up and kissed me. Lips . . . so soft . . . her tongue exploring my mouth, her right hand snaking its way past my left ear until her fingers twirled my hair, massaging the back of my skull—still sore from Dr. Becker's abuse.

And then, abruptly, she pried herself free. "Oh God, I can't do this."

Can't do what? What was she saying? Why was she pouring gasoline on the best moment of my life and apologizing by lighting a match?

"Anya, what's wrong?"

"Li-ling was right. I should have never visited you in the hospital; I don't know what I was thinking. I've been through this . . . I can't do it again. I worked so hard at the lab . . . at school. I'm not going to jeopardize my future because you had to be so damn impatient."

Impatient? She's the one who asked me to meet her backstage!

Dumbass. She's not Americanized. You're moving too fast for her. Show her your sensitive side. Tell her how you feel before she walks out that door.

"Anya . . . I love you."

"You love me? You love me! You don't get to love me. Not now, not ever. I'm not going down that path with you. This time I get to choose. This time I get to be the selfish one. So do me a solid and don't talk to me anymore. Don't text me. Don't even look at me. Just live out your life. Live it without me."

Pushing past me, she unlocked the door and darted down the hallway.

I just stood there, dumbfounded, still swooning from our shared embrace and the most amazing kiss of my life . . . and now the sudden sensation of her cold hand as she ripped out my heart and showed it to me like some ancient Mayan priest. I felt like a doe-eyed baby seal that gets lured onto land by the coos of a hunter, only to be clubbed over the head. The seal was dead, but I was in physical pain. My heart actually hurt. My insides felt twisted.

Had I misread her signals? Was this a head game? A religious thing? Did my breath stink?

I could still smell her perfume on my shirt; I could still taste her tongue . . . the impression of her lips on mine. I wanted her so, so badly—*what had I done wrong?*

I imagined Jim Morrison laughing at me. Just like his song, I had loved her madly . . . as she walked right out the door.

The bell rang, announcing the end of fifth period. Lunch was over, and I had been the main course. Mentally wiped out, a physical and emo wreck—there was no way I was going to sixth period trig.

Anya's friends with Li-ling. Li-ling has sixth period lunch. Go find her. Let her know you're confused.

I turned to face the dressing mirror, a mess. I washed my face in the water fountain, then ran my wet fingers through my hair like a comb. As I straightened my shirt collar, I noticed something in my hand.

It was a clump of hair.

Panic-stricken, I reached for the back of my head, my fingers probing the area Anya had caressed—now a bald spot the size of an orange.

That's why she stopped herself. She realized the HGH wasn't strong enough to counteract the mutation.

"I'm dying."

Rachel Solomon was on the phone when I knocked on the window of her open door. She waved me inside, motioning for me to sit.

I dropped my backpack on the floor and slumped in a chair, waiting for her to finish the call. On her desk was a glass of water. Suspended above the glass by toothpicks was an avocado seed, its lower half under water. Flowing out of the bottom of the seed were roots.

Rachel hung up the phone. "Pretty impressive, huh? From that tiny seed you scooped out of an avocado last month grows a new tree." Her hazel eyes swept over my face. "Close the door and tell me what happened."

I pushed the door shut, averting her penetrating gaze. "It's hard to explain. Everything's happening so fast. My recovery . . . the media."

"You didn't come here to deliver a State of the Union. Something upset you. Speak."

"Anya dumped me."

"Anya Patel? I didn't realize the two of you were an item."

"For about ten minutes."

"Okay, you got your heart stepped on, but that's still not what's bugging you. You seem scared. What's wrong?"

She was too perceptive, too much like my mother. *Maybe this was a mistake . . .*

"The marine lab in Miami . . . Kwan, did you ingest something that repaired your spinal cord and made you so muscular?"

I looked up, a bit stunned. "Are you psychic?"

"A little. But it doesn't take a psychic to figure out cause and effect. What did Becker give you?"

"It's experimental. I can't really talk about it. They're testing it on rats. And she didn't give it to me. I stole it."

"Kwan, why would you do something like that?"

Her voice was filled with concern, lacking all judgment. I swallowed the lump in my throat. "I knew it would either heal me or kill me. At the time, either option was better than going on."

She walked around the desk to sit next to me. "Here's a third option—talk to me. I'll give you the number of my cell phone, call me anytime. Okay?"

I nodded, gritting my teeth to prevent from tearing up.

"You weren't scared when I saw you this morning. What's happened since then?"

"My hair's falling out. It's one of the early symptoms the rats experienced before they . . . before they died."

Rachel reached out and took my hands in hers. "Listen to me carefully—you're not dying."

"You don't know. You haven't seen what I've seen."

"Kwan, you're not a lab rat. A lab rat can't change matter; it can't change its physical reality the way a human can."

"What do you mean?"

"Consciousness. Our conscious thoughts can change physical matter. Trust me, I've counseled all types, from people suffering from severe depression to stage-four cancer patients—our minds have the ability to alter our reality. This isn't me trying to cheer you up, Kwan; this is a scientific and medical fact, proven time and again. Why is it that negative thoughts often channel sickness and disease while positive thoughts can defeat the most terminal cancer? Success and failure, wealth and poverty—all predicated on cause and effect—the cause being your conscious thoughts. Still don't believe me? If you stepped up to the foul line with a chance to win or lose the game, what would affect the outcome more—your season free throw average or your conscious thoughts?"

"My thoughts," I admitted. "But this is different. The serum I injected . . . it's affecting my DNA."

"And what were your thoughts before you injected yourself with Becker's serum?"

My eyes widened. "That I would walk again."

"Exactly. Do you think those test rats thought about walking again when they received their injections? The serum is the cause; your emotional and mental state affected the outcome. True or true?"

"True. Only . . ."

"Only what?"

I pinched away tears, averting her eyes. "The lab rats mutated. I can't stop my mind from thinking about it."

"Kwan, do you believe in God? A higher power?"

"I guess so."

"You guess so?"

"I'm not really into religion."

"Neither am I. I'm strictly talking God. Because if you really believe in a Creator, then what are you afraid of?"

"I just told you."

"You saw the mutated rats before you injected the serum, didn't you?"

"Yes."

"Yet you still took the risk. What you're afraid of now is losing control of your own body—a new type of paralysis. To be paralyzed is to feel powerless. Feeling powerless, your life becomes over-whelmed with chaos. Chaos leads to fear . . . fear turns you into a victim. A victim is someone who allows the outside world or their inner thoughts to control their consciousness. Trust me; I've been in your shoes—a member in good standing at Victim.com. What I've learned is that our fears actually create what we're afraid of. The more you dwell on the negative outcome, the more you'll attract that outcome. That's how fear works. It manifests a negative energy field that brings the actual situation to life. When you're afraid or angry or anxiety-ridden you've essentially shut yourself off from God. That's the negative energy at work."

"What can I do, Rachel? How do I not be afraid?"

"Instead of drowning in fear, focus your mind on channeling positive energy to the solution. One student of mine—a fourteen-year-old girl—when she had to have chemo, she used to imagine the drug racing through her body like white knights to stab the cancer cells. Visualize the outcome you desire and these positive thoughts will connect you to the place where real miracles come from. Look at what your positive desire has already achieved. You went from being a paraplegic to one of the best athletes in school, all because of mind over matter."

She must have seen my hands shaking, because she stood next to me and hugged my head. "You're scared. It's okay to be scared. You have no idea how this is all going to turn out, and that's scary. But what if it could turn out better? What if God had a plan for you—a purpose you can't see yet? Sure, it may be a bit scary—it's already forced you to go out on a limb, but hey, that's where all the fruit grows, right?"

"What about my hair?"

"Losing your hair is more of a fashion statement; getting your heart stomped on by the pretty Indian hottie is just adolescence. No more negative thoughts. You're good, getting better." She released my head, brushing black hairs from her blouse. "Of course, it never hurts to do a little grooming before basketball practice."

Rachel opened her middle desk drawer and removed a hair clipper, shaving cream, and razor. "Last spring, I shaved half the swim team's heads—a few girls, too. You want to go Will Smith or the full Michael Jordan?"

21

An hour later, I found myself staring at my reflection in the bathroom mirror of the men's locker room, wearing a reversible Seacrest High green and white practice jersey and matching shorts.

Who was I?

The last Kwan Wilson to step onto the hardwood for basketball practice had been a boy—a cocky fifteen-year-old sophomore who weighed a buck eighty wet. The next Kwan Wilson—version 2.0—was the one I still expected to see . . . an angst-ridden, dark-haired Asian American adolescent anchored to a wheelchair by legs wrapped in flesh and frailty.

Gazing back at me was a man with a clean-shaven scalp and a sculpted physique. My former pencil neck was thick and wide, sloping past pronounced trapezius muscles to rippling deltoids and pecs that danced at my commands. I flexed my arms and my biceps exploded into tan softballs. I raised my jersey and marveled at my six-pack abs. And my legs . . . they were long coils of layered muscle that still felt alien—like a recently purchased vehicle with that lingering new car smell.

Whoever I was . . . I liked it.

"Nice haircut, douchebag." Stephen Ley slapped me across my scalp. "Don't hurt yourself out there today. My brother needs you Monday to shoot his TV commercial."

"That's not happening."

"Oh yeah, it is. Because if you don't show up, I'm going to tell all those reporters following you around like groupies that I supplied you with steroids, and it's bye-bye basketball."

I could feel my blood simmering, the muscles in my back convulsing. Gritting my teeth, I shouldered past the six-foot-seven-inch star forward, knocking over a trash can in the process.

Ley laughed. "Watch out—Asian Roid Rage'!"

Varsity basketball coach Bradford Flaig was used to dealing with postgame interviews with the local high school beat writers. Not this circus. Microphones representing every major prime-time news network were being shoved in his face. Camera crews were circling the feeding frenzy, jostling for position. A few foreign correspondents lurked along the periphery, translating the scene in their native language.

"Coach, when's Kwan's first game?"

"Seacrest's next game is Friday afternoon. Kwan hasn't made the team yet."

"Is Kwan even eligible?"

"The kid carries a 4.3 grade point average. He makes my whole team eligible."

"Steroids, Coach—is he eligible if he tests positive for steroids?"

"The Florida High School Athletic Association no longer mandates testing for steroids. Besides, Kwan has assured me he's never used them."

"Then how do you explain his muscles? The kid went from a wheelchair-bound geek to an amateur bodybuilder in two weeks."

"Look, I'm not a doctor. I heard one medical expert say that it was a rebound effect, no pun intended. A combination of his spine healing, along with the human growth hormone and hyperbaric treatments. All I know is that we're happy to see him walking again. If he can regain the All-State form he had when he played in San Diego, then terrific."

The mob rushed toward me as I grabbed a basketball from the rack and started dribbling. Coach Flaig cut them off, threatening to close practice if the media left the bleachers. Naturally, the cheerleaders decided this afternoon would be the perfect time to practice in their uniforms—which made the students filling the stands happy and the players even happier.

All except me. I was a bundle of nerves; every dribble and shot filmed and scrutinized.

Warm-ups were a disaster. During layup lines, I dribbled the ball off my foot twice, and then I jammed the little finger of my shooting hand when Ley drilled me with a chest pass at close range. The three man full-court weave was a little better, but my legs still felt disconnected from the rest of me, my brain stymied by "phantom paralysis." By the time the coaches split us into two squads (white jersey starters versus green jersey bench players), I was drenched in sweat.

Coach Flaig had the two squads walk through their offensive sets without defense while I watched from the sideline, trying to absorb the guard responsibilities. After ten minutes, the crash course ended and it was time to scrimmage, yours truly instructed to play the point for the green team.

Starting center Sal Salunitis won the tap for white. I quickly matched up with Seacrest's starting point guard, Gary Carr, who curled around a high pick set by Ley at the left elbow and hit a three-pointer.

No one had called out the screen, and Ley's defender hadn't bothered to hedge around the pick to allow me a chance to catch the quick guard.

A player in green inbounded the ball to me. I pushed it down the floor against Gary Carr, struggling to initiate the offense against the white defenders, who were cheating on the play. A bad pass led to a Carr layup and boos from the stands.

By the time the game clock dipped below the fifteen minute mark, my team was down 14 to 2. Ley had eight of the white jersey's points, and he was talking serious trash to my teammates, who were becoming more intimidated with each possession.

Dribbling the ball by the top of the key, I called for a high post screen. Ley knew it was coming and switched off on me as I drove the lane, clubbing me over the bridge of the nose with a flagrant foul as I attempted a layup.

Woozy, I remained on my back, blood dripping from both nostrils into my mouth. For a long moment the crowd remained silent, wondering if I had reinjured my spine.

Coach Flaig was taking no chances and pulled me from the game with 11:37 left on the clock. For the next three minutes I sat alone on the bench, pinching a blood-soaked towel to my nose as the bleachers slowly began to empty.

And then something happened.

It began in my chest, a steady pounding that sent my rib cage vibrating like a pile driver hammering concrete. It raced up my carotid arteries along either side of my neck and into my temples, driving the blood into my brain.

And suddenly my senses were on fire—my awareness of my internal and external environment magnifying into what I can only describe as a four-dimensional perception.

I could track every player on the court by his distinct sweat.

I could feel the acoustic vibrations of the ten bodies in motion, and somehow I knew predator from prey.

I could see subtle openings and flow patterns on the court as the action seemed to slow in my vision by a third.

My body responded to each of these sensory perceptions—my back arching, the adrenaline flowing, my pulse racing.

I stood up and grabbed Coach Flaig, squeezing his arm. "Put me in."

He was about to say no, only my vice-like grip cut him off. Then he saw the look in my eyes and blew his whistle. "Sub. Wilson's in for Tom Murray. Rusty, you run the point for green. Kwan, run the two."

The stands stopped emptying. The video cameras rose with the students' iPhones.

The crowd sensed something was about to happen.

The white team had the ball. I "felt" big Sal Salunitis moving behind me to set a back screen to free me from my man, who was dribbling toward me, attacking my left foot—only my left foot suddenly became my right foot as I anticipated his next dribble, my right arm shooting into the tiniest gap, my right hand intercepting the ball as delicately as a frog's tongue picks off a fly.

I was by him in a blink, racing down court for an uncontested layup—only instead of laying the ball in, I elevated four feet off the hardwood and completed a three-sixty, two-handed dunk—all as smooth as a baby's behind.

And suddenly the gymnasium came to life.

White inbounded the ball, only the two-guard was forced to bring it up the court as I refused to allow Gary Carr to breathe—anticipating every cut he attempted as he tried to free himself—his muscles foretelling each action before his body moved.

Ley called for the ball out on the wing. He pump-faked his defender in the air and drove to the hoop uncontested—never seeing my right hand, which swatted the layup into the third row of the bleachers.

Now the gym was jumping. Now my teammates were energized.

We set up on defense. The sideline inbound pass went to the six-foot-eleven-inch Salunitis, who backed into the low block—where I poked the ball free and headed down court with only one defender to beat.

I slowed to allow Stephen Ley to get to the lane ahead of me, and then I leaped from just inside the foul line, my right hand cradling the ball against my wrist, my arm whirling in a powerful arc which began at my right ankle and ended at the rim in a thunderous tomahawk dunk that sent Ley sprawling over the end line.

I stood over him, my feet straddling his waist—the crowd screaming, the coaches rushing onto the court to separate their two stars—only we never scuffled, we never exchanged blows. Perhaps it was the psychotic black pools filling my eyes, or the throbbing pulses reverberating through my neck like two garter snakes—or maybe it was simply the force of the blow that had bounced him onto the hardwood. Regardless of what it was, Stephen Ley knew better than to get up in my face and challenge me.

Coach Flaig pulled me aside, then blew his whistle. "Kwan, switch your jersey to white and play the two, Mark Maller, go green.

Timekeeper, put ten minutes on the clock and reset the score to zeroes. White has the ball . . . let's go!"

Enemies-turned-allies, Ley and I put on a clinic—the high school equivalent of LeBron James and Dwyane Wade. We hugged when the buzzer sounded, and the entire team gathered around us—the cheerleaders and students surrounding the team, the media capturing it all for tonight's news—a freakin' basketball scrimmage, for God's sake.

The hype continued downstairs in the locker room, with the talk focusing on a run to the state finals and did I want to go to a beach party Friday night after the game, and did I see Tracy Shane, the head cheerleader, eyeballing me from across the sideline? Ley, who was dating her best friend and cocaptain, Erin Smith, said he'd introduce me to the foxy brunette, and in a blink of neurons it was Anya who?

Stripping down, I wrapped a towel around my naked body and joined my teammates in the shower.

Heads turned. Eyes stared.

"Jesus, Kwan . . . how'd you get so muscular?"

"Dude, you look like the Chinese version of the Hulk."

"Arnold Schwarzenegger meets Arnold from *Happy Days*."

"That's your new nickname—Arnold!"

"He looks more like a Chinese version of Mr. Clean."

"I'm Korean" was my only retort to the time-honored tradition of "Jock Wars: Rip the Runt." Physically I wasn't a runt. But I was a minority and I was different, and that made me shark bait.

Sure, I could have flipped out. Physically, I could have mopped the flooded tile floor with their broken bodies . . . showed them who their real daddy was as I forcibly taught them how to distinguish a Korean from a Chinese from a Japanese from a Vietnamese. But these were my teammates now, and verbally abusing me was their way of accepting me.

Come Friday afternoon, the only color that would matter would be the color of our uniforms—and that was the beauty of sport.

* * *

Rusty Allen, one of the team's backup guards, drove me home after practice. Rusty was a good guy who was not a part of the Stephen Ley entourage. He warned me not to fall for the star forward's "buddy-buddy" routine. "Ley will put his arm around you while he stabs you in the back. You got the better of him today, but trust me, he doesn't like you."

I imagined he liked me even less when he watched TV later that night.

ESPN had looped my windmill dunk and defiant stance over my fallen teammate. Combined with postings to the social networks by the students in attendance, my "in-your-face" slam and "Allen Iverson" gesture had gone viral. Getting even more views was a song parody of Psy's "Gangnam Style," titled "Kwan-dunk Style," which featured highlights of the entire scrimmage.

Pushing past the media circus on our front lawn, I entered my grandmother's house to find Sun Jung and her friends watching the dunk on a local news show.

"There he is, my favorite grandson . . . what happened to your hair? Never mind. You just in time to see yourself on TV. Wait, I can replay it on the DVR."

I watched the highlights, grinning from ear to ear.

Sun Jung warmed my dinner while I signed assorted paraphernalia for her friends, only one of whom had ever been to our home, at least since I had moved in.

My grandmother had a surprise. Awaiting me in my room was a brand-new queen-size bed—courtesy of a local furniture company. Sun Jung said they'd send a photographer to take a few pictures of me lying on my new mattress; "three minutes for a free bed, no big deal."

I thanked her and leaped onto the mattress. To lie down in a regular bed after spending nearly a year in a narrow hospital bed with rails was heaven. Closing my door, I popped in a Linkin Park CD, grabbed my laptop, and spent the next two hours propped up in comfort, surfing the Internet.

I never heard the doorbell ring, so I was surprised when Li-ling entered my bedroom carrying a brown paper bag.

"And there he is, Mr. Kwan-dumb Style."

"Li-ling? What are you doing here?"

"I'm delivering an IV from Dr. Becker." She tossed me the brown paper bag. "The reporters thought I was delivering Chinese food . . . racist assholes."

"What happened to Anya?"

"Anya doesn't want to deal with you anymore."

"Why? Li-ling, what did I do wrong?"

"I can't say. At least, she asked me not to tell you . . . but I can be bribed."

"I don't have any money."

"Who said anything about money?" She took out her iPhone. "Take off your shirt and flex."

"Are you serious?"

"It's for my blog. You want to hook up with Anya or not?"

Feeling ridiculous, I tugged off my T-shirt and flexed. "Start talking."

"Anya's brother died back in India when she was thirteen."

"How?"

"Anya and her older brother, Rudy, were traveling on a bus in New Delhi when three men started getting rough with her. Buses can be especially dangerous places in India for women, so Anya and her brother got off at the next stop. The men must have gotten off, too, only Anya didn't see them until they were on top of her."

My heart pounded in my chest. "What happened?"

"Rudy tried to stop them and was stabbed. Anya woke up in a hospital with a broken rib. Her brother was on life support in the next bed."

I recalled Anya's anger-filled words: *I've been through this . . . I can't do it again. I'm not going down that path with you. This time I get to be the selfish one.*

"Her brother died, didn't he?"

Li-ling put the phone away. "It doesn't mean you're going to die. Use Becker's IV and I'm sure it will help stabilize the mutation."

"It's not stable?"

"It's fine. But if something comes up just call me and I'll drive you down to the lab. Thanks for the pics, you really do look hot . . . you know, for a Korean dork."

Help me welcome my first guest. Straight from Miami Beach ... ladies and gentlemen, Mr. Kwan Wilson."

My pulse raced as I stepped out from behind the curtain of the Ed Sullivan Theater and into the bright lights. I glanced to my right and waved at Paul Shaffer, who was leading the band in a middle-aged, Jewish white man's rendition of "Kwan-dunk Style." Crossing the stage, I stepped onto the carpeted riser to shake hands with talk show legend David Letterman—the moment surreal.

"Thanks for being here, young man. Now, yours is an amazing story. From what I understand, you were paralyzed in a car accident about a year ago."

"Yes. I was driving and text messaging, which I shouldn't have been doing."

"Your mother was in the passenger seat and she was killed?"

"Yes."

"Geez. So then what? You wake up in the hospital and you're paralyzed from the waist down. And I read where you had some other serious injuries?"

"Yes."

Dave reached across the desk to touch my arm. "This isn't an interrogation, Kwan. Feel free to give us more than a one word response."

"Sorry."

The audience laughed.

"So, you wake up, you're in the hospital, tubes everywhere I imagine. You find out mom's dead, you can't walk . . . what goes through your mind?"

"To be honest, I wanted to die."

"And so it's left to your dad to console you. Your father is Admiral Doug Wilson, is that correct?"

My back reflexively arched as the muscles along my spine tightened. "Yes."

"As someone who's been on the battlefield, I'm guessing he probably has had to console a lot of folks. What did he say to you?"

"First, he asked me what happened. Then he yelled at me for texting. Then he said it should have been me who died, but at least I'd suffer for the rest of my life."

"Ouch. Tough guy, the admiral."

"Yes."

"Was he always like that?"

"Yes."

"So then what? You spent some time in rehab . . . how was that?"

"It was hard. They have you in a large carpeted room with other patients and some have been going to rehab for twenty years, and you start to think . . . how am I going to do this? Because you never imagine that this can happen to you. It smells like urine and disinfectant, and bad sweat—stress sweat. There are trainers stretching and moving people around on mats, and you're one of them. It's like an out-of-body experience except your spine aches, like there's a hot coal sitting on top of the place where your spinal cord's been damaged, and the hurt's always there, which is why a lot of people get addicted to their pain meds. But the therapists are real nice—most of them, anyway, and you just . . . you just do it."

"Did you ever think you were going to walk again?"

"I did."

"After rehab, you moved to Miami Beach to live with your maternal grandmother—"

"Delray Beach."

"Delray Beach. And how did granny take to caring full-time for the guy who killed her daughter?"

What did he just say? My blood pressure jumped. My pulse pounded in my ears to the point of distraction.

"Kwan . . . your grandmother?"

"She's been an angel to me."

"Checking my notes, I realize now why I got confused about you living in Miami. Miami's actually the location of the lab where you received injections of stem cells from live sharks."

A veil passed over my vision, tinting the stage lights olive-green.

"Hell of a thing, injecting yourself with shark stem cells. What kind of shark was it, by the way? Great white? Lemon?"

"Vool." I had meant to say bull, but my upper and lower gums were suddenly inundated with a row of half-inch, serrated triangular teeth.

"Something in your mouth, Shark Boy?"

My pulse grew louder, blotting out the audience's laughter, until I realized it wasn't my heart I heard beating . . . it was Dave's! His right hand was resting on the desk that I was leaning on, the rhythm dancing across the wood finish.

"Let's talk hoops. We spoke with your old basketball coach—the one you played for before the accident. Coach Reinfeld told us back then you were built like a bean pole—that you could barely touch the rim. Are sharks good leapers? Is that why you can jump so high now?"

I shrugged, afraid to open my mouth.

"And what about your muscles . . . my God. Are sharks that muscular? Hey Paul, how 'bout we inject some shark stem cells into your puny ass?"

"Let's do it, Dave. Hook me up with a pint of mako."

I could feel Dave's pulse twitching in his neck; I could see the tantalizing movement of his jugular vein just above the collar of his white shirt. Fighting to maintain control, I gripped the chair until my fingers punctured the suede material.

"Kwan, you seem like a nice guy . . . do you see yourself as a role model? Do you think other sharks will take up basketball because of your success?"

Leaping across the desk, I grabbed the host by his lapel, hyper-extended my jaws, and sunk my teeth into the side of his neck, blood exploding in my face . . .

"Ahhh!"

I sat up in bed, my heart racing, my body lathered in sweat. I wiped my mouth with the back of my hand—no blood. I shoved an index finger around my gums—no shark teeth.

Asshole. It was just a dream.

The laptop had fallen between my legs. I wiggled my toes, just to make sure everything was still working down there, then reached for the computer and checked the time—1:57 a.m.

Must have fallen asleep after Li-ling left.

On my night table was the brown paper bag from the lab. I opened it, removing a plastic IV bag and a line connected to a capped butterfly needle. There were also several packages of alcohol wipes and a roll of white medical tape. What was missing was any indication of the drugs contained within the clear elixir. No list of ingredients or warnings. No instructions. Just a quart of liquid that would take all night to drain into my bloodstream.

Rolling off the bed, I grabbed a coat hanger from my closet and used my floor lamp as an IV stand. Then I tore open an alcohol wipe and swabbed my forearm. I thought of calling my grandmother to stick me, but why wake her? The veins in my arm were popping out, rendering them a far easier target than the last time I had attempted this same maneuver.

I was about to pierce my blood vessel with the needle when I recalled Jesse Gordon's warning: *"Do you know who funds Becker's lab? It's DARPA, as in the Defense Advanced Research Projects Agency. You seriously think the psychopaths at the DoD are gonna allow you to go on Letterman? You're already flying way above the radar. My advice? Walk now before they make you run. Disappear before you disappear."*

What to do?

Dr. Becker had told me mutating cells preferred an acidic environment; that the IV she'd prepare for me would raise my pH. I thought for a minute, then left my room and entered the laundry room, turning on the lights to search the cabinet under the sink.

During the summer, Sun Jung had purchased an aboveground swimming pool for the backyard so I could exercise in the water while she worked. She had taken it down when I had made the comment about offing myself.

I found the pool test kit in a small blue plastic container. Returning to my room, I separated the IV line from the butterfly needle, allowing drips of the clear elixir to fill the pH side of the tester. Following the instructions, I added a phenol red tablet, capped the vial, and shook it.

The small sample of elixir turned pinkish-red, the color approximating that of a 9.7 reading, the pH high on the alkaline side.

Okay, Dr. Becker, I guess I'll trust you . . . for now.

I swabbed my forearm again with an alcohol pad and slid the needle inside a vein, anchoring the connection with a few strips of medical tape. Then I shut off the light and climbed in bed.

Lying on my back, staring at the ceiling fan, I reached for my cell phone to text my agent.

Annie, cancel Letterman. Let's do Jon Stewart instead.

23

The next two days were a blur. While my coronation continued as "King of Seacrest High," Annie set out to conquer the entertainment world, leveraging a bidding war between Showtime and NBC to land a million-dollar payday with OWN—Oprah Winfrey's network. By Thursday night the deal was signed; by Friday morning two OWN trucks had arrived on campus, their camera crews setting up in the gymnasium to film my first official basketball game.

The other networks were politely asked to leave.

It was sick. Rock star sick. Students flocked to me like I was Michael Jackson returned from the dead. Girls I had never met before hugged and kissed me in the halls. Guys who had treated me like a diseased leper only a month earlier high-fived and knuckle-punched me and wished me good luck in the big game. Teachers waved and called out my name, and Mr. Hock greeted me like a long-lost son. The only hitch occurred when a producer interrupted his first period lecture on how Monsanto was earning billions as they systematically monopolized the agriculture industry and mutated our crops . . . a speech we had heard four weeks earlier.

"Sir, do you have a different lesson we could film? Maybe one that won't end up in a lawsuit?"

Oprah's producer, sound people, cameraman, and two assistants followed me everywhere, and everywhere there were students Bogarting the lens . . . all except for Anya, who cut first period, Jesse Gordon, who stayed away from my roving entourage, and Rachel Solomon, who refused to be interviewed.

Dr. Lockhart got in his fifteen minutes of fame when Oprah showed up in his office to interview the principal, and word of her arrival sent the school into orbit. She stayed only long enough to film B roll of the two of us moving down empty corridors between periods, and then she left to "prep" for our one-on-one marathon session scheduled in her hotel suite on Tuesday.

Me? I was already in orbit, swimming in glitter—Jay-Z cool. And as good as it was, this was only the appetizer. The main course was this afternoon's game where I was going to "feast" on the visitors from Palm Beach Lakes High, and tonight . . . tonight was dessert— a wild party on the beach featuring some serious alone time with the lovely Ms. Tracy Shane.

The sexy brunette "10" and I had eaten lunch together Thursday with a few of her fellow cheerleaders and some of my newfound friends from the team, and a million text messages later she was practically telling me what brand of condoms she preferred. I know what you're thinking, but Tracy was far more than luscious lips, exotic eyes, and a Playmate body, she was actually a really sweet person with luscious lips, exotic eyes, and a Playmate body.

I no longer thought about Anya, or anyone else for that matter. From the darkest depths, I had fought my way to the summit, transforming myself from the most exiled bag of flesh in high school to the most desired, and I was enjoying every intoxicating minute of my blossoming celebrity. And why not? God had blessed me with this miracle; to not partake of his bounty would be like spitting in his eye.

I was Kwan Wilson—stud athlete. Ahead of me lay fame and fortune. I was "the man," and when you're the man everyone wants a piece of you, so you have to be a little bit selfish in order to survive. If you signed everything they wanted you to sign, you'd be signing for weeks. If you replied to every text, you'd burn down your battery. Interviews? Call my agent. Seventh period? Please . . . I gotta get ready to ball.

Rachel Solomon? Now? Yo, tell the counselor I'll call her later.

My home jersey, shorts, and warm-ups were folded in my locker. Coach Flaig had assigned me #42, my number back in San Diego.

Seeing the white tank top brought the emo. Mom had been in the stands for every game since I had played Pee Wee Hoops back in second grade. Before each contest, she had made it a point to offer me one of her "pearls of wisdom." Sometimes it was basketball related, but mostly it had to do with a life lesson.

"Got the butterflies?"

I turned to find Coach Flaig standing behind me, dressed in his game-day sports jacket and tie. Rusty had told me Coach wore the same tie until he lost. Seacrest High's record was eleven and five, our school ranked fifty-seventh in the state. The visiting team, Palm Beach Lakes, was fifteen and one and ranked number seven. Coach was going with a red, black, and blue striped silk tie—the colors of the South Korean flag.

"Butterflies? Yeah, a little."

"There's no pressure. We're twenty-point underdogs. PBL has a senior shooting guard, Liam Naysmith, who's being recruited by Duke. Lot of college recruiters in the stands today. If you can hold Naysmith under eighteen points and ten assists, you'd be making a statement."

"Goose eggs."

Coach smiled nervously. "What do you mean?"

"That's what Naysmith's box score will look like. Goose eggs. Zeroes. Except for his turnovers."

"Sure, kid. Just do your best and have fun out there. Oh, I'm supposed to give you this." He reached into his jacket pocket and removed a folded piece of paper, handing it to me. "It's from Mrs. Solomon. She said I was to make sure you read it or else."

"Or else what?"

"I don't know. In eight years I've never had the balls to say no to the woman, and I'm sure as hell not starting today. You'll read it?"

"Yes, sir."

"Good. Just remember, it's your first game back from a serious injury, so don't try to be Superman out there. If I see you hobbling, I'm taking you out."

"Goose eggs."

He shook his head, muttering something as he walked away.

I opened the stapled note. It was a page photocopied from a book titled *The Monster Is Real* by Yehuda Berg.

An old Cherokee was teaching his young grandson one of life's most important lessons. He told the young boy the following parable: "There is a fight going on inside each of us. It is a terrible fight between two wolves. One wolf is evil. He is anger, rage, envy, regret, greed, arrogance, self-pity, guilt, resentment, lies, false pride, and ego. The second wolf is good. He is joy, peace, love, hope, serenity, humility, kindness, empathy, truth, compassion, and faith."

The grandson thought about this for a moment. Then he asked his grandfather, "Which wolf will win this fight?"

The old Cherokee simply replied, "The one you feed."

I read the note several times. Then I refolded it, shoved it into my pants pocket, and stripped down to change.

Liam Naysmith never knew what hit him.

From the moment he touched the basketball, I was on him like brown on rice. My hands were so quick that, after I picked his pocket twice for breakaway slams, he was afraid to face up on me. When a guard has to turn his back to his defender, he's no longer much of a passing threat. When a three-point shooter does it from beyond the arc, he's no longer a shooting threat. And when your scoring leader can't free himself from his defender to get the ball, he's no longer your scoring leader.

For forty-eight minutes, I hounded Naysmith. He never scored, he didn't have an assist, and he couldn't defend me, as I scored thirty-one points, collected twelve rebounds, and had seven assists.

We lost 67 to 63.

With their shooting guard and leading scorer taken out of the game, Palm Beach Lakes fed the ball inside to their six-foot-ten-inch man-child, Levi Godwin, who beat Sal Salunitis like a rented mule. Sal fouled out midway through the third quarter. Our backup center, Chris Coriasco, was five inches shorter and fifty pounds lighter than Godwin, and played "turnstile D," meaning the big man used him like a turnstile. Ley was bigger than Chris and would have defended the low post better, but with college scouts in the stands, the team captain wanted no part of PBL's star center.

Replaying the game in my mind, I realize now that there were at least eight possessions where my man was on the same side of the court as Godwin when he received an inside feed from his guard. On those occasions, I could have dropped into the lane to help Salunitis and Coriasco, but to do so would have left Liam Naysmith open, and I couldn't risk it—not if I wanted to shut him out.

And so we lost.

You wouldn't have known it from the crowd's reaction. As the final buzzer sounded, the student body rushed onto the court—to do what, I don't even think they knew. A few attempted to lift me onto their shoulders; when I shoved them away others joined in. When a bunch of older nonstudents violently grabbed at my jersey, the Seacrest students charged to my rescue and a fight broke out, with yours truly at the center of the melee. The players on both teams were ushered to their locker rooms as the cops joined in, the pepper spray flying. Two people were arrested, a female student was taken to the hospital for bruised ribs, and Oprah's people documented everything.

At some point, I made it downstairs to our locker room. My jersey was gone, having been torn off me, and I was physically spent. Coach Flaig hugged me and then offered me to the media as if he were feeding me to a volcano to keep it from erupting.

I answered questions for thirty minutes, and they still weren't satisfied. Finally, Coach Flaig cleared the locker room. I went home without showering, fearing the camera crews were lurking outside, preparing to storm the bathroom.

The local cops gave me a ride home, wedging me into the back of their squad car. It was embarrassing.

Night arrived to soothe the day. Having avoided me at school, Jesse Gordon graciously "volunteered" to pick me up at my grandmother's house and drive me to tonight's beach party.

"I thought you didn't want to be seen with me."

"Not on camera. The men in black are always watching. So listen, I know you're into Tracy, so if you could hook me up with any of her friends then I would owe you my firstborn. Literally, dude, you can have him."

I guess even paranoid, guitar-playing conspiracy theorists are willing to compromise on a Friday night.

It was ten thirty by the time we found a metered parking spot on A-1-A, half a mile south of the Marriott Hotel on East Atlantic Avenue. The junior class had rented Anchor Park and its grills, picnic area, and showers. The cops were there to loosely enforce the one a.m. curfew and no alcohol rule, ignoring all but the obvious pot smoke.

Jesse and I smelled the beer and pot the moment we got close to the bonfire.

There were fifty to sixty students hanging out by the lighted picnic area, God knows how many were partying in clusters on the beach. We stuck to the shadows as I searched for Tracy—and ran into Li-ling and Anya.

"Hey."

"Hey. Jesse, you know Li-ling and Anya."

"Hey."

I glanced over at Anya. She was wearing a black cashmere sweater and jeans, nursing a can of beer. With her hair down and no makeup she looked incredible.

Our eyes met, locked for a brief second, then she looked away.

Li-ling punched me on the shoulder. "So? Quite the celeb. When's the Oprah thing?"

"Tuesday. At the Ritz-Carlton."

"Cool. You feelin' good?"

"Never better."

Anya looked up. She was about to say something when someone leaped out of the shadows onto my back, her perfume and silky thighs identifying her as my favorite cheerleader.

Tracy hugged me around the neck and bit my right earlobe. "Kwan, where've you been? I've been looking for you all night."

"We just got here. Tracy, these are my—"

Before I could get out the word *friends*, the intoxicated senior was in my face, in my mouth, groping my chest . . .

And then it was raining beer.

Tracy turned to face Anya, venom in her eyes. "What's your problem, bitch?"

"Sorry. I thought I smelled silicone burning."

I grabbed Tracy before she could reach Anya, who never flinched.

Jesse yelled "cat fight!" and within seconds we were surrounded by a crowd of people who pushed and prodded and demanded to know who was fighting whom. And then they recognized me and the gathering doubled, which brought the cops—whose presence immediately drove away the drinkers and partying members of the crowd, thinning the herd to maybe a dozen—Anya not among them.

"What's going on here?"

"Nothing, officer."

"Some bitch dumped beer in my hair."

The cop shined his light on Tracy's wet scalp, then in my face. "Kwan Wilson? Hey, Garrity, it's the kid from ESPN. You played a helluva game today."

"Thanks." I felt Tracy slip her arm around my waist.

"No drinking and driving, kid. You got some future ahead of you."

"What about me?" Jesse said, offering a goofy smile. "How's my future looking?"

"Don't be a wiseass." The police officer took out his iPhone and handed it to his partner. "One quick shot, me and the kid."

We posed together, the cops switching places for another shot; then they left us to break up another fight.

Tracy wiped at her arms. "I need to wash this beer off. Walk with me down to the water?"

"Sure."

She detoured us to a picnic table to get her beach bag while I removed my sandals; then we walked hand in hand to the shoreline.

We had the whole thing planned—not the Anya thing, but the rest. Tracy had brought towels and a blanket. We'd find a secluded area away from the crowd, take a quick dip in the ocean, and then hook up under the stars.

We walked for ten minutes, leaving the streetlights and bonfire behind. Tracy droned on about school and taking the SATs and which colleges was I looking at, but only part of me was listening.

The rest of me was attuned to something else entirely . . .

The ocean at night has always affected my soul. The way it moves in pulsating waves of sound and foam, its salty hot breaths washing cold with the wind. At night, beneath the stars, the ocean was the only thing that could cleanse my mind of stress.

The shark stem cells acted like they recognized the water. My nostrils flared as I inhaled its saline fragrance; my skin tingled as my bare feet sank into its sandy, wet embrace.

Growing jealous, Tracy pulled me in for a kiss—the sensations of nature overruled by my anticipation of losing my virginity.

We walked another hundred yards before setting the blankets on a rise created by the last high tide. It was dark and deserted; the bonfire in the distance. Tracy kissed me again, then slowly stripped down to a string bikini, her barely concealed breasts beckoning me in the moonlight.

I had been paralyzed a virgin and a virgin I remained. Standing before me was a goddess who was offering to guide my journey from innocent adolescence into manhood . . . and boy was I ready!

I was down to my bathing suit in two seconds flat, my heart pounding in sync with hers, my hands gliding across her milky soft flesh, her scent of beer and perfume intoxicating. When she slid her hands between my legs it was as if I was jolted with electricity. She took an incredible five second inventory of my groin that rolled my eyes in ecstasy and rocketed way past Anya's kiss as the highlight of my seventeen year existence . . . then she broke away and walked toward the ocean, teasing me to follow.

I ran in after her.

The sea was calm, the temperature more refreshing than cool. Tracy waited for me in chest-deep water and we embraced again, our hands exploring one another beneath the incoming four-foot swells.

Our mouths locked in lust, our legs followed, our groins grinding beneath our bathing suits, my fingers exploring her breasts as she slipped her hand inside my swim trunks.

"Oh my God, Kwan! Oh my God, I've never felt anything like this before."

I smiled proudly.

Kwan Wilson—porn star.

She groped me again, intent on doing it right there in the water—and then her expression changed. "Oh . . . God."

My heart stopped. "What's wrong?"

She backed away. "What's wrong? Did you think I wouldn't notice?"

"Notice what?"

"Stay away from me, you . . . you freak!" She turned and stumbled to shore, while my hands frantically touched my privates—the blood rushing from my face as I felt something protruding from between my legs that wasn't what I expected—

—*and there were two of them!*

Male sharks don't have penises. What they have are claspers—grooved sexual organs located between their pelvic fins that resemble the long legs of a ballerina pressed together while she's standing on her tippy toes. When the act of mating occurs, the male shark positions itself belly-to-belly atop the female, securing its distressed mate in place by biting her pectoral fin. One clasper then pirouettes away from its twin and inserts itself into the lucky female's oviduct. The clasper is held in place by gruesome barbed spurs located near the tip of the organ—which may account for the female's reluctance to mate.

Kneeling in the wet sand, I stared at the freakish twelve-inch paired organ now hanging between my legs, fighting the urge to pass out. The clasper felt like my penis, it moved like my penis—it just wasn't *my* penis.

Don't panic don't panic don't panic. If saltwater caused the mutation, then get the saltwater out!

Hearing voices, I turned. Advancing toward me a hundred yards down the beach was a horde of students, led by Tracy. They were carrying flashlights and tiki torches, and for all I knew pitchforks.

Fear caused my bladder to tingle. Standing up, I peed like a racehorse—make that a seahorse, since the urine was seawater. Miraculously, the more I peed, the smaller the claspers became, until gradually the divided organ shriveled back into my human penis.

"Oh, God, thank you!"

"Kwan, you all right?"

It was Rusty, the crowd gathering behind him.

"Yeah, man. Just drank a little too much."

A dozen flashlights caught my penis as I tucked it back into my boxer shorts like a redeemed gunslinger.

All heads turned to Tracy.

"You think I'm lying? There were two of them!"

I laughed. "That's the last time I wear a ribbed condom in the ocean. Sucker filled with water . . . geez."

I breathed a sigh of relief as people teased Tracy. Jesse handed me my clothes, then left with the dispersing mob—leaving me alone with Li-ling.

"So . . . how's it hanging, champ?"

"Funny. Very funny."

"Was it a clasper?" Anya stepped out of the shadows, her tone more analytical than endearing.

"It's fine."

"If you don't tell us what happened, we can't help you."

I stared into her eyes—radiant pools in the moonlight. "It mutated while I was in the water with Tracy. It was my first time . . . I guess I got overstimulated. It reverted when I, uh, peed."

The ladies turned to one another, arguing. "Seawater enters the syphon sac—it's what propels the shark's sperm."

"How'd it get inside his bladder?"

"Who said it did?"

"Hello? I'm standing right here."

Li-ling took charge. "Anya, walk Kwan back to the party—act like you guys just made up. I'm going to get my car; I'll meet you in the Marriott parking lot. I'll call ahead to Dr. Becker—let her know we're on the way."

"We're going to the lab? Now?"

"You're right," said Anya, sarcastically. "Let's wait to see what else pops out of you. Maybe next time you'll give your little cheerleader bimbo a ride on your dorsal fin . . . idiot."

I could have argued, but I was still in shock. Instead, I dropped to my hands and knees in the wet sand and puked.

The three of us arrived at the lab around one in the morning. I had texted my grandmother's cell phone during the drive, letting her know I'd be sleeping at a friend's house. The girls did the same with their parents.

Dr. Becker let us in through the front entrance of the lab. She greeted me by shoving a light in my eyes as she examined my pupil. "Bring him downstairs to BSL-4. I want a full blood workup, hair and urine samples . . . what happened to your hair?"

"I shaved it off."

"He was losing it," Anya snitched.

"Fine. Get an EKG and tissue samples, too. And start a pot of coffee in the break room. It's going to be long night."

"Did you say anything to my father?"

"Hell, no. But you're all over the news, and the Admiral's no fool. I'm sure he'll be in touch."

Space and Naval Warfare Systems Command, San Diego, California

Before he had been promoted to assistant deputy general counsel of the US Navy, Jim Miller had spent thirteen years in the major leagues as a relief pitcher. Miller's last appearance had been a memorable one, pitching the ninth inning for the New York Yankees in game seven of the World Series.

Baseball closers and lawyers are like predators—cold-blooded and full of bite. Miller had visualized himself in this manner whenever he took the mound, growling beneath his breath before each pitch like a wolf hunting Bambi. Now, as he approached Admiral Douglas Wilson's office door, he clenched his jaw to steel himself once more for battle, lest the predator become the prey.

He reached out to knock. Changed his mind and entered, unannounced.

My father looked up from his laptop, his right index finger casually shutting down the com-link he had been using to contact the *Malchut*. "Jim? What brings you by on a Friday night?"

"We need to talk about your son. Helluva thing."

"Yeah."

"Did you know he had been interning at ANGEL?"

"Becker told me weeks ago while I was in DC. She let him go that morning."

"Obviously not soon enough. Did you know he's interviewing with Oprah on Tuesday? Her producer called to arrange an interview with you."

"Christ. What'd you tell them?"

"I told them you were involved in other pressing matters and could they wait a few weeks. I figure they'll give us one pass before they air this thing, and you know Kwan's internship will come up."

"What do you want me to do?"

"I don't know, but you're flying way above the radar on this thing. How's your relationship with Kwan? Think you can muzzle him until a new news cycle knocks him off prime time?"

"Kwan never listened to me while we were living under the same roof; I seriously doubt he'd even take my call."

"Then that only leaves us with one option." Miller turned his attention to a series of framed photographs hanging from a wall. He took his time admiring a few, then straightened a picture of my father standing on the deck of a US destroyer. "We need to shut down ANGEL. Consider it a temporary solution to prevent some nosey investigative journalist from—"

"No! I mean, no—we can't do that. Becker's getting close to a breakthrough; I don't want her to lose any momentum. As for the investigative journalism—that threat died out with the Internet. Besides, you of all people should know there are legal ramifications in play; technically ANGEL's listed as an independent contractor, not a military lab. Even if you closed the doors they have animals on the site, requiring—"

"Fine. ANGEL stays open for now. But you need to monitor the situation; make sure there's no trail of breadcrumbs. I don't want any blowback on this thing . . . or anything else you may or may not be working on. You reading me, Admiral?"

My father gritted his teeth. "Loud and clear, Mr. Miller."

ANGEL Lab, Miami, Florida

In retrospect, they probably shouldn't have shown me anything. Not the blood test results. Not the video images of my white cells, magnified a thousand times. And they could have kept me away from Joe Botchin, who was checking the medical tank for leaks while the observation aquarium was being drained for cleaning. "Doc says we're expecting a new species coming in on Monday. Must be something exotic for me to be collecting time and a half. When she called, I was in the middle of a technicolor yawn. Shoulda never gotten rotten on that cheap Milwaukee beer. Then again, it coulda been the oysters and cream."

Or maybe all those things wouldn't have added up to a hill of beans had I not seen the rats.

Racks of cages, all encoded with numbers that began with BS-MGH.

Bull Shark—Mouse Growth Hormone. These were my peeps—the little rodents that had given me the courage to inject myself . . . to venture alone down a road less traveled.

They were dead. Every last one of them.

And from the look of their mutated carcasses, they had died painfully.

Rachel Solomon had told me to use my mind to control the fear . . . mind over matter. My mind was in free fall, manifesting negative energy so palpable that I could taste its acidic breath in my throat.

Oh, no . . .

Exiting the lab, I sprinted down the empty corridor and entered the closest bathroom I could find. Standing before a mirror, I turned my head from side to side, my body shaking uncontrollably.

Appearing along either side of my neck were five gill slits. They were sealed shut, but they were there—six-inch long, vein-thin purple-colored folds of death.

I opened my mouth—and it got worse. A membrane, covered in a gook-like saliva was lodged in my throat—cutting off my airway.

And suddenly I couldn't breathe!

Fleeing the bathroom, I ran down the corridor for help . . . unable to speak, unable to gasp. I felt my lungs collapsing. I felt like I was drowning in air . . . literally like a fish out of water!

My muscles were lead by the time I found my way into the observation area. The room was spinning as I dragged myself up the circular stairwell to the catwalk bordering the open top of the five-thousand-gallon shark aquarium—an aquarium Joe had not yet begun to refill.

Staggering forward, I blacked out . . . flopping face-first into the medical tank.

25

A speck of consciousness, I drifted beneath a surface awash in moonlight and became one with the sea. It flowed through my mouth and I could breathe. It filled my nostrils and I tasted its soul. Down my throat and out my neck and the burn of my near asphyxiation became a distant memory.

Open wide and breathe.

Open wide and breathe.

So soothing. So simple. The sea cooed in my brain and reverberated in my bones, and Kwan Wilson disappeared.

Ahhhhhh . . .

And then the moonlight became lights and the oasis of calm was shattered with an avalanche of sound as I was violently dragged from my womb back into the world of chaos.

"His gills appear to be functioning."

"Mr. Roig, use the dental wedge to pry open his mouth. Anya, shine your light down his throat. Li-ling, get a shot of the esophageal membrane."

"Hurry up, he's getting cranky!"

"Got it."

"Li-ling, put the hose in his mouth so he can breathe."

"He's fighting it."

"Mr. Wilson, I need you to remain calm. Mr. Wilson—"

"I can't hold him up much longer, Doc!"

"Anya, you try."

"Kwan, it's Anya. Look at me, Kwan. Let the hose drain down your throat so you can breathe. Breathe, Kwan. Breathe and stay calm; we're going to help you."

Blue eyes . . . so familiar. Pulling me out of the void and into her azure sea.

"Good, that's good. Now listen carefully, but stay calm. You can't speak because there's a membrane sealing off your esophagus. Your lungs are intact, but they've collapsed. To inflate them, you need to collapse the membrane located deep inside your throat. I want you to focus on that membrane—you can feel it below your Adam's apple. When you're ready, we're going to remove the hose. I'm going to count to three to allow your gills to flush your throat; then you're going to collapse that membrane by inhaling a deep, lung-inflating breath. Nod if you can understand."

I must have nodded, because she smiled.

"Good, Kwan, very good. Are you ready to breathe air again? Okay, I'm removing the hose . . . nice and easy, and we count one . . . two . . . three and breathe! Big deep breath!"

I opened my mouth and sucked in a massive gulp of air which lodged in my throat and sent me into a state of panic.

Anya grabbed my face in both her hands and her eyes held mine. "Kwan, the membrane acts like a muscle. Take another short breath and swallow it open."

There was a part of me ready to fight the two men anchoring my arms in theirs—to submerge back into that container of sea, but I knew Anya couldn't follow. And so I gulped another bite of air and imagined my throat yawning open—and the air passed through my esophagus into my chest.

And now I was suffocating.

"Breathe again! Deep breaths! You need to inflate your lungs enough to be able to engage your intercostal muscles and diaphragm."

My mouth became a bellows, inflating my chest with short bursts of air until I could inhale and exhale. . . inhale and exhale.

The blue eyes teared up. "Good, Kwan. Very good. Can you speak?"

I cleared my throat and collected a load of phlegm, which I turned and spit into Joe Botchin's face. "Let . . . me . . . go, asshole."

The vice grips on my arms eased.

We were standing in the medical pool, waist-deep in water. Anya put her arm around me and we climbed out onto the catwalk.

Dr. Becker sat me down, then peered into each of my eyes using a retinoscope. "Get him downstairs to BSL-2, I need to check his corneas. Joe, I want the main tank cleaned and filled in an hour or I'll feed you and Mr. Roig to Taurus."

"Yes, ma'am."

The dead rats I had seen in Lab 4 were the first test subjects that had been administered mouse growth hormone as part of stem cell protocol. The MGH injections had established a temporary equilibrium between the shark mutations and the rodent's DNA, but the patients had still died when their respiratory systems had evolved gills, collapsing their lungs in the process.

Dr. Becker explained that, like human lungs, gills consist of a dense network of thin-walled blood vessels that are conducive for gas exchange. As water flows through the gills, oxygen is extracted from the water molecule and enters the bloodstream while carbon dioxide is expelled from the bloodstream back into the water.

Becker told me that evolution had endowed mammals with an epiglottis—a flap that seals the trachea in order to prevent food and liquids from entering our lungs when we eat. In the same way the shark mutation had generated an esophageal membrane to prevent seawater from entering the rat's esophagus and drowning the host. Composed of an elastic cartilage, the membrane moved into place when the gills were engaged.

Dr. Becker explained to me that the rats in Lab 4 had suffocated because they weren't in water when their metamorphosis had occurred. Once she realized this, she had the next group of rodents placed in five-foot-long glass tanks that offered a dry island habitat surrounded by water.

Of course, it would have been nice if she had mentioned her findings to me *before* I had nearly suffocated.

I followed Dr. Becker and Anya inside Lab 3, my expression no doubt incredulous as I gazed at racks of these multihabitat aquariums. Hairless rats were swimming underwater like rodent-fish, breathing through their gills and paddling with webbed paws. Occasionally a rat would climb out of the water to eat, at which time it would regurgitate a mouthful of mucus—an act that reopened its esophagus and inflated its lungs.

"This is sick. Look at that one—it's swimming like an otter."

"Yes, Mr. Wilson. They adapt quickly."

Anya seemed distracted, but I didn't care. I needed to know what my own limitations were. "Dr. Becker, are these saltwater or freshwater tanks?"

"Both. Bull sharks can live in freshwater and saltwater, so can rat-fish . . . shark-rats—whatever we eventually call them."

"What do you call me?"

Anya turned to me, squeezing my hand. "There are things you need to know . . . things I need to tell you."

"Tell him later," said Dr. Becker. "Right now I need to look at his eyes before they revert. Put him on the keratometer."

Anya led me to a small desk situated between two stools. Mounted to the tabletop was an instrument that resembled a large microscope, except its lens was pointed at eye level. Anya had me sit down and place my chin onto a guide cup while Dr. Becker adjusted the machine to my face, peering through her end of the scope into my right eye.

"What I'm doing, Mr. Wilson, is checking your cornea. Shark and human corneas are surprisingly compatible, which is why we use them in cornea transplants. The difference is the presence of a membrane that protects the shark's cornea . . . which I can't see in your eye."

"Is that good?"

"It's inconclusive. If you had it during your metamorphic episode and you already reverted, it means your ability to use your amphibious features is hyperkinetic. If your cornea failed to generate the membrane, it may mean you're hypokinetic—slow to adapt. The only way we'll know for sure is to let you spend some time in the observation tank."

"No!" The suddenness of Anya's objection ruffled my already shot nerves. "Kwan needs to know everything before you use him as your guinea pig . . . fish."

"What's she talking about, Doc?"

"What Anya is saying is that, among rats, the mutation isn't limited to their respiratory system. The longer the test subject remains in the water, the greater their metamorphosis. Turns out our injected rodents seem to prefer their new environment."

"Good for them. As long as my lungs inflate when I need them to I don't mind being able to breathe underwater using my neck."

Anya turned to Dr. Becker, her turquoise eyes insistent.

The scientist sighed. "Show him."

They were in BSL-2, which was on night habitat. Anya handed me a pair of night vision goggles, then led me to the rows of tanks.

The rats in these aquariums had been the first test subjects exposed to water—their mutations, therefore, the most advanced. In place of their hairless skin was a thick, grayish-brown shark hide. Their arms and legs were still in place, but the limbs were weak and atrophied. Compensation came from the rodents' tails, which had thickened and were being used to propel the creatures through the water like a crocodile. On some of the rats, a calcium deposit had formed midspine—perhaps a precursor for some kind of dorsal fin.

There were other more subtle anatomical changes, but overall nothing startling . . . yet.

Anya reached into a large terrarium filled with white mice and extracted one of the squirming little guys by its tail. "The rats used to eat a specially formulated diet of rodent chow. The shark-rats prefer their meals with a pulse."

Selecting an aquarium, she unceremoniously tossed the mouse in the water.

The mouse doggy-paddled its way toward the floating plastic island located at the far end of the tank.

The shark-rat immediately homed in on its prey, circling below its churning legs. Just as it was about to strike, Anya scooped the little guy up in a goldfish net and deposited him on the island.

I breathed a sigh of relief.

"Keep watching," Anya said. "The mutations have developed shark-like senses that allow them to feel vibrations in the water. The rat can hear the mouse's heart beating through the plastic island."

As I watched in horror, the shark-rat circled twice, then propelled itself out of the water onto the island and grabbed the mouse along the scruff of the neck in one sickening, blood-squirting bite.

It did not feed on dry land. Instead, the mutant slid backward into the water, dragging its twitching meal underwater where it shook it until it mercifully drowned.

"A little depraved, but impressive."

Anya turned on me like I had been the one who fed the creature its meal. "Don't you get it? The mutated species' physiology is determined by its environment, but the rats clearly prefer the water—directly defying their instincts as land mammals. This new behavioral pattern indicates the shark DNA is far more dominant. Behavioral patterns are also directly linked to one's personality. These once docile, warm-blooded lab rats have become cold-blooded predators—and the same thing may happen to you."

Dr. Becker lived on the third floor of the building that housed ANGEL. She had a full kitchen, den, three bathrooms, a library, and six bedrooms—not including the master suite.

It was after four in the morning by the time Anya, Li-ling, and I made our way up the private stairwell to the guest quarters. Any hope of spending the night with the beautiful Ms. Patel was dashed the moment I saw my room.

"A hospital bed? For real?"

Her response was cut off by Nadja Kamrowski, who entered pushing an IV stand. "The accommodations on this floor were intended for cancer patients. If there is a problem, Joe Botchin has a sofa bed in his trailer."

"No thanks. What's in the IV?"

"Human growth hormone, vitamins, and something to allow you to rest. Get in bed. I need to start your drip and hook you up to a heart monitor."

Kamrowski's left eye was squinting more than usual, and the last thing I wanted her doing was jabbing my vein with a needle. I glanced at Anya, who came to my rescue. "Get some rest, Dr. K., I can handle it."

I removed my shirt and climbed into bed, awaiting the IV.

Anya closed the door, then surprised me by removing her own shirt.

"Anya?"

"If you're going to lose your virginity, Kwan, gift it to someone special." She climbed in bed with me and we kissed, her tongue flirting with mine. Before I knew it we were naked, and yet everything felt different from my groping encounter in the ocean with Tracy . . . lust and love worlds apart.

I always imagined what my first time would be like. You see stars hooking up in movies and they're moaning and their eyes are rolling and everything's choreographed and perfect, and then there's porn and that's a whole different animal. I didn't know if Anya was a virgin, but she sure felt like a virgin. Me? I was clumsy and panting and trying my best to force myself inside her before I totally lost control. She finally climbed on top of me and guided me in and I lasted about seven seconds . . . seven seconds of heaven I never thought I'd ever get to experience after my car accident.

When I was done Anya laid down on top of me, resting her head on my chest. "How was it?"

"Best moment in my life."

"Mine, too. But now I have to hook up your IV drip and say good night."

"You can't stay here with me?"

"Dr. Becker would have a fit. Besides, this bed can barely hold you, and we both need our rest."

She kissed me; then we climbed out of bed and dressed. I lay back down in my bathing suit, allowing Anya to adhere the EKG leads to my chest. I tried not to wince as she slid the IV needle into my vein.

"Kwan, before I leave I'll fill the bathtub with water—just in case your gills spasm."

My heart pounded, my mind suddenly consumed in fear. "Is that something I need to worry about?"

"It's something we obviously need to prepare for, but worrying does no good. Your mind needs to stay focused so you can remain in control."

"What happens if I can't control these changes? What happens if I become psychotic, like those rats? If that happens, will you be there to save me?"

She squeezed my hand. "I'm here for you."

"That's not what I meant. If things go bad, I don't want to end up suffering like those rats with the fangs and nasty dispositions . . . or be an exhibit in Becker's aquarium of horrors. If the human Kwan disappears, I need to know you'll put me out of my misery."

"Kwan—"

"Please, Anya! You have to promise me that if things go too far you'll end my life."

Hot tears ran out of her blue eyes and onto my hand. "I promise."

I couldn't sleep, my thoughts ping-ponging from Anya to the basketball game to the scene on the beach, and finally to the sudden, frightening gill transformation that had nearly ended my life. The fear refused to allow my mind to shut down, and when I finally drifted off the urge to pee shook me out of my dream.

Damn IV. I must have gone to the bathroom five times over the next three hours, each visit requiring me to unplug my heart monitor and wheel the IV stand to the toilet—my bladder refilling throughout the night as the meds continued draining into my vein.

It wasn't until daylight that exhaustion finally pulled me under . . .

The surface undulates above me like liquid mercury. Curtains of sunlight dance before me, bleeding into the depths below. I move through this liquid universe and the liquid universe moves through me. I can see it and taste it; I can hear it and inhale its scents, but most of all I can feel it. Everything. From the tiniest flick of a shrimp's tail to the cry of a twenty-ton whale. The sea is a world of vibration, and my body is a tuning fork.

A moray eel pokes its head out of a hole and I can sense the sand grinding beneath its belly. A school of fish feeds on krill in the distance, and their gnashing jaws become my overture. The harmonics attract an audience—a gray whale and her calf. The pair expels thunderous breaths through the surface—the chuffing of their lungs reverberating along the sides of my body, the beating of their hearts taking residence in my blood.

Kwan . . .

Now, it is the deep that beckons. Driven by primordial instinct, I curl into a steep dive, harboring neither thought nor worry nor fear. Blue becomes olive-green as the darkness closes in around me, my eyes accommodating the swift descent into the abyss.

Kwan . . .

The empty carcass awaits my presence, bobbing upright along the bottom. There is no vibration, no scent. No movement, no pulse. I have been summoned into the void by food which lacks sustenance—a scavengers' banquet.

I circle the dead creature, my current disturbing its slumber.

The dead woman's eyes flash open.

"Huh!" I shot up in bed, my heart racing, my mind holding fast to the image of my mother, her face pale in death—melding into Anya's, my girlfriend, hovering over me.

"Kwan, are you all right? You were yelling in your sleep."

"Nightmare. Anya, get this IV out of me; I've had enough. What time is it?"

"Almost one in the afternoon. Dr. Becker sent me in to wake you. They're discussing ways to fix your DNA."

The conference room was located on the second floor. It was small and still smelled of last night's Chinese takeout. Seated around an oval table that looked as old as the building was Dr. Becker, her assistant, Nadja Kamrowski, Joe Botchin, Li-ling—and a new but familiar face.

Jeff Elrod was a heavyset man in his midfifties. He had blond hair that had whitened with age and he wore it long to cover a receding hairline, and I suppose because wearing a ponytail probably made him feel cool. He had thin lips and a wide smile that reeked of ego, but the eyes were dangerous—hazel lasers that locked onto you and burned a hole into your soul.

I knew Mr. Elrod—he associated with my father, but never with others present. It would be a midnight visit for a walk in our backyard or a chance meeting at the mall with "Uncle Jeff." I had last seen him four years ago lurking in my father's study at some ungodly hour of the night and it was his presence that compelled me to hack into the Admiral's e-mail where I managed to cross-reference a rough identity. Elrod's waistline had thickened since then, but I doubted the former CIA field operative had moved to a desk job.

His eyes locked onto mine the moment Anya and I entered the room.

Dr. Becker stood to make the introductions, but Elrod cut her off. "That's unnecessary, Doctor. Kwan and I are old friends, aren't we, Kwan?"

I took a seat across from him, his smile unnerving. "You were my father's friend. We spoke twice in fourteen years."

"Three times, actually. You're forgetting about the time you and your pal Clark Newsom hacked Dad's computer. Good times, huh?" And he smiled at me like a serpent.

"Why are you here?"

"Why am I here? Well, I'm here as a friend. And I'm here representing a group of investors. See, kid, Dr. Becker led us to believe that she had finally developed a cure for cancer—an immune system booster we expected her to be mass-producing by now. Thanks to you, we know this cure still has a few bugs in it. Of course, Dr. B. wasn't exactly volunteering that information, but we have other means of obtaining updates. Isn't that right, Dr. Kamrowski?"

Nadja Kamrowski turned to Dr. Becker. "I'm sorry, Barbara. But time is of the essence. Like it or not, we have a human test subject. We need to use him."

"How?"

"We place Kwan in the observation tank and allow the full effects of his metamorphosis to come out. Then we use the filtration system to feed him high doses of the three beta-blockers we've been working with. Whichever drug or combination of drugs causes his symptoms to abate gets added to the protocol. It'll take ten days to complete the tests, during which time we can bring in the extra personnel and equipment needed to mass-produce the sharks' stem cells."

Jeff Elrod's eyebrows rose. "Wow, Kwan. Looks like your involvement in this project could shortcut a cure for cancer and make you a national hero, except no one can know about it."

"Why not?" Anya asked innocently.

Elrod's eyes took her in. "Anya, right? My, you're a pretty young thing, just like your mother, Elizabeth. No wonder your father fell in love with her at Cambridge. How is Dad? Still teaching economics at FAU? A tenured professor . . . you and Mom must be so proud. And look at you, following in the old man's footsteps. The future sure looks bright for our young immigrant . . . unless, of course, you overstep your boundaries. Then it's bye-bye citizenship, bye-bye Boca, hello New Delhi. But hey, there are worse things than being deported. By the way, my condolences about your big brother—his death was a real tragedy . . . but I digress. You asked me a legitimate question about keeping our work here a secret, and I went off on one of my famous tangents."

Anya reached beneath the tabletop and squeezed my hand, her limb trembling.

"See, sweetheart, sometimes it's better for business not to air your dirty laundry. Growing gills . . . that's dirty laundry. Dunking a basketball—that's good stuff. Which is why your boyfriend here is going to be allowed to be a star athlete after he cooperates with Dr. Kamrowski. By the way, Kwan, I spoke to Oprah's people and let them know you'd be rescheduling your interview while we finished doing all the necessary medical testing—that way our biotech partners can help other paraplegics dunk basketballs, too. But, hey, let's not put the cart before the horse—first we've got to get those beta-blockers in your system, right Dr. B?"

Dr. Becker nodded nervously. "Yes, right. Kwan, we ordered breakfast for you—why don't you and Anya eat while we—"

Jeff Elrod slapped his palms on the table, the acoustic blast causing everyone to jump. "Breakfast . . . the most important meal of the day. Except my watch says it's already thirteen hundred hours, which means breakfast is over. And since lunch is for union workers and other useless dregs of society, why don't we get junior here in the freakin' tank and if he gets hungry you can feed him a fish."

I turned to the black ops agent, my eyes burning into his, the muscles in my upper back contracting. "Maybe you should join me in the tank, asshole."

Anya held on to me, Joe Botchin and Dr. Becker hurrying around the table to join her lest I grab Jeff Elrod by his throat. "He's testing you, Kwan. Remember what we spoke about last night? Stay in control. Let it go."

I took a deep breath—only to find myself wheezing through the partially closed esophageal membrane in my throat.

Dr. Becker probed the side of my neck. "His gills are more pronounced. Get him into the tank—now."

Anya dragged me out of the room, Jeff Elrod's smile unnerving.

27

I was in serious trouble by the time we made it out to the cat-walk. Johnny Roig was standing by the open top of the forty-foot-wide, thirty-foot-deep cylindrical aquarium, the tank's water level nearly reaching the rim.

"We've had the heater running all night; if it's not warm enough for you—"

I pushed the man aside and jumped in.

For an anxiety-filled thirty seconds I couldn't breathe, my chest on fire. And then I burped a long belch of air that seemed to squeeze my stomach flat and crushed the cavity beneath my rib cage as my lungs collapsed, sending a sizzling trail of bubbles out of my mouth.

With every molecule of air gone, I opened my mouth and inhaled my briny surroundings until my gills opened and I could breathe again. The instant the air was purged, I sank feetfirst to the bottom of the tank.

Within seconds, my body adapted to my underwater environment. My sinus passages pinched beneath my nose and eyes, flattening the contours of my face. My ear canals pressed together until the cavities were sealed. Protective membranes slid over my cornea and eyes and my fuzzy liquid world came into focus as if I were wearing swim goggles.

I kicked off my shoes and socks, then pulled off my jeans and shirt and stood on the Plexiglas bottom to take inventory of myself and my surroundings, still wearing the bathing suit I had worn to the beach party.

I was neutrally buoyant, standing on a grilled surface that vented filtered water into the aquarium. The slightest push off the bottom and I rose ten feet, the slightest twist and I spun.

How did I feel? There was a part of me that felt petrified . . . I mean, after all, I was changing both internally and externally, and that's pretty scary. At the same time I was breathing underwater, and that was just beyond sick.

The tank was cylindrical for a reason—the shape allowed sharks to swim in a perpetual circle in order to breathe—something that I could accomplish simply by opening and closing my mouth. Above my head, the circular opening revealed the catwalk and the ceiling lights above. Otherwise, I was surrounded by the aquarium's curved glass walls, which distorted the periphery of the observation room, rendering it a convex fish-eyed world.

Turning slowly, I discovered my audience.

Dr. Becker and Dr. Kamrowski were jabbering away, though I could hear nothing. Joe Botchin was setting up folding chairs for himself and Li-ling. Jeff Elrod paced back and forth, his eyes wide with wonder, even as he videoed me on his iPhone.

Looking up, I saw Anya descend from the catwalk's spiral stairwell. Pushing away from the bottom, I swam up to her—and was suddenly overcome by the bizarre sensation of my skin thickening over my entire body. I opened and closed my hand, the muscles taut. The pigment along the back of my arms appeared to be darkening to a grayish-brown, and it felt almost alien in texture—like rubberized sandpaper. A closer inspection revealed triangular-shaped dermal denticles that rubbed smooth from head to toe but bit when stroked the opposite way.

Within seconds my flesh had become living armor. Not only was it protective, but it seemed to channel the water! With a flurry of kicks, I felt myself accelerating across the width of the tank as if it were filled with oil.

While my new shark skin gave me speed, I still swam like a human, and humans are awkward in the water, certainly no match for sharks. Worse, I looked freakish and felt like a sideshow exhibit—all of which contributed to a building sense of anxiety.

How long did I have to remain in here?

How soon would those beta-blockers start to kick in so I could go home?

I torpedoed over to Dr. Becker and her colleagues—and suddenly realized I had no means of communicating. Their voices were muffled—until I pressed my hands to the acrylic wall and discovered something else about my skin: my shark epidermis possessed neuroreceptors that registered the tiniest vibration, acting like an inner ear.

Touching the aquarium glass, I could hear everything outside the tank.

"Becker, what's he doing?"

"It would appear, Mr. Elrod, that he's trying to communicate."

"He wants to know how long he has to stay underwater," said Li-ling, reading my lips.

"You think he can hear us?" Joe asked.

Dr. Becker shook her head. "The glass is far too thick. Besides, look at his ears—his ear canals have sealed to prevent damage from the water pressure."

I was about to correct Dr. Becker when Jeff Elrod pulled her aside. "By pressure, you mean he's capable of diving into deeper waters. How deep?"

"That's impossible to say."

"Well, how deep can a shark dive?"

"As far as I know, there aren't any limits."

"Does the kid have limits?"

"Again, it's impossible to say."

Elrod's face was reddening. "Let's play a game, Doctor. Let's pretend your life depends upon you providing me with accurate answers."

"Are you threatening me, Mr. Elrod?"

"Very much so. Now how deep can the kid dive?"

Dr. Becker appeared flustered. "Whether it's ten feet or ten thousand feet, water pressure only affects things possessing air cavities—lungs, sinuses, and ear canals in humans; steel hulls in submarines. In order to breathe from his gills, Kwan's air cavities must collapse."

"Then he may not be susceptible to the dangers of extreme depths?"

"In theory. The only way to know for sure is to subject him to hydrostatic pressure testing. For our purposes, that's not necessary. We want to reverse the mutation, not quantify it."

"What would it entail, this hydrostatic pressure testing?"

Dr. Becker was about to object, but thought better of it. "When you test a dive watch, you place the watch in a container of water inside a hyperbaric chamber and increase the pressure to simulate submersion at depth. With a human—it's never been done."

Jeff Elrod smiled, patting the geneticist on the back. "Good talk. You can go now."

I heard tapping sounds and traced them to Anya. She had typed a message to me on her iPad, dictated to her by Nadja Kamrowski.

Dr. Kamrowski says you must remain in the tank at least ten hours. We cannot begin the beta-blockers until your metamorphosis is complete; otherwise any latent symptoms may become resistant to the drugs.

Seeing my despair, Anya pressed her hand to the glass as a gesture of support. I did the same—the nerve endings in my dermal denticles so sensitive that I was able to feel the vibrations of her pulse.

It was going to be a long day.

Three hours passed. I had held out hope that the mutations had ceased when my feet started to change. The deformity began as a hunk of cartilage which protruded from the back of my heels like a two-inch spike, only it continued to thicken and grow. By five in the afternoon, the prominence had peaked into a pair of gruesome fourteen-inch-long bony structures—my feet now resembling a miniature pair of concave skis, the curvature preventing me from standing.

I was petrified. *Would my entire body begin sprouting these mutant growths?*

My handlers were perplexed. None of the rats had developed these foot deformities.

Finally, it was Li-ling who suggested a potential purpose. Tapping on the glass to get my attention, she held both of her arms in front of her, then pressed her palms together before moving them from side to side.

It took me a moment to comprehend. With my feet and legs pressed together, the protrusions along the back of my heels formed the curved upper lobe of a tail fin!

Rising off the bottom, I pressed my legs together and attempted moving my hips back and forth like Li-ling suggested. It was awkward, sort of like twirling a hula hoop, and my body kept rolling sideways until I figured out where to position my arms. But the combination of streamlining my legs while swishing my feet east-west propelled me through the water so efficiently that in no time it became second nature, and I found myself circling the periphery of the tank, my body undulating like—well, like a shark.

Kwan Wilson—Sharkman.

The more I swam, the better I felt. At some point I closed my eyes, entering a Zen-like state that shut down part of my brain, allowing me to sleep—my skin's neuroreceptors feeling the interior walls of the tank as I glided and breathed . . .

Glided and breathed.

Glided and breathed . . .

Izzzzzzt. Zzzzzzzzt.

The electrical discharge zapped in my head . . . well, not in my head as it turns out, but from within hundreds of tiny, dark pores which covered my scalp like a crew cut. Filled with a gelatinous substance, this shark sensory system, known as the ampullae of Lorenzini, formed a network of neurons that enabled my rewired brain to detect the faintest electrical fields—electrical fields generated by the moving muscles or beating heart of other life forms.

The disturbance was originating above me. I circled the intruder warily, my rational human mind disconnected from my suddenly dominant predatory instincts.

I was hungry. I needed to feed.

This was food.

A triangular row of teeth hidden within my gums rose into position along the outside of my human molars. Like a torpedo going active, I launched my attack.

"Kwan—stop! Stop it!"

It was not Anya's scream that snapped me from my predatory state, but her scent—an alluring chemical pheromone. I circled her, rubbing my belly-skin against her flesh until she reached out and violently pinched my throat, ending the courtship.

Anya?

"Kwan, snap out of it! We only have a few minutes—I need you out of this tank."

Grabbing my wrist, she kicked for the rim of the aquarium, dragging me with her.

With a powerful downward thrust of my legs, I launched my body out of the water and landed on the catwalk—Anya in my arms. I set the stunned girl down, then purged my gills and gasped a voluminous breath of air.

My lungs inflated, opening my sinus passages and ear canals with an internal pop. My blurred vision sharpened—my eyes widening at the sight of Anya's body, exposed in her bra and panties. I continued to stare while my skin shed its density, the grayish-brown pigment quickly fading away.

My scalp tingled as the ampullae of Lorenzini pores sealed closed. I hocked up phlegm and spit it into the tank—and I could speak—the triangular teeth squeezed back inside my gums.

"Anya? Where is everyone?"

"Eating. We only have a few minutes, so listen. That Defense Department guy—he wants to run some kind of crazy experiment on you . . . something involving your father. The Admiral's flying in—he'll be here in the morning. Get out of here, Kwan. Don't come back, don't go on TV anymore. You need to disappear."

She leaned in and kissed me.

"He's on the catwalk! Don't let him escape."

I looked down and saw Jeff Elrod pointing at me. To my left, two men dressed innocuously in blue blazers and khaki pants were sprinting up the spiral stairwell, each CIA assassin sporting a 9mm Glock. The exit door that led outside to the back of the facility was being chained shut by John Roig—and Joe Botchin was approaching me cautiously from the other end of the catwalk, the wrestler-turned-shark wrangler holding a heavy fishing net.

"Easy, Kwan. No one wants to hurt you, only we can't let you bail out on us. Dr. Kamrowski will explain everything."

I looked one last time into Anya's eyes, then sprinted down the catwalk at the Aussie—leaping over the rail at the last second into the flooded channel that connected the medical pool and aquarium with the shark paddock. Holding my breath, I ducked underwater and swam my way through a dark, enclosed tunnel . . . emerging outside . . . surrounded by the night sky and dozens of moving bodies.

Sharks . . . I was in the shark paddock. I could sense them and they could sense me, and yet none of the predators took much interest. It was as if we were strangers sharing a crowded sidewalk.

The real threat was unchaining the back doors to come after me.

I climbed out of the canal and looked around. Biscayne Bay was a mere stone's throw away, its glistening moonlit waters guarded by a steel perimeter fence. I ran to it, and with a grunt, tore the chain link from the nearest support post.

Then I heard Li-ling . . .

"Hey genius—we ordered two pizzas and three salads. You forgot one of the salads. And I asked for a two-liter bottle of Coke. This is Diet Coke."

"Yeah. Sorry about that. My manager said he'll send another driver out with it. He's not charging you for the salad."

"Whoopee, we saved six bucks. Hey, on the drive back, make sure you use your seatbelt. That's your tip. I'm sure it's not what you expected either."

She slammed the front door of the lab, sending the pizza delivery man back to his car, grumbling to himself. "Bustin' my hump on a Saturday night . . . for this? Dwayne can kiss my ass . . . I quit."

Climbing inside the 1997 Toyota Tacoma pickup truck, he blasted the night air with Metallica's "Bleeding Me" as he accelerated out of the ANGEL complex—yours truly hidden in the flatbed.

I huddled in back, shivering in my wet bathing suit. *What did the Admiral want from me? Where could I hide? And what good would it do to run anyway? Becker had the cure to my freakish condition, and Jeff Elrod had stopped her from administering it. At some point, I'd have to return or face the consequences.*

Unless I could control it. Maybe I could. As much as my body changed in the water, once out of it, I seemed to be able to resume my human form without any lingering side effects. It was only when the gills randomly struck without rhyme or reason that I found myself in serious trouble.

Was it a random response, or had I done something to cause it?

I tried to recall what had happened back in the conference room before the last attack had sent me jumping in the aquarium. Everything seemed fine—until Jeff Elrod had pushed my buttons.

Anger . . . I was angry.

And what about the first time . . . in the lab? I had been looking at all the dead rats. I wasn't angry that time; I was scared. Filled with fear.

What had Rachel Solomon told me about fear?

"Kwan, the more you dwell on the negative outcome, the more you'll attract that outcome. That's how fear works. It manifests a negative energy field that brings the actual situation to life."

What did fear and anger have in common? What was it about these two emotions that caused my DNA to circumvent my respiratory system?

Both emotions engaged the body's "fight or flight" response. Heart rate, blood pressure, and respiration all increased, while the adrenal glands flooded the body with stress hormones.

Stress hormones? Which ones were being secreted?

I had studied this back in tenth grade health class. What was the mnemonic device I had used to study for the final?

Adrenal glands. Adrenaline and gambling. Gambling in Vegas—no, no, not Vegas. Atlantic City. AC. A was for adrenaline, what did the C stand for?

I closed my eyes to think . . . and then suddenly it came to me, and it all made sense!

Cortisol.

During fight or flight, the adrenal glands released cortisol to suppress the immune system. Conversely, the shark stem cells were designed to supercharge the immune system.

When I had been afraid and angry, my adrenal glands had flooded my system with cortisol, weakening my human immune system, creating a void for the shark stem cells to take control of my respiratory system.

Rachel Solomon was right. If I could control my emotions, I could control the mutation.

It really was mind over matter.

The pickup truck had driven west over the Rickenbacher Causeway to Interstate 95. The signs passing overhead indicated we were heading east on the MacArthur Causeway to Miami Beach.

After twenty minutes of driving in traffic, the driver parked the truck. I remained in back while he changed his shirt inside the cab. With a whiff of cologne, he exited the vehicle, slamming the door shut.

I waited another minute before sitting up to gauge my new surroundings.

Crowds, music, neon lights . . . flavored by a thousand scents carried on a warm ocean breeze.

I was in South Beach.

Located on the southernmost tip of Miami Beach, South Beach is a mecca of seaside hotels and brightly painted stucco buildings, street cafés, and nightclubs. Stroll down Collins Avenue and you may spot a pop star or an actor sharing the scene with local artists and European tourists, scantily clad women and men flashing their six-pack abs. Hit the beach, lunch at a café, dine at a five-star restaurant or hit a pizza joint or sushi bar . . . then party until dawn at dance clubs where the women dress to possess. Tattooed flesh, wild hair, no inhibitions . . . and it's all fabulous.

South Beach may also have been the only populated area east of San Francisco where I wouldn't stand out.

The pizza guy had left his passenger door unlocked. I found his grease-stained T-shirt in the cab and put it on, only my shoulder and arm muscles tore the fabric at the seams. Still barefoot, I walked out of the 10th Street parking lot onto Collins Avenue.

I was in survival mode, my needs simple. I was beyond hungry—my last meal thirty hours ago. I needed shoes and a change of clothing, and I needed sleep.

I continued walking east another block to Ocean Drive. It was after two in the morning, the night was still young, and I was flying way above the radar. Beyond the lights and cafés and bumper-to-bumper traffic was a wide stretch of pristine beach and the Atlantic—a dark void that seemed safer than the crowded streets of SoBe.

"It has to be him, Spencer; look at his body. How many Asians are built like that?"

I turned to face the woman with the British accent and found myself face to face with a family of three. The husband, whose hairless scalp resembled mine, apologized for his wife's comments. "Forgive Gail, you're her first celebrity since we arrived on Thursday. Really, we're big fans. Especially my daughter, Zoey."

"Dad!" The teen rolled her eyes at her father.

I looked down at the man's sandals. "Want a picture—me and your daughter?"

"Would you mind? That would be incredible."

"A photo for your shoes."

"My shoes?"

"Spencer, give him your sandals."

"I just bought these sandals."

"Dad, you're embarrassing me. If Kwan Wilson wants your sandals, then you give Kwan Wilson your sandals."

"They probably smell," said Gail, nudging me. "He's been wearing them the entire trip."

"That's because you forgot to pack my kicks. Where's your shoes, Kwan?"

"I lost them on the beach."

"Really, Dad? Like it's any of your business."

"Fine. You want my shoes, take them, only I'm getting in the photo, too." The Englishman freed his feet from the Velcro straps and handed me his sandals. "Hope you didn't lose your underwear on the beach."

Gail took a photo of Zoey and me with her iPhone; then we had a passerby take one of the four of us, and I had my shoes . . . and a growing crowd.

Seeking anonymity, I headed south where a line of people had gathered beneath turquoise-blue awnings.

* * *

Mark Coney was twenty-eight, his wife, Shaina, twenty-three. While I was bartering for shoes, the couple from North Carolina was waiting in line a block away outside Mango's Tropical Café, one of the most popular destinations in South Beach.

Mark Coney felt uneasy. There was a certain vulnerability with having a hot wife, and Shaina was hot. Her wavy, thick brown hair fell down to her tight waistline; her scantily clad athletic figure attracted looks from every guy and gal who passed by.

None of that bothered Mark. It was the three Cuban men waiting in line behind them that made him feel uneasy.

The big man whom the others called Jorge was buzzed and physically imposing. His mate, Paco, had cocaine eyes and a handgun tucked into his waistband. But it was Raul, the vocal ringleader, who Mark feared the most.

"Hey, *mami*. Why you hangin' with this *págaro*?"

Mark positioned himself behind his wife. "Ignore them. We'll be inside in five minutes."

"Hey, white boy. You gonna let us buy the *chica* a drink? Hey, *chica—Oye asere, que bola?*"

The three men laughed.

"Mark, maybe we should go?"

"It's okay," he said, searching Ocean Drive for a cop.

Mark Coney would have left with his wife long ago, only he knew the three men would follow them to his car, which was parked half a mile away on a far less populated block. With their leader growing bolder, he was no longer sure the crowded bar offered sanctuary.

And that's when he saw me.

"Shaina, wait here a second, I'll be right back."

"You're Kwan, right?"

I looked up to find an Italian-looking man with jet-black hair and a desperate look blocking my way.

"Mark Coney, big fan." He pointed to an attractive woman standing in line. "My wife and I wanted to know if we could treat you to dinner at Mango's."

"Sorry, man. I'm not really into that."

"No, no, it's just dinner. See, there are these three Cuban guys harassing us, and I just thought if you joined us, you know . . . maybe they'd back off. I'll even buy you a new shirt."

I glanced down at the filthy cloth pinning my biceps. "Okay."

"Really? That's great."

He led me over to his wife, who was being bumped from behind by a Hispanic man with a pencil-thin mustache.

"Shaina, this is Kwan Wilson . . . you know, that basketball player who was paralyzed. Kwan's going to be joining us for dinner. That's okay, right?"

"Sure." She held out her hand, relieved. "Shaina."

The man behind her leered. "Shaina. I got Shaina on the braina, eh, Paco."

I wedged myself behind Mark's wife so that I was standing eyeball to eyeball with the drunk.

What to do? What to say? There were so many options to choose from. I could have growled at him while I gave him the Clint Eastwood squint. I could have grabbed a handful of his testicles like Tony Soprano, or smashed his skull against his bigger friend's head and knocked the two of them out like Moe Howard from the Three Stooges. I could have pulled a Mike Tyson and bitten his ear off, or crushed his shoulder muscle clear down to his clavicle like Arnold Schwarzenegger in *Terminator 2*.

And after I "Hulked out," then what? The anger would cause my adrenal glands to release a wave of cortisol, and I'd end up sprinting across the street to make it to the ocean in time before my emerging gills would suffocate me.

So instead of losing it, instead of proving to the world how tough I was, I looked into the Cuban's psychotic eyes, pursed my lips, and lisped, "You fellas come here often?"

"Huh?"

"When we get inside, you can buy me a drink. Something sweet . . . like you." I pinched his oily cheek, causing him to stumble backward.

"Coney, party of two?"

Mark turned to the hostess. "Right here, only we're three now."

I blew the three men a kiss, and followed the couple inside.

Mango's was loud salsa music, strobe lights, wall-to-wall people, and bikini-clad girls dancing on bars in their knee-high boots. We were seated upstairs and handed menus. A waitress came by and Mark ordered a pitcher of mojitos and a plate of barbequed rib appetizers for the table; then he excused himself and left me sitting with his wife.

"It must be amazing to be able to walk again."

"Yes," I said, my eyes searching the crowd for Elrod's thugs. "So, what does your husband do?"

"He manages a Hampton Inn. Kwan, are you looking for someone?"

"Huh? No. I mean, just those guys who were harassing you."

She pointed. The three men were drinking at the bar, their attention focused on the bikini-clad dancers. "I think we're safe now. You don't have to stay if you don't want to."

"I don't mind. Actually, I'm hungry. Plus my wardrobe can use an upgrade."

Mark returned, handing me a Mango's tropical print Tommy Bahama shirt. "Hope this fits. It's the biggest size they had."

"Thanks. I'll go try it on." Targeting a restroom sign, I squeezed through the crowd, the dance music's heavy bass pounding in my ears. I entered the men's room and an empty stall, then tore off the frayed remains of the T-shirt and slipped my arms through the short sleeves of the shirt.

The fit was still tight, but at least I didn't stick out in the crowd as much.

I expelled what seemed like a gallon of pee that smelled like seawater mixed with sewage. Then I washed my hands and gave a quick biceps flex in the mirror—which was stupid because my muscles tore the fabric.

Chiding my ego, I left the bathroom, exiting to the pulsating music.

The food had arrived, but Mark and Shaina had left. Dancing, I assumed. I searched the dance floor, but it was wall-to-wall people. And so I ate.

Twenty minutes, a plate of ribs, and a cheeseburger later and they had still not returned. I stood and searched the dance floor again; then I scanned the bar.

That's when I noticed the three Cuban men had left.

I pushed my way down the stairwell and crossed the dance floor to the exit, emerging outside. There were still people waiting to get in, but no sign of Mark and Shaina.

Nothing I can do now. Besides, I completed my end of the deal; it's not my fault they cut out early. Forget about them and find a place to sleep.

Crossing Ocean Drive, I headed for the sand dunes.

Maybe it was a gnawing sense of guilt, I don't know, but suddenly I didn't feel so good. It wasn't my respiratory system—I could breathe just fine . . . it was my belly. Seeking privacy, I ran toward a dark stretch of beach, bent over, and puked.

Everything I had consumed—ribs, cheeseburger, fries, mojitos—erupted out of my mouth, followed by something else . . . *my stomach!* It was as if I had blown a bubble gum balloon and sucked it back inside my mouth, only this balloon was the size of a grapefruit and it was rubbery and flexible, and it happened so fast I didn't realize what it was until I inhaled it back down my throat.

I staggered away from my regurgitated dinner, then dropped to my knees in the cool sand and rolled over on my back, staring at the night sky. I had read that sharks could remove indigestible items from their stomach, things like license plates and human limbs, through an act known as stomach eversion that literally sent the lining of the belly out of the body. If that's what had just happened, then the shark stem cells had succeeded in mutating my digestive organs as well as my respiratory system, and God only knew what else.

What could I eat that would stay down?

Asshole. You should have ordered the fish.

And then I heard a scream.

They had walked Mark and Shaina out of the club by gunpoint. Crossed the street to the beach and disappeared behind the dark stretch of dunes.

Mark was lying on his back, bleeding from a head wound. The big Cuban was standing over him, his booted right foot on top of his wrist, preventing him from moving. The addict was removing Mark's watch from his other wrist—both attackers watching Raul, their pulses racing with cocaine and lust.

Raul was on his knees in the sand, hovering over Shaina. One hand held a gun to her head; the other was fighting with the woman to remove her skirt. "This is going to happen, *chica*. Now you be a good girl or I'll have Jorge shoot your honey."

Shaina's cries quieted to whimpers as Raul turned and aimed his gun at her husband. Mark tried to fight the bigger man, only to be stomped in the gut.

Standing in the shadows, an eyewitness to evil—I felt a wave of adrenaline coursing through my bloodstream like hot magma . . . only this time I refused to flee; this time I needed to stand and fight—not by ceasing my transformation, but by channeling it.

Gurgling softly in my throat, I traced the insertion of the muscular membrane in my esophagus and forcibly flexed it open, preventing my gills from taking over my respiratory system. Harnessing my rage, I willed my denticle skin to manifest . . . my flesh thickening as quickly as a chameleon changed colors.

I blinked my eyes . . . and I could see in the darkness.

I inhaled the night . . . and smelled Mark's blood in the air.

My lips receded and my tongue ran across the sharp tips of my triangular teeth.

The muscles of my upper back arched . . . and I attacked.

An athlete tapes his ankles to secure a weak joint; he wears an elastic sleeve for strength and speed. Multiply these shared effects by a factor of a hundred and you might begin to imagine the torque a human muscle can generate when enveloped in denticle-encased shark flesh. To describe the feeling . . . it was as if each muscle had its own miniature set of pistons.

One stride and suddenly I found myself airborne, forced to reach back to grab the gunman on top of Shaina as I hurdled the two of them. I landed on Raul and rolled off him and onto my feet, the startled Cuban's gun flying from his hand as I used his body like a gymnastics mat.

The other two men never moved—they knew something was wrong, only they couldn't see me, so well did my gray-brown skin blend in with the night.

Leaving Raul, I stepped toward the big man and unleashed a right roundhouse punch that shattered Jorge's jaw and separated his mandible from his skull—the man's mangled screams renting the night air.

I turned to confront the third assailant and winced at a bee sting as a bullet grazed my left shoulder. In a haze, I remember tearing the gun from the shooter's hand—only to realize later that I had torn the gun *and his hand* from his wrist.

Regaining his bearings, Raul attempted to crawl away, only I saw him, grabbed him by the ankle, and jerked him face-first into my knee, which rose to meet his nose and front teeth.

For a long moment there was just the ocean breeze blowing over the dunes, Mark and Shaina comforting each other, and the sound of three crippled men moaning in the darkness. Then the cops arrived and what happened next . . . I could only piece together later.

See, there was blood . . . lots of blood. It was on my knee and in my hand, and in my nostrils . . . and in my brain. I didn't know that I had bitten the Cuban until I read about it in the paper, but I guess I did, because the man screamed and flashlights flashed and a swarm of bees stung me across the back and suddenly I was running . . . racing across the beach and into the ocean.

Ducking beneath an incoming wave, I expelled a lung-flattening gasp from my lungs, sending streams of bubbles fluttering out the sides of my neck. Sinking to the shallow's muddy bottom, I pulled myself into deeper water, burping out the remains of my air. I cringed as my sinus cavity sucked my nose flat against my skull and cheekbones and as a deformity of cartilage curled out the back of my heels.

Thirty feet below a moonlit surface, I rested on my knees on the seafloor and took inventory of my wounds. To my surprise, there was a 9mm slug lodged in my left deltoid muscle. The gun had been fired at point-blank range and the bullet should have blown off most of my shoulder, only my dermal denticles had acted like an organic suit of armor, sealing off my underlying muscle. Gripping the hunk of lead between my thumb and index finger, I twisted until the slug popped free, its removal releasing a trail of blood.

I inhaled the dispersing plasma into my nostrils and down my throat, my innards trembling from weakness.

Immersed in survival mode, I needed to eat—something I could digest.

Pushing away from the bottom, I leveled out and began slow, sweeping movements of my hips and legs, my feet propelling me through the sea. With my denticle skin channeling water, it took almost no effort to generate speed. As I watched, the shallows plunged beneath me and I entered deeper water.

At some point the hundreds of sensory pores along my scalp opened, and suddenly the olive-green void came alive.

The effect was indescribable. As a human, my five senses worked independently of one another; as a gilled man (or whatever I was becoming), my sensory system was multilayered. I could hear in surround sound, smell every taste, and pinpoint the precise location of every living creature over a half-mile radius simply by isolating the telltale electrical impulses of its beating heart. More than that, I could *feel* the animal's girth by the amount of water it displaced when it moved and measure its distress levels by its residual odors.

Turning my head, my right nostril inhaled something tantalizing . . . *blood.*

My pulse raced, my belly ached. Using my nose as a GPS, I headed off in the direction of the scent.

My prey was somewhere ahead, its movements erratic. A line of dermal denticles from my armpits down to my ankles were buzzing with vibrations. Even though I was still a football field away from my intended meal, I could register its blood being stirred in the water by the wounded fish's tail.

Homing in on the creature, my movements suddenly became more rigid, my acceleration so rapid that particles shot past my eyes like stars at warp speed. I was moving through the scent trail—and then I felt something else . . . another shark! It was clearly a challenger, and it was advancing on *my meal* from the opposite direction. From its voluminous water displacement I could sense it was bigger and faster than me.

I didn't care; I needed to eat. And then I saw my competition, and the rules of the food chain quelled my hunger pangs.

The great hammerhead was three times my size and outweighed me by at least seven hundred pounds. It was so big that I was closer in size to the three-foot tuna we were both pursuing. The albacore was zigzagging thirty feet below the surface, fighting from being reeled backward through the sea, its lacerated mouth bleeding from the fisherman's hook.

The recognition of a human presence in this life-and-death arena snapped me out of "predator mode." Altering my course, I cruised along the bottom, circling eighty-five feet below the fishing boat, my senses keeping vigil on the hammerhead who was also circling, waiting for the right moment to snag the wounded albacore.

The lull allowed my human side to overrule the predatory stalking response, and once more I was governed by rational thought.

I needed to feed, but my targeted meal had been hooked by a fisherman and was being circled by a monster I had no interest in challenging. The charter boat, however, offered its own menu of delicacies.

Rising away from the bottom, I ascended toward the forty-eight-foot hull, giving a wide berth to my competition. From the location of the struggling albacore, I knew the fisherman would be positioned along the portside rail. Targeting the starboard engine, I poked my head above the waterline, keeping my mouth and gills underwater.

A mouse-gray dawn identified the eastern horizon, separating the night from the Atlantic. The fishing charter bobbed before me in five-foot seas. I could hear voices on board—two men encouraging a third.

". . . there ye go, Anthony, there ye go!"

"I see 'em. He's a big boy. Another albacore."

"Good thing I went with the twenty pound test. Skipper, get ready with the gaff."

Quietly, I reached for the gunwale, pulling myself out of the water. All of the action was along the portside deck where three men and a woman had lines in the water, and an authoritative dude, most likely the charter's captain—was standing by the rail with an eight-foot-long gaff.

Focusing on the aft deck, I saw what I was after—a horizontal storage locker filled with ice . . . and fish.

Holding the water in my mouth, clenching my gills shut, I climbed on board, took one step onto the fiberglass deck with my elongated bare feet . . . and slipped, landing hard on my back. The blow knocked the seawater from my mouth and released my gills, and suddenly I couldn't breathe!

"What was that?" The captain, a burly man, headed for the stern, the eight-foot pole in his hand ending in a six-inch hook.

Move!

On all fours, I scrambled across the deck to the open storage bin—only to have the lid slammed shut.

"What in the holy hell are you?" The captain's mate loomed over me, a beer in one hand, and a machete in the other.

My vision suddenly blurred. The protective membrane was still in place—my eyes no doubt appearing bulbous, reflecting alien-green in the darkness. My skin tingled as the thirty-inch blade whistled in the night air, the plunging steel intended for my brain . . .

"Ahhhhhhhhh!"

The captain never saw his first mate until the screaming man's airborne body struck him chest high and both men tumbled over the rail into the Atlantic.

Searching the ice chest, I grabbed a dead albacore by the base of its tail and jumped feetfirst into the water, gasping a life-giving mouthful of ocean. A few deep inhales and the burning sensation subsided, my gills pumping again.

Hovering beneath the keel, I sensed the erratic movements of the two men flailing along the surface. The hammerhead sensed them, too, the eighteen-foot shark rising to attack!

Releasing my fish, I torpedoed beneath the hull into the path of the ascending monster. Grabbing the beast by its mallet-shaped head the way a rodeo clown intercepts a charging bull, I straddled the hammerhead's back, twisting its eye sockets backward as I wrapped my legs around its muscular torso.

The two of us breached the surface.

For a surreal moment, I found myself staring into the startled face of a middle-aged redheaded woman, and then my mount and I plunged sideways into the sea, the hammerhead's girth writhing violently on top of me as it tried to shake me loose.

Instead of releasing the muscular behemoth, I held on, rolling it onto its back as I had seen Joe Botchin do with Taurus. Within seconds, the animal became docile.

I remained pinned upside down to the shark's back until I no longer registered the two men's racing heartbeats. Uncurling my legs, I rolled the hammerhead dorsal-side up, watching the shaken predator dart into the depths.

I inhaled the sea into my nostrils, searching the vicinity for my hard-won meal, only to realize the dead tuna was gone—claimed by a swarm of smaller sharks. Diving toward the feeding frenzy, I located a fist-size chunk of meat and quickly shoved it into my mouth. I chewed it into tiny bites, the action purging the seawater from my gullet—allowing me to gulp the mangled hunk of tuna down my esophagus. The protective membrane opened and closed behind it . . . my first meal underwater.

Satiated, I dove deep, hitching a ride on a northeasterly twist of current. The river of rushing water carried me effortlessly along the bottom. The shoreline thundered softly in the distance, my troubles a million miles away . . .

nnie, it's Kwan."

"Kwan? Where the hell have you been? Oprah's people have been blowing up my cell phone for three days. Why did you cancel the interview? You hired me to represent you and—"

"I didn't cancel. Someone else made that decision without asking me."

"Who? I'll rip their throat out."

"A guy who works for my father. It's a long story, and I'm telling it all to Oprah tomorrow as scheduled, only it has to be a live interview."

"Live? You can't do it live. The interview isn't scheduled to be aired until next week. They've been promoting the hell out of it."

"Annie, we either do it live tomorrow or the powers that be will shut it down. Once it airs they can always show it again, but this is the way it has to be. Make the arrangements; I'll call you in the morning."

"Kwan, wait—"

I hung up the cell phone and handed it back to Ryan Davis. Pulling the hood of the Florida State University sweatshirt low over my head, I followed the hotel manager through an Italian Renaissance courtyard past tropical landscaping to the waterfront.

The sun had just set, casting a golden-orange glow over the pool deck and a stretch of private beach to the azure ocean that dominated the postcard view.

Five-star accommodations, spas and pools, bikini-clad women . . . this was the lifestyle I yearned for.

The Breakers Resort occupied one hundred and forty acres of oceanfront property in the heart of the barrier island of Palm Beach. I had staggered onshore three hours earlier, having spent the better part of the last day under water, traveling close to one hundred nautical miles.

My plan was simple—I'd tell the truth on live TV to Oprah. Everything from my relationship with my father, to the texting that had caused the car wreck that killed my mother and caused me to be paralyzed, to my internship at ANGEL—even the side effects. By exposing everything, I'd force my father to call off his dogs and help Dr. Becker raise the funding to support her research. Most of all, by exposing what had happened, I'd be able to force the lab to treat me with the beta-blockers without Jeff Elrod or some other CIA black ops assassin messing with my cure.

Mr. Davis led me past another pool and over a small bridge to a private oasis where the resort's twenty-five bungalows were located. He keyed into Bungalow Seven and handed me the magnetic card. "You can stay here until noon, Kwan; then we need to clean it for a three p.m. check-in."

"Noon's great. Thanks again, Mr. Davis. And remember—"

"I know, I know. Not a word to anyone."

I entered the bungalow, which was more of a plush cottage, featuring a living area, kitchen, master suite, and bath. I slipped off my sweatshirt and matching sweat pants, and climbed into the king-size bed, exhausted.

It was not the journey from South Miami Beach to the Breakers Resort in Palm Beach that had worn me down; it had been the willpower to become human again.

Back in tenth grade health class, I had spent a semester being lectured about the dangers of addiction. The sensation of pleasure, whether from sex, drugs, rock and roll, or a mouth-watering cheeseburger is caused by the release of the neurotransmitter dopamine. The area of the midbrain that releases dopamine is known as the reward pathway in that it rewards a desired behavior. Evolution utilized the reward pathway so that we humans would feel good when we engaged in behaviors that were necessary to our survival—stuff like eating and making babies. Whether natural or artificially stimulated, the release of dopamine is what gives us the sensation of pleasure.

Substances like alcohol and nicotine, as well as drugs like pot and heroin, also cause the brain to release dopamine, only in powerful surges. A drug's level of addiction is directly related to the speed, intensity, and reliability of that release.

In much the same way, the act of using my new underwater senses caused my rewired brain to release high levels of dopamine—the more predatory my action, the greater the jolt.

Consuming the hunk of tuna had not only staved off starvation, it had excited my pleasure center, telling me I needed more food. Revisiting the charter boat was out of the question, which meant I had to hunt and kill live prey for myself.

The manta rays were scattered along the bottom, camouflaged by sand. My first six attempts to capture one of these three-foot bat-like creatures must have resembled Rocky Balboa attempting to catch a chicken. Swapping speed for stealth, I was finally able to snag one of the elusive creatures . . . and promptly bit its head off à la Ozzy Osbourne.

Manta ray was tough eating; turtle meat was a delicacy. I had homed in on the green turtle at first light, attracted by its deep, hypnotic pulse and a scent that no doubt rendered it a desirable feast for bull sharks. Unable to bite and crush the shell with my weak human jaws, I grabbed the back end of the lower casing with both hands, then wedged my feet against the upper shell and pried the entire tank-like armor off of the stunned wounded reptile. Then I ravaged the calipee—the fat attached to the lower shell—the main ingredient in green turtle soup.

If these acts sound gruesome, well, I suppose they would be to a human . . . even a gilled human. But I had changed. Swimming in a tank was one thing, inhabiting the ocean something quite different. The ocean is a liquid jungle; you're either hunting prey to survive or you are prey trying to survive.

At first I was the latter. Endowed with four awkward human limbs, I moved far slower in the water than most of the fish I was trying to catch or avoid being eaten by. Hunting alone also left me quite vulnerable, and while possessing sharper-than-human teeth may have allowed me to chew through raw fish, my jaws were far too weak to be considered a threat to another creature.

It wasn't until I had to defend the turtle meat from a barracuda that I realized the shark stem cells had endowed me with two lethal weapons.

A shark's dermal denticles are actually miniature skin teeth that are ribbed with longitudinal grooves. As I discovered back in the tank, these grooves channeled water and propelled me through my liquid environment. When I flexed a certain body part, say my knee or elbow, the denticle teeth became more pronounced.

Nowhere was this more prominent than when I made a fist. The flexed knuckles along the back of my hand formed three-inch spikes that were as tough as nails and as sharp as blades, and suddenly I was a very dangerous creature.

It was about that time that I began *thinking* like a dangerous creature.

Consuming living flesh was far different than eating the cooked meat of a dead animal. Living flesh was warmed by blood. Blood had a pulse and a rhythm when I bit into it that made it . . . well, addictive. With each successful kill and succulent bite of living flesh, I found myself losing more of my human consciousness, until I no longer knew my own name.

Ironically, it was a shark that forced me to confront my own predatory addiction and save my soul.

Bull sharks are solitary hunters. Extremely territorial, they prefer to hunt in the shallows, a fact that makes them the species most dangerous to human bathers. It was a bull shark that ventured up a freshwater river in New Jersey in 1916 and went on a killing spree, and it was a bull shark that intercepted me as I approached the barrier island in Palm Beach.

The predator was a female, about nine feet and a thousand pounds. She had been trailing me since late in the afternoon when I had ventured into the sun-drenched shallows, lured in by the hypnotic break of the waves. Moving to within a mile of shore, I found myself suddenly aware of not only the bull shark but of something far more familiar . . . the presence of humans.

I could smell their suntan oil; taste their telltale urine. I could feel their plodding movements and discern their trepidation by their fluctuating pulses.

The female bull shark could sense them, too. Moving parallel to shore in only ten feet of water, she targeted an adult and a child.

I felt the predator's movements quicken. She was in attack mode, her aggressiveness fueled by the presence of a competitor in her territory . . . *me!*

Lost in the fog of darkness, my consciousness lit a candle and I remembered who and what I was.

Shortening my own kicks, I soared inland like a bronze torpedo, hell-bent on intercepting the bull shark before she slaughtered the unsuspecting bathers. Ten feet from her intended target, the female detected my bold challenge and circled out to meet me, her senses assuring her that I was smaller and slower—an easy kill.

I felt her coming and stopped swimming. She appeared in the murky, sun-drenched shallows seconds later—a gray, blunt-nosed devil racing toward me at twenty knots.

I settled upright on the bottom, offering her an easy target.

Her back muscles arched, her jaws opening as she launched her attack.

I balled my fists—and ducked.

Momentarily blinded by her protective nictitating eyelids, the half-ton behemoth soared inches over my head—the bladed edges of my denticle-covered knuckles slicing open her exposed soft underbelly like an electric knife carving through a Thanksgiving Day ham.

The agitated bull shark continued another ten yards, then circled back and forth through a crimson cloud of blood, never realizing the meal she was consuming was her own eviscerated entrails.

Sensing my predatory instincts returning, I continued gliding inland, away from the tempting taste of blood. Locating a deserted stretch of shallows, I rose out of a breaking swell and trudged toward shore. I expelled seawater from my gills, then inhaled a lung-inflating gasp of salty air as my vision cleared. I felt my porous scalp tighten, and my flattened nose pop back into place as my sinus cavity returned, my flesh continuing to thin as I shed my shark armor.

Naked and alone, I collapsed to my knees on the deserted resort shoreline.

Kwan Wilson . . . fugitive.

"Hey, Dad, I found a naked man."

"Don't go near him, Blake."

I opened my eyes to a cobalt-blue sky and a man in bathing trunks who was covering his six-year-old son's eyes. "This isn't a nude beach, fella."

"Sorry. I . . . uh, I must have lost my bathing suit in the surf."

He tossed me his towel, which I wrapped around my waist. "The waves are rough today. My son and I had to come in." He uncovered the boy's eyes. "See the man's big muscles, Blake. Eat your veggies and one day you'll be big and strong like him."

"Why aren't you big and strong like him, Dad?"

"Because Daddy doesn't use steroids. Wait a sec . . . you're him! The crippled fella who plays basketball. Gordon Walpole, nice to meet you . . . ?"

"Kwan."

"Kwan, right. Our family's down from Canada; the wife and I saw you last week on the evening news. Can you wait here? I want to get my camera."

"Think you can bring me some clothes, Gordon?"

"Clothes? Sure. There's a shop by the pool. Do you have any money? No, I guess not. No problem, happy to come to your rescue. Say, what happened to your knuckles?"

I looked at the back of my hands, which were bleeding, the skin scraped clean off. "Must have sliced them on some corral."

"That's dangerous, you could draw sharks. Wait here, then; I'll only be a minute. Come on, Blake, Daddy needs to get his wallet."

Annie Moir knocked on my bungalow door at five minutes before nine the next morning. In one hand she held a suit bag containing a freshly pressed pair of black dress pants and a matching polo shirt, in the other were dress shoes, a leather belt, and clean underwear. She entered the cottage, kissed me on the cheek, laid the clothes out on the bed, and then sniffed the air. "What is that God-awful stench?"

"Sorry. Must've been something I ate."

"Teenagers. You have cast-iron stomachs. Before I forget, your grandmother said not to call her until later this afternoon, something about working in the OR."

"Was she upset about me not calling her yesterday?"

"She was furious. I told her we were prepping you for your interview and she calmed down."

"Good one."

"Don't make me lie for you again. Better get dressed, the network's sending a limo for us at nine thirty."

"Turn around." I slipped out of the sweat suit Gordon Walpole had purchased for me, pulling on my boxers and pants. "The interview's still live, correct?"

"Live at eleven a.m., just like we discussed earlier. They're pre-empting a taped interview with Justin Bieber, which is perfect—the viewer demographics should be close."

"I've been watching Oprah's network all morning and didn't see one announcement."

The publicist frowned. "You said you wanted it live to avoid your father shutting us down. What's the point if we let the world know hours before you go on?"

"Right." I smiled, embarrassed. "Okay, you can turn around."

"My God, every time I see you your muscles look bigger. Stop working out so much; it's tough to find shirts that fit you."

"Did you try calling Anya's parents again?"

"Three times. I finally got through to her father's graduate assistant at FAU. He said the family left for London last night to attend a cousin's funeral. They'll be back Friday."

"Did he give you the cousin's name?"

"Kwan, the cousin's dead. Why do I need a name?"

I felt my blood pressure rising. *What if they deported Anya's family . . . or worse?* I forced myself to take a few long, deep breaths to cool off. *Fear and anger—stay calm.*

Annie's cell phone rang. "Moir Agency, Annie speaking." She paused to listen. "You're early. We're in Bungalow Seven." She hung up. "The limo's here."

"Who were you talking to?"

"I hired a security guard. If there's really a threat to keep you off the air, then we may need him. Plus it adds a little intrigue to your story . . . whatever it is."

"You don't believe me?"

"You haven't told me anything, Kwan. Tell me something not to believe."

"You'll hear everything when Oprah hears it."

I went into the bathroom to brush my teeth and make sure my gill slits weren't showing. I was anxious about Anya, worried Jeff Elrod might endanger her life in order to flush me out of hiding.

Relax. In less than two hours you'll be the one flushing.

I heard a man's heavy knock on the bungalow door.

Mark Edward Burton sported square-cut glasses and a brown goatee that matched his short-cropped hair. He had some size to him, was dressed like a South Beach businessman in loafers with no socks, and was carrying a 9mm Glock in a holster beneath his white sports coat.

He walked past my handshake to search the bedroom and bath, adding to my annoyance by sniffing the air. "Something reeks like bad fish."

"It's your mother. She was over last night."

Burton shot me a snarky grin. "They said you were a wiseass."

A jolt of adrenaline shot through me. "Who's they? Elrod? My father?"

His smile disappeared, his eyes darting to Annie.

My publicist's expression dropped, along with my heart. "There is no interview scheduled with Oprah, is there, Annie?"

"Kwan—"

"The Admiral's people got to you, didn't they? Didn't they?!"

Burton reached for his gun, only he miscalculated my quickness—my front thrust kick meeting his chest like a sledgehammer striking concrete, cracking his sternum while sending him flying backward across an end table, shattering a lamp.

They were through the bungalow door before his body hit the floor—two assassins armed with dart guns. One projectile hit me in the chest, the other penetrated my right thigh.

Refusing to go down, I plowed through them and into the suddenly brilliant tunnel of daylight, the ocean sparkling thirty yards away.

Get to the water!

I searched for the path, my legs moving in slow motion . . . everything spinning. My breathing became labored as I toppled sideways over a shrub . . . into darkness.

Pain forced open an eye. I was in an ambulance. I tried to move, but my wrists were handcuffed to the sides of a gurney. There was an IV and it was spinning like a carousel, and one of the bungalow dudes was speaking in distorted echoes over a cell phone.

Hey, Bungalow Bill. What did you kill . . . Bungalow Bill.

"Kwan?"

A familiar male voice dragged me out of a drug-induced sleep.

"Open your eyes."

I opened them. I was lying on my back in a blue collar office, staring at a water-stained drop ceiling and fake wood-paneled walls. Someone had dressed me in a camouflage-colored neoprene body suit. For a frightening moment I feared I was paralyzed again—I couldn't move my arms and legs—until I realized my wrists and ankles were shackled to the gurney.

"It's good to see you, son."

The face now looming over me belonged to a man in his late fifties, his rugged features giving him a slight resemblance to Liam Neeson, the actor who played the kick-ass dude in *Taken* . . . a guy who had been kicking my ass for most of the last seventeen years.

"Admiral?"

"I'm your father, Kwan. Why don't you try calling me Dad."

I grinned, barely conscious. "Why don't you try treating me like a son instead of an enlisted man . . . or a prisoner of war. Do I get an attorney, or are you sending me to Gitmo?"

"The restraints were necessary. You crushed Mr. Burton's chest and nearly killed him. As for treating you like a son—you're right, I was too hard on you. But it's not too late to make amends."

"By kidnapping your only child? Not off to a great start, are we, *Dad*?"

"Do you know why you can walk again, Kwan? You can walk again and run like a deer and dunk a basketball because I funded the research that healed your spine . . . research that one day may heal a lot of paralyzed people's spines. Had you only waited until Dr. Becker completed her work you would have been one of the first chosen to receive the stem cell injections. Instead, as always, you had to do things your way."

"Hey, you were the one who kicked me out of the internship program."

"That's because I know the way you are, and your actions proved me right. Why is it that the basic rules of society don't seem to apply to you? Hacking into my e-mails . . . texting while driving—your mother's dead because you couldn't follow a simple rule. Stealing Becker's stem cells . . . injecting them into your body with no regard for protocol—all you ever cared about was yourself."

I swallowed a lump in my throat, feeling the cartilage in my esophagus. My old man may have been a bastard, but he was right.

"Believe it or not, Kwan, I'm here to offer you a chance to earn your cure and redeem yourself in my eyes and in the eyes of our Lord and Savior. First, however, we need to do a little test. You won't be in any danger; Dr. Kamrowski and I simply need to know the limits of your mutation. Depending upon how well you do, I may offer you a mission that utilizes your newfound aquatic skills. Complete the task and Dr. Becker will administer the beta-blockers that will neutralize your mutation. Once you're cured, you can return to the life of fame and fortune that awaits you."

"What's the test?"

"Nothing strenuous or dangerous. We just want to see if your mutated state can handle a little water pressure."

My heart pounded in my chest. "How much is a little?"

He patted me on the chest. "Just do your best, son."

Geez . . .

The two men who had tranquilized me wheeled my gurney out of the office and down a short corridor into an empty warehouse—empty, save for a massive hyperbaric chamber.

Waiting for me by the pressurized door was Nadja Kamrowski.

"Kwan, inside this hyperbaric chamber is a sphere. After I release you, you'll enter the chamber and climb inside the sphere, sealing the hatch. Inside the sphere is a control panel with a green button and a red button. Push the green button once and the capsule will begin filling with seawater. Allow your respiratory system to mutate. Once the capsule is filled with water and you feel ready to proceed, press the green button twice more and we'll begin gradually increasing the pressure within the hyperbaric chamber which will raise the water pressure inside the sphere. If you feel like it's too much, press the red button and we'll dial it back and get you out of there. Even though your gills won't allow you to talk, we'll be communicating with you through the entire process. We'll also be monitoring your heart rate and blood pressure using instruments built into your neoprene suit. Do you have any questions before I uncuff you?"

"Where's Anya?"

"Somewhere safe. She'll be released after you complete the test."

The two guards raised their weapons while Dr. Kamrowski keyed my restraints. I stood up, rubbing my wrists, peeking inside the hyperbaric chamber. Inside was an eight-foot-in-diameter metal sphere, the hatch propped open on top.

I hesitated, then entered the chamber. Stepping over a spider's web of hoses and cables, I mounted the sphere and lowered myself through the open hatch, twisting it shut behind me.

The interior was padded—small, but not claustrophobic. I sat down on a bench seat that faced two colored buttons and a digital pressure gauge set at 0.00.

Would they hurt Anya if I refused to cooperate? I didn't think so. Still, there was a desperateness in my father's eyes that suggested now was not the time to test his boundaries.

The question was—how far did they intend to test mine?

I took a few deep breaths, then pressed the green button.

Seawater entered from a floor vent, jump-starting an unexpected wave of anxiety. The sudden sensation of claustrophobia was overwhelming—the human condition refusing to release me from its stranglehold. My esophageal membrane spasmed, unable to close. For a three-minute eternity I remained in the near darkness, still gulping air—hyperventilating as the water continued to rise. I waited until it had reached my neck, then slammed my palm against the red button.

Dr. Kamrowski's voice crackled over a speaker. "Kwan, what's wrong?"

"Dunno. Can't . . . calm myself."

I heard my father's muffled voice in the background. "Isn't it obvious? Look at his vital signs—he's panicking."

He was right. I tried submerging, and still nothing was changing. It was as if the mutation refused to reveal itself to my father.

And then I heard the Admiral say something that changed the game.

"I've had enough. Drown the little bastard and be done with it."

Within seconds the seawater rose above my head, stealing the last few inches of air. I pounded the tank—enraged—then burped out a belly of bubbles that collapsed my lungs and caused my gills to flutter to life.

Within thirty seconds the transformation was complete, my skin thick with dermal denticles, my air cavities having internally pancaked.

With far too much strength, I struck the green button, shattering the mechanism.

"Kwan, it's Dr. K. Your vitals have calmed significantly; I'm assuming your gills are functioning again. If you're ready to proceed, hit the green . . . never mind, it looks like you may have disconnected it. If you're up to beginning the water pressure test, gently tap the red button three times."

I complied—for all the wrong reasons.

Drown the little bastard? Now they couldn't drag me out. I wanted to show my father what I was made of. I prayed the pressure would kill me. I'd stay in this container until my skull imploded, just to teach the heartless jerk a lesson.

My eyes adjusted, casting the dark confines in an olive aura.

As I watched, the pressure gauge began rising: 100 psi . . . 200 psi . . .

Water has weight. To calculate water pressure you start with the weight of the Earth's atmosphere at sea level, which is 14.7 pounds per square inch. Each additional 14.7 pounds under water equates to 33 feet, a standard measurement known as an atmosphere. Applying the math—every foot of depth under water weighs .445 pounds. A depth of one thousand feet therefore equals 445 pounds per square inch . . . the equivalent of two adults sitting on top of you.

Yesterday, my maximum depth had probably been less than five hundred feet. I felt nothing then and I felt nothing now—even though the depth gauge was passing 2,000 psi—the equivalent of descending nearly five thousand feet.

Minutes became hours. My mind grew restless.

I thought about what happened back at the resort. Annie had betrayed me . . . or more likely, she worked for Elrod and had been monitoring me from the first day I met her in the hospital. The CIA was always two steps ahead of the game, and the boys in black ops had money to burn. They had probably spent a hundred grand on the hyperbaric chamber and sphere, and would end up leaving it in this warehouse to rot.

Still, they needed me for something . . . and I had nearly failed. Would my father have allowed me to drown? Had he issued his second Do Not Resuscitate order, or was it one of his mind games to get me to perform?

And what of my performance? Anger and fear usually jump-started my adrenal glands, causing my mutation to take over physically. Why, then, had I had so much trouble engaging my gills in the sphere?

Anxiety was far different than fear. Anxiety was neither fight nor flight; it was a paralysis of the mind and body. Overcome by the panic attack, I found myself unable to function, barely able to draw a breath. It was only when my father had flooded the tank that my adrenal glands had finally taken over to rescue me from myself.

The tank creaked around me, the pressure in the hyperbaric chamber testing the sphere's integrity.

The depth gauge passed 13,000 psi . . . and stopped.

Dr. Kamrowski's voice reverberated through the water. "Congratulations, Kwan, you have the intestinal fortitude of a fish. Hang tight; we'll have you out of there soon."

Alone in the control room with the Admiral, Jeff Elrod slapped my father on the back. "Congratulations. Looks like you can recover the package and still keep us on schedule."

"That's the problem with you spooks, Jeffrey; you're always assuming what tests well in the lab performs well in battle. It doesn't. Diving to the bottom of the Puerto Rico Trench is a lot different than sitting in a steel canister and watching numbers flash by on a pressure gauge. Out there the real pressure comes from that little voice screaming in your head. You saw what happened when the water began rising—Kwan panicked. His mind shut down, rendering his mutation useless. Believe me, my friend, I've seen enough 'deer-in the-headlights' paralysis to know you don't rely on an inexperienced operator to fly solo on a mission like this."

"What choice do we have? Woods Hole's pushed back their subs' availability for another five weeks. We can't wait that long . . . unless?"

The Admiral nodded. "Unless someone more experienced—more trustworthy used the stem cells the way Kwan did, and mutated."

"Sabeen?"

"The two of them have more in common than you know. Sabeen's haunted by her past, just like Kwan."

"True. But psychologically, they're on different ends of the spectrum. Sabeen's motivated by revenge, not guilt."

"She hates her life, Jeffrey, and that's all that matters. E-mail her the video of Kwan swimming in the aquarium, then send a chopper to bring her to Miami."

"What about Kwan? He's a celebrity now, which makes him dangerous. We can't risk releasing him."

"Sedate him for the flight out to the *Malchut*."

"But you just said—"

"I said we can't rely on him to complete the mission; I didn't say I wouldn't give him a chance. After all, he is expendable."

Kwan Wilson Suffers Drug Overdose
in Florida Resort

WEST PALM BEACH, FL (Associated Press). Kwan Wilson, the seventeen-year-old paraplegic wunderkind who regained full use of his lower body to become an overnight celebrity and basketball sensation was taken by ambulance Tuesday morning to an undisclosed medical facility after a hotel chambermaid found him lying unconscious in his private bungalow at the Breakers Resort in Palm Beach. Unconfirmed reports suggest a drug overdose may have been involved, possibly cocaine.

Wilson's publicist issued a statement following the incident. "Kwan has undergone a tremendous amount of physical and emotional change in a very short period of time, with everything magnified by being in the public eye twenty-four seven. Neither Kwan's family nor I have any evidence indicating drugs were involved in his collapse, or that his condition is related to his dramatic physical transformation. His location is being kept secret so he can deal with his situation in private."

According to a Breakers employee, Wilson checked into the resort Monday evening to prepare for a Tuesday morning interview with Oprah Winfrey. A spokesman for the Oprah Winfrey Network claims the previously scheduled interview had been canceled two days earlier.

Seacrest High School

While I was being forcibly reunited with my father, Anya was back in school. She was struggling to make it through first period when she was summoned to the guidance counselor's office.

She knocked on the open door and entered. "Mrs. Solomon, you wanted to see me?"

Rachel Solomon looked up from reading the file on her desk. "Come in and close the door. You missed school Monday and Tuesday. Were you sick?"

"Not exactly."

"Then where were you?"

"I can't talk about it."

Rachel Solomon said nothing, allowing the intense gaze of her hazel eyes to do its job.

"I can't talk about it, Mrs. Solomon, because it involves my internship. There are things you don't understand. I signed nondisclosure agreements."

"Where's Kwan?"

Anya looked away. "I don't know."

"You don't know, or you can't disclose his whereabouts?"

"I don't know. Honestly."

"But he was at the lab with you and Li-ling this weekend?"

"Yes."

"What happened?"

"I don't know."

"I don't believe you, young lady. I also don't believe the story that was posted on the front page of today's *Sun Sentinel*. Neither does Kwan's grandmother, who is hiring a lawyer to find out where her grandson was taken, and by whom. You know exactly what happened this weekend, and if you don't tell me, you can tell the police."

Anya broke down in tears. "He told me they'd deport my family if I said anything."

"Who told you that?"

"This guy. I can't tell you his name . . . even if I knew his real name. All I know is that he does some kind of work for Kwan's father."

Key Largo, Florida

Located an hour's drive south of Miami, Key Largo is the largest and first of the islands that make up the Florida Keys. Bordered by Florida Bay to the west and the Atlantic Ocean to the east, Key Largo is home to the John Pennekamp Coral Reef State Park, a seventy-square-mile underwater sanctuary encompassing coral reefs, mangrove swamps, and the *Spiegel Grove*, a 510-foot-long naval vessel sunk in one hundred and thirty feet of water as a dive attraction.

The Sikorsky S-434 light chopper raced west over emerald-green shallows, its pilot slowing as he located his destination—a private estate on the east side of the island on a three-acre lot facing the ocean. Hovering over a stretch of manicured lawn within walking distance of the mansion's swimming pool, the pilot touched down just long enough for the female passenger in the copilot's seat to jump out with her duffle bag.

Instead of ducking, Sabeen Tayfour stood defiantly against the gale-force winds created by the chopper's circulating rotors, the teen's raven-colored hair whipping past her face, her coal-black eyes glittering in the sun as she waited for the helicopter to lift off.

"Sabeen?"

The Syrian freedom fighter turned to find a woman in a blue lab coat, her left eye squinting badly.

"I'm Nadja Kamrowski; we've been expecting you."

"You are the geneticist?"

"One of them, yes."

"You are the one who can transform me into this?" Sabeen held up her cell phone, set to the video she had been watching almost nonstop over the last twenty-four hours.

"Well, yes and no."

Dr. Kamrowski winced as she was dragged to her knees by her ponytail, Sabeen pulling her down to the ground. "What means 'yes and no'? You think this is game?"

"Let me explain. Yes, we can do it, but Kwan—the subject in the video—was mutated using stem cells from a bull shark. Since then, those particular stem cells have lost their potency. We have new, very potent shark stem cells we want to give to you, only these were taken from a tiger shark."

"Tiger shark?" Sabeen released Dr. Kamrowski's hair. "My skin . . . it will have stripes?"

"Dermal denticles only appear when you're underwater, but yes it's possible."

"I will lose my hair?"

"Yes. But that's because your scalp will harbor a sensory organ capable of detecting the electrical impulses produced by a beating heart or moving muscle of any living creature over great distances."

"How long before I am transformed?"

"By placing you in a hyperbaric chamber we can accelerate the effects. Assuming we begin the first dosage right away, we're estimating two to three days."

"And my muscles? Will they grow as large as this man's muscles?"

"We have to stabilize the stem cells using human growth hormone. Being a woman, you won't have huge muscles like Kwan. Then again, female sharks are far larger than their male counterparts, so . . ."

Sabeen reached down and helped the geneticist to her feet. "Give me stripes, Kamrowski. Long, beautiful stripes over large, powerful muscles."

Nadja smiled. "Come inside the house; we have everything waiting."

Twenty minutes after dropping off Sabeen in Key Largo, the Sikorsky S-434 helicopter landed at a private helipad in Homestead, Florida, where three more passengers joined the pilot for his return trip across the Atlantic.

Jeff Elrod rode in the copilot's seat while my father and I sat in back. Perhaps "slumped in back" would be a better description, since I remained semiconscious for the first hour of the flight. I finally came to about halfway to Puerto Rico, only to discover my wrists were shackled to the seat.

The Admiral positioned the straw of a container of orange juice to my lips and I drained the cup. He then adjusted a pair of headphones around my ears, speaking through his headset. "Back in February 2013, the Iranian government announced they had installed a new set of machines in one of their fortified underground facilities designed to enrich uranium. Enriched uranium, as you probably know, is the key ingredient needed in both the generation of nuclear power and nuclear weapons. The mullahs, of course, continue to insist they only want to enrich uranium for nuclear power—as if these oil-rich bastards need it.

"While the Iranian mullahs and their puppet officials continued to play cat and mouse with representatives of the International Atomic Energy Agency and the United Nations, our contacts in Tehran confirmed that Iran's nuclear scientists had produced enough enriched uranium to destroy major cities in Israel and Saudi Arabia. Though they're capable of it, Iran won't launch a nuclear missile at Israel. The Israelis air defense system is top-notch, and their own nuclear arsenal is far greater than the Iranians. Launching a nuke at an Arab nation carries its own blowback.

"The real threat is that the Iranians will provide suitcase bombs to a terrorist organization like al Qaeda, or Hezbollah and Hamas, making September eleventh look like a fender bender. The Bush Doctrine holds the country who supplied enriched uranium to a terrorist organization responsible for a terrorist act—assuming you can prove the enriched uranium used in a suitcase nuke came from that country's reactor.

"When a nuclear device is detonated, it leaves a trail of isotopes that can be used to trace it back to the reactor that produced the enriched U-235. The key is to obtain a sample of the enriched uranium before it's detonated. Just showing the rest of the world that we have a sample can be enough to dissuade Iran from providing nuclear material to these nut jobs."

I glanced at Elrod in the copilot's seat. "I assume that's why he's here."

The Admiral nodded. "A few months ago, we managed to sneak one of our retired Los Angeles attack subs into the Strait of Hormuz. A private militia was used to obtain a sample of enriched uranium from one of the Iranian black sites. The sub made it all the way back to the Atlantic, but sunk before we could rendezvous with its crew."

"It sunk?"

"We don't know what happened. The remains of the sub, its crew, and the enriched uranium are lying at the bottom of the Puerto Rico Trench in 28,373 feet of water."

"Where the water pressure's—let me guess—13,000 pounds per square inch."

"Twelve thousand, six hundred pounds, to be exact. Well within your mutation's physical capabilities. The question is whether it's within your mental parameters."

"You know me pretty well, Admiral. What do you think?"

My father turned to me, looking me straight in the eye. "We wouldn't be having this conversation if I didn't believe in you, son. The question is whether *you* believe you can do it."

I drained the bottle of orange juice, the sugar rush shaking the cobwebs loose from my brain. "After all the crap you've put me through over the years, diving into a sea trench sounds like a vacation trip to Disney World."

* * *

It was dusk by the time we landed on the deck of the fishing trawler *Malchut*. My father had released my shackles during the flight, citing his need to be able to trust me. He talked about my mother and how they had met while he was stationed at the Commander Fleet Activities Chinhae naval base in South Korea.

"CFAC is a big base, lots to do, plenty of recreational activities for a guy like you. And Chinhae is a lovely city, surrounded by mountains on one side and the harbor on the other. I used to love looking at the cherry blossoms set against the backdrop of the sea. Anyway, it was my second week at the base—a hotshot captain, full of piss and vinegar. One night I walked into the base club and there she was tending bar—the most beautiful woman I had ever laid eyes on. And I wasn't the only one who thought so, there were sailors lined up three deep to get her attention. She was only nineteen at the time, but she handled herself like someone far more mature. I remember pulling rank and clearing out the drunks, then I said the only Korean I knew, '*Young-oh hahm-nee-ka?*' . . . Do you speak English? And '*Ee-ru-mee moo-ot-shim-nee-ka?*' . . . What is your name? She told me her name was Mi Yung and that her boss said she wasn't allowed to speak more than two sentences to any customer or she'd lose her job. I later found out her boss was her father and that his company supplied the base with alcohol. I stayed until closing and helped her clean up, and I refused to leave until she agreed to one date. It wasn't until our fourth date that she allowed me to kiss her good night, but it was worth the wait."

I told him about seeing Anya for the first time and our first kiss, and suddenly my father and I were actually talking to one another. He introduced me to a few of the internationals, then escorted me below deck and gave me a tour of the vessel. I was surprised to find a modern galley and crews' quarters that were far more comfortable than I imagined and a workout room that he said I could use anytime. In fact, my father gave me complete freedom to explore any part of the ship—except the lab, which he said was the private domain of one Professor Presley O'Bannon Gibbons.

We found Professor Gibbons eating pizza and playing video games on an iPad in a corner of the galley. An average-looking white guy, the dude never looked up from his screen, even when we were hovering over his table.

"Gibbs, this is my son, Kwan."

"He's been briefed?"

"Just the basics. I thought you'd handle the rest in the morning."

Gibbons finally looked up, scrutinizing me as if I were a horse being evaluated for either the Triple Crown or the glue factory. "You probably think those muscles make you more efficient. They don't. They weigh you down. Wastes blood circulation. Forces your liver to overcompensate. In ten hours, when you find yourself five miles below the surface in oxygen-low waters paralyzed with hypothermia and you can't remember who you are or what you're doing, you can blame those Captain America muscles of yours."

And then he returned to his video game.

"Nice to meet you, too."

We grabbed a plate of chow from the kitchen; then my father walked me to my stateroom. "Don't let Gibbons get inside your head. He's not a bad guy; he's just spent too many hours alone in the lab."

"He's creepy. And what did he mean when he said I'd be paralyzed with hypothermia?"

"The deeper you descend, the colder the water. Temperatures in the trench drop to near freezing. But don't worry—I've never seen a fish wearing a sweater."

We stopped at my door and he gave me a hug that wasn't awkward or forced. "Get some rest, son. I'll wake you in the morning."

Maybe it was the salty air blowing in from the portal, maybe it was the unexpected budding relationship with my dad, but that night I slept better than I had since before the car accident.

My father knocked on my door at first light, carrying a breakfast tray. "I brought you a ham and egg sandwich and a few bananas for potassium. I didn't know if you drank coffee."

"No, but maybe a Coke—just to wake me up."

"We'll grab one on the way to the lab. How'd you sleep?"

"Surprisingly good."

"You've got sea legs, just like your old man."

"I've got more than sea legs, Dad; I've got gills and fins."

My father wiped a tear. "You know how long it's been since you called me Dad? Fourth grade. I remember because you got in trouble in school."

"Do you remember what I did? A teacher's aide said I was talking during a fire drill. Turned out to be a Filipino kid who was suspended a week later for bringing a switchblade to school. When I tried to explain what happened, you grounded me for a month."

"It was excessive, I know." He stood by the open portal, breathing in the briny air. "My father was a military man, his father and two uncles before him. The Wilsons have always believed in the virtues of discipline. You think I was tough? My old man used to take a hickory switch to my behind if I was so much as late to supper. It was a different time—the world always at war. Guess it's the only world I've ever known."

For my father, it was as close to an admission of guilt as I was going to get, and for some reason it made me think of Rachel Solomon. She had told me that her father couldn't get past being a victim; as a result, he died an angry, bitter man. After seventeen years, my father had just apologized the only way he knew how . . . and his confession lightened my soul.

"Come on, Dad. Let's go retrieve your uranium."

Gibbons's lab was located in the lowest of the three decks, aft of the engine room. To enter the sealed-off chamber you had to proceed through two pressurized doors which created an airlock that was similar to the BSL-3 safety measures back at ANGEL.

Entering the lab, I realized the compartment served a far different purpose.

At the center of the chamber was a diving well—a volcano-shaped resealable opening to the sea that peered straight down into the abyss. Only the pressurized air inside the chamber prevented the ocean from flooding the hull.

The rest of the lab held worktables and lamps attached to magnifying glasses and an assortment of luggage, including several small suitcases and an army backpack about the size of my Doors bag. There were also supplies packed in stacks of military crates that gave me the distinct impression that Professor Gibbons had sanitized the lab before allowing me inside.

"Sit." He pointed to a folding chair, addressing me as if I were the family pet.

I glanced at my father, who nodded.

Gibbons opened a folder and removed two glossy images. "Look closely at this first photo—it comprises the debris field of the sunken submarine. Note the position of the bow; you'll use that as a reference point as you approach the wreckage. This second image is a thermal sensor, taken at the exact same angle. See the dark outline of the bow? Everything is cold and black—except for this orange speck right here. That speck is your target; the enriched uranium is radiating heat."

"What are these blurry red things circling the orange speck?"

"Probably just some fish attracted to the warmth." Gibbons retrieved one of the camouflage-green canvas backpacks. "This backpack is reinforced and lined with lead; it will protect you from the radiation. Your target is a crate marked in Arabic writing. Inside you'll find an object composed of thick plastic—about the size of a basketball. Don't open it; inside is the enriched uranium. Just shove the object in the backpack, strap it on your back, and surface straight into the diving well. Understood?"

"Understood."

"Admiral, did you tell him about the injection?"

"Not yet. Kwan, Professor Gibbons is going to give you a B-12 injection which contains a stimulant we offer our Navy SEALs before they embark on missions in cold waters. It may give you the edge you need to withstand the near-freezing temperatures."

"We need to make you more efficient," Gibbons reiterated as he extracted a hypodermic needle and an alcohol swab from a medical kit. "Drop your pants and pick a cheek."

I lowered my sweat pants and pulled down the edge of my boxers, allowing him to inject me in my left butt cheek.

"He's set, Admiral. I suggest we allow him to mutate before you give him the depth gauge."

"Depth gauge?"

Gibbons reached into a pocket of his lab coat and removed a device shaped like a large-faced watch. "The digital display calculates depth as well as direction. Course zero-nine-zero is straight down; adjust to course zero-zero-zero to surface. It's easy to become disoriented down there."

"Dad, I don't need this. I can hear the surface; I can feel the bottom—even five miles down. The electronics will just annoy me."

Gibbons started to protest, only my father cut him off. "Let him do it his way."

He walked me over to the edge of the diving well, his arm draped over my shoulder. "Remember, son, it's a marathon, not a sprint. Steady pace; keep your wits about you. If you feel the need to surface—"

"I'll be fine." Stripping off my clothes, I fastened the empty backpack around my shoulders and waist, then climbed over the edge of the diving well and slid feetfirst into the water.

The sea was warm and incredibly clear. Sucking in my gut, I forcibly exhaled, causing my rib cage to flatten as a steady burst of air vacated my lungs, sealing my esophageal membrane behind it. Gills fluttered in my neck as I inhaled the ocean, my secondary respiratory system fully engaged.

I looked up at my father as my blurred vision wiped clear. He gave me a thumbs-up, and I returned the gesture with some difficulty—my denticle skin thickening quickly, the rigidity restricting my range of motion. Waiting for my heels to deform, I continued to sink so that my eye level was just below the hull.

The water was a brilliant royal blue, sparkling with shards of sunlight. I took note of a strange looking device attached to the ship's keel—no doubt responsible for the two images taken of the sub—and then it was time to go.

Ducking my head, I settled into an easy seventy-degree descent, my swaying lower limbs propelling me down a shaft of light until it faded into a deep burgundy shadow some six hundred and fifty feet below the surface.

Growing up in San Diego, living near the Pacific, I became addicted to oceanography. As I descended, years of watching the Discovery Channel came back to me, my inner voice describing ocean realms normally visited by the episode's narrator aboard a submersible.

I was leaving the epipelagic or sunlight zone, entering the mesopelagic region. The sea darkened into shades of gray until the depths extinguished the last speck of light, casting me into the eternal night of the bathypelagic zone.

Luminescent lights twinkled all around me, blinking in and out of existence as if I had entered another universe. I slowed my descent, momentarily disoriented by flashbulbs of color—greens and blues that were visible over great distances to attract mates, reds and yellows that flared like fireworks in order to confuse predators.

A fluorescent-white entanglement of limbs floated by, resembling a hydra's head.

Perceiving me as a threat, a scarlet vampire squid turned itself inside out, casting a false glowing turquoise eye upon yours truly before it expelled a cloud of bioluminescent mucus, executing a magician's vanishing getaway.

My eyes adjusted to the dark, turning the starry night sea into an olive-green minefield of ugliness and evil. A thousand shadows materialized around me in every direction, becoming bulbous eyes and jaws that unhinged, and bizarre fish with frightening teeth, casting bioluminescent bulbs that dangled before their open mouths like bait. They were everywhere—viperfish and gulper eels, fangtooths and dragonfish, and angler fish with teeth that would put a piranha to shame.

And then my senses identified a far more terrifying presence as it descended through the bathypelagic zone two thousand feet above me—closing fast.

I heard its *clickity-click* of echolocation—a beacon of sound that grew louder as it descended. I felt its heart pumping swimming pools of hot blood; its fluke displacing a steady river of seawater.

Petrified, I raced into the depths, chased by the most formidable predator in the sea—a monster the size of an eighteen wheeler that possessed a toothed lower jaw capable of crushing a small boat in half. There was no outmaneuvering it, nowhere to hide. The bull sperm whale was sixty feet and seventy thousand pounds, and it was plunging through the darkness toward me like a runaway locomotive.

I had one chance—I needed to reach a depth beyond the bull's limitations.

How far could a sperm whale dive?

I racked my brain, tracking down a speck of memory from eighth grade marine biology. *Sperm whale . . . deepest diving mammal. Mature bulls could reach the deepest part of the bathypelagic zone—about twelve thousand feet down.*

Regretting not taking Gibbons's depth gauge, I closed my eyes, fighting to ignore the charging predator closing quickly from above—willing the senses flanking my dermal denticles to register the vibrations caused by the undersea current rushing along the bottom of the canyon. Locating the telltale disturbance, I triangulated my position using the surface and seafloor some twenty-five thousand feet down.

I was a third of the way down, maybe less. Figure seven thousand feet.

That translated into another five thousand feet before the bull sperm whale would be forced to turn back. That didn't bode well—the leviathan had already closed the gap to a thousand feet and was descending at twice my speed.

There was nothing I could do, the math did me in—I had no chance.

And then I sensed them . . . squid—thousands of them—racing through the depths somewhere below me.

I changed course, aiming for the center of the school, my hip and leg muscles on fire. Altering the angle of my descent allowed the whale to gain on me, but like a camper running through the forest from a bear, I didn't have to be faster than the bear to keep from being eaten, I just had to be faster than the slowest camper.

Minutes became seconds. The monster's clicks became clanging bells, tolling my death. Tucking my chin, I looked back and saw my swishing feet—outgunned by a giant fluke undulating steady and true, driving a gargantuan head that occupied my entire field of vision—a head scarred white from a hundred battles.

And then its mouth opened and I was inhaled backward in a sudden, terrifying suction that separated my legs and ceased all forward propulsion. I caught a quick glimpse of cone-shaped teeth and a dark, cavernous gullet—igniting a final jolt of adrenaline.

One arm thrust is all I had time for . . . one powerful downward stroke that sent me flailing chest-first into the sperm whale's head like a bird hitting a windshield.

My arms and legs stretched wide to embrace the wall of blubber, my teeth gnawed into the flesh, securing my face to the charging bull's rostrum . . . anything to avoid being eaten.

Whap! Whap . . . whap! Whap!

Jelled bodies slapped against my back, shards of tentacles adhering to my denticle-covered limbs as the whale plowed through the school of squid like a mad bull, rolling out of its two-mile descent to feed.

I hung on, waiting until the majestic beast slowed.

Hovering in eleven thousand feet of water, the monster clicked once more, sending a bone-rattling reverberation through my body. With a tremendous shake of its mammoth head, it shook me loose, sending me into a desperate dive to avoid its flapping thirteen-foot-wide fluke as it righted itself to return to the surface.

Exhausted, I watched it ascend. The behemoth had altered my marathon dive into an energy-depleting sprint. Fortunately, I didn't have to exert myself nor travel far to feed—the surrounding sea a battlefield of bleeding body parts and torn tentacles.

For the next twenty minutes I fed on fresh calamari, desperate to regain my strength while I prepared myself mentally to continue my descent—another three miles to go until I reached bottom.

While I was descending to the bottom of the Puerto Rico Trench, Rachel Solomon was using her GPS to locate the home of Jeffrey and Gay Gordon. She arrived after seven in the evening, her knock answered by their son, Jesse.

"Hey, Mrs. Solomon. Everyone's in the den."

She followed Jesse through the house to a rec room where a very tall, lanky man was speaking to half a dozen familiar faces seated on two matching sofas.

Rachel hugged Sun Jung, nodded to Principal Lockhart and Coach Flaig, and accepted a folding chair offered by the speaker. "Sorry I'm late. Mordechai needed a ride to practice. Mr. Gordon, I'm Rachel Solomon, the school counselor."

"Jeff Gordon, Jesse's dad."

"We appreciate your firm looking into this case."

"I'm happy to help. Unfortunately, as I told Kwan's grandmother, there's not a lot my law firm can do at this juncture. Because Sun Jung was never appointed by the court to be Kwan's legal guardian, his father maintained all parental rights. That includes the right to provide his son with medical care without having to reveal his whereabouts to the public, or to his grandmother."

"He's not in rehab, Dad. They disappeared him."

The attorney turned to his son. "Jess, just for argument's sake, let's say that's true. How do we prove Kwan's parent—an admiral no less, kidnapped his own son? Even if we filed criminal charges, the admiral's attorney would ask the court for thirty to ninety days so Kwan can rehab out of the public eye. Most judges are going to grant it—especially for an admiral."

"I understand where you're coming from, Mr. Gordon," Rachel interjected, "however, I have to agree with your son. Kwan wasn't doing drugs; he did, however, tell me he had a terrible relationship with his father. Contact the hospital in San Diego and you'll find Admiral Wilson only visited his paralyzed son twice after the car accident—once to sign a Do Not Resuscitate order. Is that the kind of loving parent Sun Jung should entrust to care for her grandson?"

"No. Absolutely not. Sun Jung, when was the last time you spoke with Kwan?"

"Friday night. He said he was spending the weekend with friends."

"Anya was with him Friday night," Jesse said. "He was supposed to hook up with Tracy, this super-hot cheerleader, only Tracy freaked out, saying Kwan was deformed or something. So everyone marched down the beach to see if he really had two . . . um, if he really was a freak. Turns out Tracy was lying, only maybe something really was wrong with Kwan because Anya and Li-ling rushed him out of there in Li-ling's car, except Kwan left his Doors backpack in my car, and Kwan never goes anywhere without that backpack."

Sun Jung nodded, tears in her eyes. "He love that stupid backpack. Something definitely wrong if he leave that stupid backpack behind."

The attorney jotted a few notes on his legal pad. "Sun Jung, how long have you been taking care of Kwan?"

"Let me think . . . nearly four months."

"We may be able to convince a judge that Admiral Wilson granted you physical custody of his son; that you assumed he'd be filing custody papers to that effect in California. I know one of the judges over at the Fifteenth Judicial Court . . . Kamilla Cubit. Her father, Tommy, and I are old friends; his son's in the navy. I'll get a copy of that DNR order and show it to the judge. We'll try to establish that the admiral had forfeited his legal rights and that Sun Jung had assumed physical custody. At the very least, Judge Cubit should force Admiral Wilson to provide Kwan's location and grant her visitation rights. If the admiral refuses, it would give us grounds to file criminal charges—"

"Which would not sit well with the navy," said Annie Moir, jumping in. "I could issue a press release about the resuscitation order that would cause the public to demand the admiral release Kwan's whereabouts."

Rachel turned to the petite brunette. "Excuse me, but who are you exactly?"

"Annie Moir. I'm Kwan's manager."

The high school counselor's intense hazel eyes seemed to burn straight into the woman's brain. "The manager who mentioned cocaine might be involved to that AP reporter?"

"I never . . . who told you that?"

"A former student of mine works for the Associated Press. The question is—who do *you* work for, Ms. Moir?"

Puerto Rico Trench, Atlantic Ocean

The abyssopelagic or abyssal zone covers 13,124 to 19,686 feet of the ocean depths, an expanse that includes much of the planet's seafloor. The water temperature is near freezing; there is no light and very few fish.

Fish can handle the extreme water pressure far better than the frigid environment. Cold-blooded vertebrates tend to avoid the deep; their core body temperature dropping with their surroundings. The exception are large-bodied sharks like the great white, a species that adapted to the extreme cold by developing a web-like structure of veins and arteries located beneath its swim muscles. This blood-warming adaptation, known as gigantothermy, utilizes the heat generated by the great white's working muscles to transport hot venous blood into the arteries, allowing the shark to maintain a core temperature far warmer than its environment.

I was not a great white, but I was warm-blooded, a factor that allowed my mutated cardiovascular system to transport heat to my internal organs in a similar fashion. Still, my prolonged exposure to these thirty-four-degree-Fahrenheit surroundings had numbed my dermal denticles to the point that my movements were becoming alarmingly sluggish.

Of greater concern was the crushing depth. I hadn't felt the water pressure inside the hyperbaric chamber, but I sure felt it now as I sank headfirst into the abyss, my legs barely moving. My bones ached. My skull hurt worse. And the deeper I went, the harder it was to breathe.

I was barely functioning by the time I plunged into the hadal-pelagic zone, the ocean realm that plummets beyond 19,686 feet, encompassing the world's sea canyons and trenches. The deepest point on the planet is located in the Mariana Trench in the Western Pacific. Seven miles down . . . 35,797 feet. The water pressure is an incredible eight tons per square inch—the weight of forty-eight Boeing 747 jets. And yet life had found a way to exist.

The Puerto Rico Trench reached a depth of 28,373 feet. The dark chasm appeared below, its depths formidable, its canyon wall rising to meet me like a coffin.

No longer swimming, I was simply sinking headfirst with my mouth open, my gills struggling to inject life-giving oxygen into my condensing bloodstream. At my present rate of descent, I would hit bottom in a matter of minutes—my final resting place.

My field of vision narrowed. Olive-green became shades of lead gray.

I began to hallucinate, my mind in free fall. I looked to my left and saw a mermaid endowed with Anya's face. *"I'm here for you, Kwan."*

"Are you, Anya? You promised me if things went bad, you'd put me out of my misery."

"Soon enough." She looked at me with those turquoise eyes and winked.

I reached for her . . . and she was gone.

I have no idea when the object distinguished itself from the black valley below or how long I had been staring at it before I realized it was the bow of the sunken submarine.

Paralyzed by the cold, I no longer cared. I was back in ICU, on life support, my father having issued the Do Not Resuscitate order.

And then a pulse of sensation trickled into my vegetating brain, forcing me from my stupor. Something was alive down there. Something dangerous.

Four hundred and thirty feet from the bottom of the Atlantic, I spun myself around and slowed my descent, the sudden shot of adrenaline shocking my consciousness awake.

There were hundreds of them, perhaps thousands; it was impossible to tell. Translucent bodies . . . six to seven feet long. Some glowed rose-red, others preferred albino-white, the beasts changing colors at will as they converged into a frenzied kaleidoscope of swirling, seemingly mindless madness over an unseen section of seafloor.

Diablo Rojo—the Red Devil.

Humboldt squid.

A cannibalistic carnivore, the Humboldt squid possesses eight lightning-quick tentacles, two longer sucker-equipped feeder arms, and a razor-sharp parrot-like beak that can slash and devour its prey like a buzz saw. It can jettison itself through the water at speeds up to twenty-five knots and stop or change direction on a dime. Ferocious fighters, Humboldts have been known to attack every species in the sea . . . including man.

And then my senses alerted me to the presence of another predator.

The goblin shark circled the chaos a hundred feet below me, biding its time. Eleven feet long from its surfboard-shaped snout to its rounded tail, the creature resembled a sand tiger shark, only with blue fins and a pink belly—the latter color caused by an abundance of blood vessels located beneath its semitransparent skin. I couldn't see its dagger-sharp teeth or its stomach, but I could *hear* the hunger gnawing at its insides . . . *feel* the electrical impulses running along its back as its muscles coiled to attack.

As I watched, the goblin shark made a sudden descent, targeting a wounded Humboldt bleeding from the remains of three missing tentacles.

In a blink, dozens of agitated squid rose tentacles-first to engage the outnumbered challenger.

The goblin shark spun away in retreat . . . too late.

Tentacles bloomed like exploding fireworks, distracting the shark even as pairs of feeder arms grabbed the overmatched predator and drew it into the snapping beaks of the voracious killers.

My heart pounded irregularly in my pressure-impaled chest. Within seconds the squid had eaten all but a few bloody morsels of the goblin shark. Still in the throes of their feeding frenzy, they battered one another, probing for weakness among their peers.

And then they stopped.

My heart pounded, my life hanging in the balance—as the creatures rose as one to feed upon me! With a burst of speed I descended, heading for the submarine wreckage, seeking cover within the twisted caverns of steel. Racing parallel to the seafloor, I soared past sixty feet of hull before locating a gap large enough for me to squeeze through.

It was large enough for the Humboldts, but they didn't pursue me, their senses perceiving the submarine as a larger predator.

Safe for the moment, I took in my new surroundings.

The submarine was resting on its portside, tilting every apparatus that remained bolted down. I inspected a rack of torpedoes stacked sideways, moving carefully past a maze of crushed computer stations and an open watertight door.

Thankfully, there were no human remains to be seen.

There was, however, a Geiger counter, its glass cracked, its metal box flattened—and now I realized why the Humboldt squid were congregating along the bottom.

It's the uranium. They're attracted to the heat.

The flooded chamber started spinning. I gasped mouthfuls of seawater, struggling to compensate for the flow needed to keep me

conscious. My body convulsed—*if I couldn't swim, I couldn't breathe
. . . I couldn't create enough heat to keep my internal organs functioning.*

If I didn't leave the sub, I'd die.

If I left the sub, I'd be devoured.

Do Not Resuscitate. My father had been right after all. Suffocation . . . it was more humane.

Facing death . . . it's a scary thing. But I was done, my mind was baked. Every breath burned, every labored beat of my heart threatened to be the last. I was freezing and alone, surrounded by a darkness that was closing in rapidly. Buried beneath five miles of ocean, there was no hope, no escape . . . now it was just a matter of seeking my final resting place.

I made my way slowly through the open hatch of the torpedo room, somehow comforted by my human surroundings. The corridor led to a rush of ocean where the bow had split open upon impact with the seafloor, depositing its payload of Tomahawk missiles across the trench floor.

I scanned the debris field—a graveyard of technology, flattened by five tons per square inch of water pressure. The only recognizable remnants of the attack sub were sections of the titanium vertical missile silos.

The ampullae of Lorenzini became a five-alarm fire in my brain. I looked up and saw hundreds of Humboldt squid racing for me—red and white darts of death.

Desperate, I squeezed inside a five-foot length of titanium pipe lying along the seafloor. The fractured missile silo was open on one end; the other end was covered by a hatch that was intact but suspended open. Crawling toward the spring-loaded opening, I reached out and grabbed the round metal door by its interior wheel and slammed it shut—severing two intruding tentacles in the process.

I was trapped and far from impregnable—my feet exposed at the other open end of the tube. Relentless killers, the Humboldts reached in and tried to drag me out of my makeshift titanium shell by my ankles. I kicked at them, attempting to defend the thirty-inch-in-diameter opening.

Hold on . . . few more minutes . . . before you . . . suffocate.

Their sucker pads had barbs, forcing me to squirm closer to the sealed hatch.

In my delirium, I popped open the silo door just enough to reach my arms out. Allowing the metal disc to rest on the back of my head, I pushed against the sandy seafloor with every ounce of strength left in my body until the fractured missile silo levitated horizontally away from the bottom.

I changed my flutter kicks to the now-familiar east–west hip swivel and the titanium casing lurched forward, the curvature of the silo actually channeling the current more efficiently, like the hooded propeller used on the latest nuclear submarines. Using my back, I managed to keep the nose of my armored hull level as I crawled straight into the maelstrom of squid.

To the enraged Humboldts, I was simply a crustacean moving along the bottom in a protective shell. They battered it, attempted to pry it loose, but in the end the predators were forced to yield to it.

The overexertion heated up my muscles, thawing my dermal denticles. Breathing became easier, the casing around me lighter— until I realized it wasn't just me—the water was noticeably warmer.

With renewed vigor, I kicked and propelled and pulled my way into the whirling dervish of invertebrates until the seafloor beneath me became the crushed remains of a wooden crate and then—eureka!—a plastic object the size of a basketball, encasing the enriched hunk of uranium.

Reaching down, I grabbed the precious object, which warmed my hands like a roaring fireplace on a cold winter's day. I slammed the hatch and locked it, then peeled the lead-lined backpack off my shoulders and shoved the radiating sphere inside, zippering the lead-lined casing shut.

And then something unexpected happened . . . the missile silo went vertical, rising away from the bottom!

It was the uranium. By heating the water inside the sealed tube, it was causing the missile silo to become buoyant.

To aid the process, I positioned the backpack between the hatch and my head. I held on as the titanium shell plowed through the dispersing school of Humboldt squid—the nasty creatures never realizing I had just made off with their magic orb.

The water inside the tube went from warm to hot in minutes, increasing the silo's rate of ascension. Looking down, I watched the dark canyon disappear from view—the open end of the silo spinning wildly in my head . . . *need to breathe!*

Reaching up, I secured the backpack's straps to the inside wheel of the hatch, then slid feetfirst out of the back end of the rising silo until my head was free. Maintaining a grip along the inside of the titanium tube, I shoved my face into the current of water and opened my mouth to the rushing sea.

I had lived seventeen years, but that moment right there—that was the best. To have escaped death so many times, to be surfacing with my life and a gift for my father—I wanted to scream to the heavens.

Ascending fast . . . the water pressure easing, the pain in my skull gone, my chest expanding. Rising higher, the waters were growing dense again with life. Viperfish and gulper eels, fangtooths and dragonfish—no longer ugly, no longer gruesome—beautiful creatures, miracles of creation and adaptation—mutations, like me . . . all of us just trying to survive.

The sea remained in nocturnal-olive, yet I could feel the warmth of the shallows and the lapping waves, and suddenly I was rocketing free of the water, falling sideways onto the titanium shell, which started to sink. Ducking back inside, I untied the backpack, popped open the hatch, and squirmed back outside.

Relieved of its buoyancy, the empty shell fell away, beginning its return descent into the abyss. Glancing up at the starry night sky, I thanked my mother's soul for guiding me to it.

I searched the horizon, locating the *Malchut* half a mile to the east. Her crew must have been tracking my ascension on sonar because she was heading my way.

Slinging the backpack over my shoulders, I expelled water from my esophagus and inhaled a chest-inflating breath, forcing air into my collapsed lungs. My skin softened to flesh—the flesh burning with frostbite. My eyeballs ached as my sinus cavity squeezed open. My ear canals popped, causing my head to ring with tinnitus. My leg muscles spasmed. My stomach contorted, my heart raced.

Exhausted, hungry, writhing in pain, I was Kwan Wilson . . . human.

Waiting for the boat, I nearly drowned from the exhaustion of treading water.

The crew mercifully lowered a rescue ring and hauled me onto the deck. My father barked orders while Professor Gibbons tore the backpack from my shoulders and looked inside.

"Sonuva gun . . . it's here. He actually did it."

"Of course he did! He's my kid, isn't he?"

My father may have hugged me—I can't be sure. Relieved of my burden, I passed out.

Daylight burned red behind closed eyelids. I opened them, moaning in pain.

I was in my stateroom, propped up in bed. A doctor was peering into my left eye with an annoying light. A nurse was applying an ointment to my raw, bare feet.

The physician spoke in a Hispanic accent. "You're my first frostbite patient. How long were you locked in the galley freezer?"

"Whaa?"

"Seventeen hours," I heard my father say.

"He's lucky to be alive. We'll start him on an IV for the pain, but he really should fly back with us to San Juan."

"He'll be fine, Doc. We appreciate you coming. Can you stand next to him for a moment? I want to get a quick photo of my son receiving medical care . . . you know, just in case we need to sue that freezer manufacturer."

Through heavy lids I saw my father aim his iPhone at me. Then he handed the doctor a wad of cash and I passed out.

Key Largo, Florida

The patient was propped up in bed. Her complexion was sickly pale, her forearms bruised from multiple intravenous needles and injections. An IV bag dripped steadily into a vein in her right hand, the toxic liquid having vanquished the woman's jet-black curls days ago. Long strands of hair littered her bedsheets.

Dr. Kamrowski leaned over Sabeen, inhaling her noxious breath as she removed the thermometer from beneath the teenager's tongue.

The Syrian rebel gazed up at her through feverish dark pools. "How bad?"

"A hundred and one point five, same as yesterday. Open wide; I want to check your throat again." Aided by a wooden tongue depressor, Dr. Kamrowski shined her light into Sabeen's mouth, noting the creamy-white lesions. "The thrush has gotten worse. We need to boost your immune system."

"I thought the shark stem cells were supposed to be doing this?"

Ignoring her, Dr. Kamrowski moved to the end of the bed and lifted the blanket and sheet to examine Sabeen's feet. What had been petite size 7s had mutated into knotted size 13s that curved sharply from toe to heel.

"They have grown larger?"

"Sabeen, every subject reacts differently to a new drug."

"Answer me!"

"Yes, but it's okay. Your internal organs are changing, too, preparing you for an amphibious existence, which is what we wanted. The problem is that the HGH isn't stabilizing your human DNA the way it did with Kwan. It may be that the tiger shark stem cells are more aggressive, or it might be the difference in the male and female testosterone levels. Whatever the reason, I feel our best course of action is to get you stronger . . . allow your immune system to stabilize before we inject you with any more human growth hormone."

"Stabilize me how?"

"By getting you into the water sooner than we planned. We'll allow the mutation to run its course at an accelerated rate, which is what it seems to want to do. If it works, you should feel much better."

"And if it doesn't?"

"Let's not go there." Dr. Kamrowski removed a walkie-talkie from her belt. "Joe, are you ready for Sabeen?"

"On my way."

The early afternoon was thick with humidity, the South Florida sun veiled behind gray islands of stratocumulus clouds.

Sabeen Tayfour squinted through feverish eyes at the emerald-green horizon of ocean spread out before her. Shallows littered with pockets of coral reefs led to darker patches of deep water.

Her teeth rattled as the Australian man pushed her wheelchair across a stretch of boardwalk, then down a ramp that ended ten feet of rock and sand short of the waterline.

Joe Botchin made it one revolution on the beach before the wheels became hopelessly buried. Gently, he leaned over and scooped the Syrian beauty up in his thick arms, carrying her down to the water's edge. The shark wrangler's boots sunk ankle-deep into the muddy bottom—his eyes behind the dark sunglasses darting to Sabeen's dressing gown as it soaked up the sea, adhering the flimsy patterned cloth to her naked breasts.

Sabeen closed her eyes to the lust-filled stare. The water was a balmy seventy-seven degrees in the shallows but still felt frigid, casting goose bumps across her feverish flesh.

The Australian moved deeper. The water rose to her neck.

And suddenly he was on top of her, his arms wrapped around her chest in a bear hug, his weight pinning her underwater!

Adrenaline coursed through her body even as the rancid air hissed from her mouth. She screamed in protest, the sound muffled in her ears. She tried to reach for his eyes . . . his private parts, only her arms were pinned and he had rolled himself on top of her. Pressing her deformed feet to the muddy bottom, she managed one massive heave of her legs, only her head never cleared the surface.

Her lungs burned. Her vision tunneled into blackness.

Joe felt the fight leave Sabeen Tayfour's body. He waited another moment, then released her, planting a boot to her lower back to keep the corpse underwater and out of sight. "She's dead."

Dr. Kamrowski nodded from the beach. "A waste of precious time and resources."

"Spooky guy, the Admiral. I'd hate to get on his bad side. Why do you think—"

"She became expendable the moment Kwan salvaged the package. The last thing Amalek's council needs now is to expend more personnel at the compound. Believe me, having seen the way those rats suffered, this was a far more humane way to—"

"Ahhhh!" Joe screamed, then fell backward into the shallows—a fountain of blood spurting across the surface.

Dr. Kamrowski ran to the water's edge and froze, unable to see beyond the Australian's thrashing limbs and the frothing pool of blood.

And then everything stopped.

Nadja Kamrowski's heart pounded in her chest as Joe Botchin's body surfaced, his corpse floating facedown in the scarlet waters. Blood pooled around two massive bite wounds—the first coming from his savaged upper right thigh and torn femoral artery, the last from his neck, which was nearly severed from his head.

The killer's face rose slowly from the sea, revealing a porous scalp and two coal-black eyes filled with hatred which remained just above the water line.

"Sabeen, I'm sorry."

Blood ran past her sunken cheekbones and flattened nose into her open mouth. Her gills rippled red with the outflow, remained underwater.

"It was the Admiral's orders, Sabeen. I don't question my Amalek superiors."

The face submerged. A moment later, a mutated pair of feet lashed the surface, splashing blood across Dr. Kamrowski's blue lab coat.

A long, dark form glided through the shallows toward deeper water . . . and then she was gone.

Aboard the *Malchut*

I was gliding in a cool blue sea, the surface above my head undulating in thick waves of mercury that muted all sound.

"He can be useful to us, Jeffrey."

"I'm sorry, Admiral, but the council disagrees."

The sea grew warmer. The voices were disturbing Queen Dilaudid, the surface rippling with sound.

"Gibbons said he was able to salvage enough U-235 to incinerate Port Everglades and the convention center. You really think Kwan's going to remain silent with half a million people dead?"

The sea boiled, the pain returned. Swimming to the agitated surface, my head popped free—sound returning with a *whoosh*.

My eyes snapped open.

The cabin was empty. The voices were coming . . . *from my forearms?*

I looked down at my arms. The flesh was covered in dermal denticles—my brain fooled by the drug-induced dream. The sensory cells beneath my shark skin were picking up reverberations of sound coming from my steel bed frame which was bolted to the wall behind my head.

Turning around to face the wall, I pressed my forearms to the plaster, eavesdropping on my father's conversation in the adjoining stateroom.

"How will you kill him?"

"Drug overdose—we stay with the rehab story. I'll inject it right into his IV bag; he won't feel a thing."

"I'm concerned about the timing. Amalek was very clear—the three Iranians arrive tomorrow at seventeen hundred hours."

"Which is why it has to be done now. We'll fly Kwan's remains to Miami tonight and hold a press conference at Jackson Memorial Hospital in the morning. You'll shed a few tears, the coroner will schedule an autopsy—that school counselor and her attorney will do whatever they're going to do . . . and none of it will matter. By tomorrow night Kwan's death will be yesterday's news—a trickle of water over a bursting dam."

Sweat poured down my face. I held my breath, waiting for my father's protests . . .

"Do it. Kill him."

My mind raced, my thoughts fluctuating between madness and panic. Hearing the door to my father's stateroom open, I climbed back into bed, ripped the IV from my vein, shoved the bloodied needle into the mattress, and then pulled the covers up over my arm to hide the evidence.

My eyes closed as the cabin door opened. I could feel the CIA assassin hovering close. Heard him remove something from his jacket pocket. Through half-closed eye slits I saw him inject a syringe of clear liquid into my IV bag.

He adjusted the drip, then traced the line back to my right arm, lifting the blanket . . .

Sitting up, I clubbed him across the face with my left fist.

It was a glancing blow, allowing me a few precious seconds to leap out of bed and grab his wrist before he could aim his 9mm at my head. And in the midst of this brief struggle something bizarre happened to me.

One moment I was consumed by a tornado of emotion—anger and rage and fear; the next I found myself in the eye of the storm, a place of calm . . . a place where my consciousness seemed to observe my reactive behavior and quell it. And within this Zen-like state I found the keys to controlling my mutation. It was as if I were an infant seeing my hand for the first time, realizing that not only did this strange five-fingered limb belong to me, but it was mine to control.

Accessing a reservoir of strength I had no knowledge of seconds earlier, I crushed Jeffrey Elrod's wrist in a vice grip that snapped his radius and ulna bones. So great was his pain that my would-be assassin let out a moan, rolled his eyes up in his head and fainted.

Releasing the swollen, deformed joint, I lifted him off the ground by his waist and placed him in bed as if he were a child. Tearing the sheets into strips, I bound his ankles and wrists to the bedrails and gagged him.

Yes, the thought to kill him had occurred to me. It would have been so easy to jab that IV death drip into his vein and justify the act using an-eye-for-an-eye justice . . . only I didn't do it. And no, it wasn't mercy or a sense of weakness as the Admiral would have called it; it was something beyond that . . . a sense that by killing this scumbag I'd be tainting my own soul.

The act of restraint strengthened my resolve to stop my father from using a weapon I had delivered to him on a silver platter—only first, I needed to collect my bearings.

Moving to the porthole, I slid back the curtains and realized that it was daylight and we were moving. That meant the diving bell would be sealed, preventing me from accessing the lab from under water.

Moving to the door, I pressed my palms to the metal surface and changed the flesh on my hands to dermal denticles, manipulating my DNA as easily as a chameleon altered its color. Using the sensitive neurons located beneath the thick skin-teeth, I could feel/hear the engines reverberating two decks below, but the corridor itself seemed clear.

Exiting the stateroom, I moved quickly down the empty passage to a watertight door that sealed a steep set of stairs. Setting my palms and instep on the handrails, I slid down the seventy-degree slope to the next landing, repeating the process to access the lower deck.

Yanking open another watertight door, I entered the engine room.

The noise of the running engines concealed the deck creaking beneath my weight as I made my way aft to the lab. Peering through the porthole window, I located Professor Gibbons. The man's back was to me as he carefully packed a spherical device the size of a volleyball into a chocolate-brown leather carry-on tote bag.

I entered the lab, quickly sealing the two watertight compartments behind me. The chamber pressurized, causing him to turn around. "Kwan? What are you doing here?"

"My father sent me down for a briefing," I lied.

"Briefing?"

"Amalek, the council, the whole nine yards."

"The Admiral discussed these things with you?"

"How else would he recruit me? I'm in, dude. We're in this thing together." I pointed to the object he was packing in the brown carry-on bag. "Is that it?"

"Huh? Yes."

"If you're half the genius my father tells me you are, then I'm sure this baby will do some serious damage."

Gibbons smiled. "It wasn't easy. Hiroshima and Nagasaki were aerial detonations; it's hard to generate that kind of blast radius with a ground device. Plus this one's being detonated on board a cruise ship, leading to all sorts of challenges. Would you like to see how it works?"

"That's why I'm here."

His ego properly stroked, the nuclear physicist stepped aside to show me the spherical device, which had a small clear Plexiglas canister strapped to it with duct tape. Inside the canister the back of a cell phone was visible.

"We call this a SADM—Special Atomic Demolition Munitions. Inside this porous metal sphere are two polished sections of enriched uranium and a brick of C-4 plastic explosive. The cell phone's battery connects to a blasting cap in the ball. When you dial the phone number, the ring will send a power surge to the blasting cap, setting off the C-4. The C-4, in turn, will blow one piece of the enriched uranium through the other, starting a chain reaction that will end in a nuclear explosion that will vaporize every object upwards of ten stories high inside a five-mile radius."

"Awesome. But what if you get a telemarketing call or a wrong number before the big boom?"

"First, no one else has access to the phone number but members of the council. Second, the device is pre-armed using a timer. I just set the device to arm itself at seven o'clock tonight. In approximately six hours and forty-two minutes, Amalek himself will place the call, and once again the world will change."

"Nice." My heart pounded as he rezippered the tote bag, my mind racing like Michael Corleone before he shot Sollozzo and that corrupt police captain in *The Godfather*. "The SADM . . . is it waterproof?"

"Of course. Why do you ask?"

Grabbing Gibbons by his arm, I flung him over a crate. Gripping the carry-on in my left hand, I reached for the sealed lid of the diving bell with the right and spun the wheel.

The nuclear physicist regained his feet in time to see what I was doing. "No!"

A fire hydrant of seawater erupted into the chamber, cutting off his screams and setting off alarms. The lab filled within seconds—by which time I had mutated into my shark alter ego. Clutching the leather bag to my belly, I jumped feetfirst into the aqua-blue hole, sinking like a rock.

The keel of the *Malchut* passed overhead, both blades churning, shredding the clothing my dermal denticles had already sliced and shed from my body. Hovering in eighty feet of water, I looked down, surprised to find the seafloor a mere hundred feet below. Darting to the surface, I spy-hopped, my eyes searching the horizon.

The *Malchut* had cut its engines, drifting several hundred yards away. Two miles farther to the west, I could see the Miami Beach shoreline.

I quickly submerged, swimming north at a brisk twenty knots.

According to Gibbons, the nuke would detonate in just under seven hours. That left me two choices. I could bury the device far out to sea, or I could bring the SADM to the authorities and have my father and his mysterious Amalek colleagues arrested and brought to justice.

I decided upon the latter for several reasons. First, if I buried the device along the seafloor, the resulting blast could wipe out any passing ships and create a tsunami. Second, unless I exposed my father and his fellow warmongers, I could never find peace—they'd come after me and my loved ones and "disappear us" as Jesse Gordon had called it.

I considered pulling out the wires connecting the blasting cap to the cell phone. In the end, I decided to let the authorities handle this, not knowing if the act might automatically arm the device or even detonate the SADM.

I sensed the *Malchut* bearing down on me seconds before my ampullae of Lorenzini detected a tiny electrical current pulsating along my left butt cheek. *Gibbons's injection . . . it wasn't intended to help me survive the near-freezing temperatures in the trench, it was a tracking device!*

Even moving at twenty knots, I wasn't about to lose the suped-up fishing trawler. Wherever I went, the ship would follow, the Admiral ready to deploy a crew to recover the device.

There wasn't enough time to make it back to the Puerto Rico Trench, so instead I went where their ship couldn't follow.

Altering my course, I trekked west . . . heading for land.

Key Largo, Florida

The creature was eight and a half feet long from the top of her pore-blemished scalp to the sickle-shaped curve of her mutated toes and heels. The additional length was a painful deformity caused by her bone softening into a lighter, more flexible, cartilage-like substance which stretched her skeleton like taffy. This sudden lack of rigidity along her spinal column had initially caused her to move through the water with inefficient serpent-like sweeps, until her dermal denticles had thickened along her dorsal surface to compensate. Black in color, these double-plated layers of "skin-teeth" were streaked gray every twelve to twenty inches with lateral lines—specialized clusters of sensory cells that allowed her to detect vibrations in the water over great distances. Set in four-inch-wide vertical canals along her dark dorsal surface, these silver-gray neuromasts resembled tiger stripes, fading as they wrapped around her pale abdomen.

Her mouth had widened to accommodate a lower jaw filled with jagged triangular teeth. Her nose and brows had flattened with the extinction of her sinus cavity. Having lost their bone density, her arms had atrophied into semi-useless T-Rex-like limbs which hung flaccid by her side when she swam.

Sabeen Tayfour had been close to death, her human DNA overwhelmed by a rapidly metastasizing army of shark stem cells that were systematically destroying her human immune system, yet remained stuck in a neutral state. Ironically, it had been the Australian brute's attempt to drown her that had released a lifesaving wave of adrenaline and cortisol, the latter's secretion instantaneously "switching on" her mutated genes.

Sabeen's transformation into a gilled species lacked the genetic balance necessary to reverse the mutation. With each passing minute she was becoming less human, and yet she was still bound to her *Homo sapien* species by her brain, her thoughts, and her tarnished memories. War had stolen her loved ones; revenge had demanded she become a freedom fighter. Her time in prison had robbed her of her dignity; her jailers' cruelty had turned her into a predator.

The final act of evil perpetrated against her had left her more dead than alive.

Ravaged by fever, Sabeen hadn't eaten in days. She had fought off her intended killer with a rush of adrenaline that was so sudden and so close to her demise that she never knew she had transformed. Held underwater, her inflicted bites had been a primordial reflex honed by a hundred million years of shark evolution.

The effort had saved her life but had exhausted her physically, all cognitive thoughts jettisoned in a state of delirium. Swept away from shore by the currents, Sabeen drifted in and out of consciousness, oblivious to the fact that she was breathing underwater through a pair of gills in her neck. Her lower body dragged along the bottom as she futilely attempted to bob to the surface in twelve feet of water to gasp a breath of air. Too weak to use her legs, she propelled herself forward by wiggling her upper torso—an ineffective maneuver that left her struggling to push enough sea down her throat for her gills to process an adequate supply of oxygen.

Hovering nearly vertically in the coral-rich shallows, her mind gone, Sabeen Tayfour was systematically drowning.

Claudia Kukowitsch had arrived in Key Largo two days earlier with her boyfriend, Andy. Born and raised in Switzerland, the thirty-seven-year-old Alpine beauty had long blonde hair, blue eyes, and curves in all the right places.

She had come to Florida on vacation with two goals: to visit Universal Studios in Orlando and to snorkel in the Keys. Andy had reluctantly joined her yesterday on a two-hour snorkeling excursion, but his back was scorched red with sunburn, providing him with an excuse to play golf.

With the basics now behind her, Claudia opted for a charter boat—a thirty-foot Pro Kat high-powered catamaran she shared with four other guests and the captain. The vessel had left the dock an hour earlier, cruising across the brilliant green-blue shallows of Key Largo's National Marine Sanctuary. Arriving at one of the park's protected coral reefs, the five patrons had donned snorkels, masks, and fins, and then it was every man and woman for themselves.

Drifting facedown along the glassy surface, Claudia gazed at the myriad of life darting in and out of soft coral beds that swayed with the currents. Toting a used underwater camera she had purchased at a local dive shop, she photographed clown fish, angelfish, a spotted sting ray, a pair of parrotfish, and a grouper that remained partially hidden within a cluster of sea grass.

Growing bored, she fluttered her swim fins, moving beyond the reef and an expanse of empty seafloor until she arrived at another contained ecosystem—and the presence of a life form that took her breath away.

The creature was immense—black with gray stripes. At first she thought it was a wounded eel, by the way it wriggled through the water. Hovering above the struggling creature, Claudia was shocked to see some seriously bizarre, almost human features. There was the shape of its skull and the hourglass spine that formed a mutilated tail. Split into two segments, the lower curved lobes resembled elongated, deformed toes.

Then it occurred to her—*My Gott . . . it's a mermaid!*

Paddling along the surface, Claudia followed the sickly creature, snapping dozens of photos, only to realize she needed to get a lot closer for the money shot. She watched in fascination as the mermaid managed to wedge itself between two coral reef formations, its open mouth inhaling a stream of current that dusted up the sand, obscuring it from view.

Claudia waited impatiently, but the dark being refused to move. She heard the dive boat sound its horn, recalling the snorkelers.

Knowing fame and fortune depended upon her next move, Claudia inhaled a belly full of air from her snorkel and tucked her head into a steep surface dive, kicking hard to compensate for her natural buoyancy. Seconds later, her knees touched down along the sandy bottom a good fifteen feet in front of the reef formation.

Before she could raise the camera strapped around her left wrist the current grabbed her—an invisible cushion of water that propelled her rapidly toward the object she desired. Rather than fight the stream she went with it, aiming her camera at the strange looking sea creature.

Goot Gott im Himmel . . .

Claudia dug the heels of her fins in the sand. This was not a mermaid; this was an alien life form! Its black eyes stared at her, its head cocked in a curious expression. Its almost human lower jaw hung open . . . filled with triangular teeth.

Near panic, the Swiss woman kicked off the bottom—only to be embraced by the alien's frail arms. One knotted five-fingered hand clutched Claudia's right wrist, the other stroked her blonde hair as it palmed the back of her skull.

Ich Fühle mich nicht gut.

Claudia's eyes widened as the voice whispered the German phrase, *"I don't feel well"* into her head.

The burning sensation in her lungs took precedence and she twisted and kicked her way free, racing to the surface—the creature hitching a ride by grabbing hold of her ankle!

Claudia's head popped free and she gasped several breaths, searching for her voice—as the being surfaced next to her, its mouth opening with a horrifying gurgle.

"*Hilfe* . . . help!" The Swiss woman pushed the listless creature away, slicing her hands on its rigid, extremely sharp skin.

Sabeen submerged, her nostrils inhaling the swirling trickles of blood. The scent jump-started her senses, burning away the fog that had been veiling her consciousness. Homing in on the symphony of beating pulses, she grabbed the shrieking woman by her throat and bit her neck, her teeth gnawing on her prey's cervical vertebrae.

Blood spurted from the severed carotid arteries into Sabeen's throat and down her open gullet, igniting a savage urge to feed. Following the blood stream, she buried her face and jaws into the blonde's fleshy bosom, shaking her head like a dog as she ravaged the fatty morsels.

Kurt Roberts heard his missing passenger's scream and knew it was a shark attack even before he saw the spreading pool of crimson thirty yards off the port bow. Yelling "hold on," he gunned the idling engines, nearly tossing a Canadian couple over the side.

The thirty-foot Pro Kat covered the distance in seconds, forcing Captain Roberts to throttle back in a tight circle. Looking down, he saw the dark presence of a shark-like creature writhing beneath billowing scarlet clouds of blood.

Roberts pulled his head back, feeling queasy. In twenty-two years of working the sanctuary, he had never heard of a shark-related fatality. As he reached for the radio, his passengers pointed excitedly at an object floating behind the outboard.

The captain grabbed a reach pole from a storage bin and staggered to the stern. Floating along the surface was an underwater camera—still attached to the severed, blood-streaked left arm of its owner.

Atlantic Ocean, twenty-three miles due east of Port Everglades, Florida

The 38,000 ton cruise ship *Prinsendam* churned west, its bow navigating along a beacon of sunlight reflecting on the surface. The Holland America Line excursion had set sail from Fort Lauderdale seven weeks ago with seven hundred and forty passengers on board. After spending eight days at sea, the ship had arrived in Madeira, a Portuguese island off the west coast of Africa. Two days in paradise were followed by twenty more port cities in the Mediterranean, including Haifa, Athens, and Venice.

Twenty-nine-year-old Christopher Stump stood in the crow's nest of the sports deck with one leg over the rail, clowning around for his pregnant wife, Kelly, who was videotaping him on her cell phone.

"Go on, honey, jump. Show your unborn child what a dumbass her father was."

"You mean *him*. And my son will respect me for the genius I am. What time are we supposed to dock?"

"Between five and six o'clock, and don't ask me again, *genius*. What are you looking at?"

Christopher signaled her over. The couple peered one level down to the lido deck where three Middle Eastern men were kneeling on small embroidered prayer rugs, prostrating themselves before Allah. "There they are again. Five times a day, like clockwork."

The three Iranians had boarded the cruise ship in Istanbul on day thirty-three of the voyage. The gray-beard and his two younger companions had kept to themselves—except for their daily ritual prayer sessions, which made many of the American passengers—especially the New Yorkers, more than a bit uneasy. By voyage end, the men's faces had been posted over a thousand times just on Facebook alone.

One level up on the observation deck, a spry man in his fifties sporting "runner's calves" watched the pregnant woman snap the Iranians' photo with her iPhone.

Allen Foster smiled to himself. In a world overrun by surveillance, the court of public opinion was easier to sway than ever—perfect for maneuvering unsuspecting players into a false flag operation.

Coined from the naval tactic of flying another country's flag to fool an enemy ship, a false flag operation was a covert action where the perpetrator lays the blame on another political party, nation, or terrorist organization, often to influence the public to go to war. In 1931, the Japanese government blew up sections of their own railway as a pretext for annexing Manchuria. In 1933, the Reichstag fire brought Hitler's Nazi party to power. Twenty years later, the United States and Britain unleashed Operation Ajax, a false flag event that targeted Mohammad Mosaddegh, the democratically elected leader of Iran. In 1962, President Kennedy shut down Operation Northwoods, a Defense Department plot that would have blamed Cuba for the hijacking and crash of a US commercial airliner.

Forty years later, commercial airliners were used in an event that led the United States into an unjustified invasion of Iraq.

In the twenty-first-century chess game known as global economics, covert intelligence officers like Allen Foster were used to manipulating the board. Terrorist organizations played the role of the knight—a chess piece convinced its actions were noble, when in reality, it was simply a lower-valued player upon which a false flag could be draped.

Was 9/11 a false flag operation? Despite a myriad of security failures and excuses, despite multiple warnings from foreign intelligence agencies, no one lost their job after 9/11 or was even reprimanded. An FAA administrator who "accidently" destroyed the recordings of the day's tragic events was actually promoted.

Any individual or organization bold enough to challenge the "official facts" was labeled unpatriotic.

Allen Foster aimed his camera two decks below, zooming in on his three al Qaeda stooges. Despite its success in leading the United States to invade Iraq, September eleventh had been a bull-in-the-china-shop event that left a huge mess to clean up. This time around, the neoconspirators' plan was far simpler. Upon disembarking from the boat, the three al Qaeda operatives would proceed to a limousine with their luggage. Instead of escaping from ground zero, they would be terminated and left for incineration. In the aftermath of the nuclear explosion, their fake passports would lead investigators on a trail that ended with an Iranian Qods Force demolition expert and several Iranian nuclear physicists—all of whom would also turn up dead.

Weeks later, Iran's leaders would either surrender or Tehran would be nuked back into the Stone Age. Either way, the nuclear threat would be eliminated, Iranian oil would flow through the Persian Gulf under US jurisdiction, and the military-industrial complex would continue to prosper.

As for the deaths of millions of innocent civilians?

Amalek had said it best: "One cannot expect to win an economic chess match without sacrificing a few pieces. On an overpopulated planet bleeding resources, there were plenty of pawns to spare."

Bal Harbour, Florida

While the cruise ship *Prinsendam* continued its westward direction on its rendezvous with destiny, I moved north, paralleling the shoreline through the shallows, shadowed by the *Malchut*. As I passed the island of Miami Beach, a current swept me into Baker's Haulover Inlet, a manmade channel that connects Biscayne Bay with the Atlantic Ocean.

Baker's Haulover Bridge is a fixed bridge with only thirty-two feet of clearance—a fact that kept the 165-foot *Malchut* from following me into Biscayne Bay. The fishing vessel remained half a mile offshore, its radio operator no doubt tracking me with GPS.

I hovered by one of the moss-covered steel and concrete supports, avoiding a swirl of bleeding bait fish attached to a hundred fishing hooks while I contemplated my next move.

My father's relentless pursuit allowed me no place to separate myself from the nuke and alert the authorities.

Perhaps by hanging out at certain locations—like the bridge—I could force the Admiral to deploy a scuba team to check if I left the SADM behind, buying me some time.

Traveling underwater was too slow. To distance myself from my pursuers I needed a car. That meant exposing myself on land . . . literally—I was naked as a jaybird.

I remained underwater by the bridge support for three more minutes before entering Biscayne Bay. Moving through the turquoise shallows, I popped my head free, inhaled a gust of air into my lungs, and reverted to my human flesh before anyone knew better.

As luck would have it, I had surfaced at the right place.

Haulover Beach Park covers the bay side to a half-mile stretch of oceanfront located between Bal Harbour and Sunny Isles Beach, representing Miami's only legal "clothing optional" nude beach. Exiting the water, I positioned the suitcase over my chest and naked groin and hustled through the park, jogging past shaded picnic facilities before crossing Route 1A to the beach . . . my bare behind exposed to traffic.

Stowing the suitcase beneath a shrub behind the public shower, I kept my head down and ventured onto the nude beach, searching for a pile of clothing I could "borrow."

Before me were a thousand bathers, seventy percent of whom were naked. They came in all colors, shapes, and sizes and no one was gawking . . . okay, maybe a few people were staring at my muscles—more guys than girls.

I scanned the horizon for the *Malchut*. Sure enough, the boat was heading for the channel, a team of divers donning scuba gear out on deck.

"Excuse me, but aren't you Kwan Wilson?"

I turned to find a brown-haired woman in her midfifties. She was wearing a one-piece bathing suit, her waist wrapped in an oversized beach towel.

"I'm Terri Browning, I teach high school English back in Oxford, Kansas, and my students just adore you."

"Can I borrow your towel?"

"My towel? Sure. Are you shy?"

"Are you?" I asked, wrapping the towel around my waist.

"Well, no, but like I told you, I'm an English teacher. English teachers from Oxford, Kansas, can't be seen strutting around a public beach buck-naked. My husband and I are on vacation and Jim . . . well, he insisted we drive down from Fort Lauderdale. 'Stop acting so old,' he said. Well, I'm not old, but I am a new grandmother and it just wouldn't be right to—"

"Wait, did you say you have a car?"

"Of course."

"I need a ride. It's an emergency. Please, Mrs. Browning."

"My goodness, don't you sound just like one of my seniors." She turned to her left and yelled across the beach, "Jim, get your damn clothes on, we're leaving!"

Ten minutes later I was seated in the back of a rental car, the leather bag by my feet as we cruised over Baker's Haulover Bridge, my father's fishing trawler less than a hundred yards away.

Borrowing Terri Browning's cell phone, I dialed 4-1-1, asking for the phone number to the local FBI headquarters. Jim Browning eyed me suspiciously in the rearview mirror as I asked to be connected to the highest-ranking official.

"Special Agent Zachary Restivo, to whom am I speaking?"

"This is Kwan Wilson, the guy who was paralyzed. I was kidnapped but I escaped. It's vital that I come in; my life is in danger."

"Kwan Wilson, huh? Last I heard, you were in rehab for cocaine."

"What? No—I've never done coke in my life."

Jim Browning shot me another look.

"Agent Restivo, I can prove to you that I'm telling the truth. Where are you located?"

"North Miami Beach. We're on NW 2nd Avenue, just past 163rd Street."

"Okay, great—see you in a few." I googled the address, calling out directions to Jim from the backseat, a big smile stretched across my face.

Got you, Admiral.

39

FBI Headquarters, North Miami Beach, Florida

Thirty minutes later we arrived at the concrete and glass structure that housed the Miami-Dade County headquarters of the
FBI. I said good-bye to the Brownings in the parking lot, posing,
of course, for the obligatory photos, then approached the entrance
wrapped in a beach towel.

Seconds later, I found myself encircled by the barrels of at least
a dozen handguns.

The two guards posted outside the building were aiming them,
the touristy-looking dude smoking by the entrance produced one,
the two yakkity women exiting the building . . . the gardener trim-
ming the hedges—it was like a bad cop show. They were joined by
other agents in suits and earpieces, one of whom confiscated the
leather tote bag, another who led me into the lobby, removed my
towel, and visually searched my naked body. Then it was down two
flights in an elevator to a windowless interrogation room where an
agent in a bad suit greeted me.

"Kwan Wilson . . . nice towel."

"Someone took my clothes."

"Your kidnappers?"

"I can explain all that, but first you need to get some bomb squad dudes in here to deactivate the nuke I stole from my father and his wacko cronies."

I cringed inwardly as I heard the words coming out of my mouth—*but hey, the SADM was real, who cared if I sounded like I was on drugs.*

Special Agent Restivo looked at me with a smirk. "Are you high, son?"

"No, man. Just check what's in the leather bag, but be careful; it's set to go off at seven."

"My agents are checking the bag, but this could take a while. Is there anything I can get you while you're waiting?"

"Some clothes would be nice."

"I'm not sure if we have anything in your size, but we'll find you something. Are you hungry?"

"Are you kidding? I could eat a whole dolphin . . . uh, pizza. You know, the kind of pizza they serve at Miami Dolphin football games, or whatever you can find . . . they didn't feed me very well."

"The kidnappers?"

"Yeah, dude. Just check what's in the bag—you'll see I'm telling the truth."

Agent Restivo shook his head and walked out, leaving me seated alone at a small conference table, staring at my reflection in a large framed wall mirror. From watching all the cop shows on television I knew it was one-way glass—my captors observing me from the other side.

Maybe coming here was a mistake . . .

The door opened and a woman entered, holding an armful of clothing. "Official FBI T-shirt and sweat pants; double extra large is the biggest we had, Mr. Muscles. We're still working on the shoes."

I waited until she left before I removed my towel to dress, finding a small area of wall along the outer edge of the one-way glass for a bit of privacy.

What's taking so long? Once they saw it was a nuke, they should have been in here, questioning me about my father. I turned, eyeballing the observation glass. *Maybe I can eavesdrop on them . . .*

Focusing inward, I closed my eyes and found the island of tranquility in my mind's eye—causing dermal denticles to appear across my entire right arm. With my back to the one-way glass, I casually pressed my right palm and forearm to the smooth surface, "hearing" through the sensory cells in my shark skin.

"... *yes, sir. He said exactly what you told us he'd say. Yes, sir, I totally understand. I had a cousin who was bi-polar. No, sir, the bag remains sealed as per your orders; in fact, it's sitting right next to me. Ten minutes, yes, sir. I look forward to seeing you.*"

My blood pressure soared, the internal heat converting impatience to rage as I spun around and punched the one-way mirror with my right fist, the emptying framework raining a thousand shards of glass.

Seated in the dark observation room was Special Agent Restivo, his eyes wide in shock. "That's bullet-proof glass. How the hell—"

I grabbed him by the back of his neck and lifted him out of his chair as I reached for the brown leather bag with my free hand and tore it open. "Open your eyes and see for yourself! It's a nuclear bomb!"

Agent Restivo hesitated, then looked at the spherical device. "Sweet Jesus."

"Yeah, sweet Jesus. And there's going to be a lot of innocent people meeting sweet Jesus in about three hours if you let my father have this back."

"He's on his way with my section chief. I don't have anyone on staff trained to deactivate this, even if I had the authority to stop them."

"Do you have a chopper? We can drop it far out to sea. Hello?"

He was inspecting the device again, pressing his nose to the sphere and inhaling.

"What are you doing?"

"SADMs require an explosive component to set off the nuclear chain reaction. C-4 has an oily odor when mixed with butyl mercaptan." He inhaled again. "Smells like a skunk, which is good for you but bad for the rest of us. There's a Miami PD chopper on the roof. I'll instruct the pilot to dispose of this in deep water away from the shipping lanes. He'll bring you back after the drop; then we'll have a sit-down with your father and my section chief, who will no doubt drill me a new asshole."

"You're letting me go with him?"

"Technically, you're escaping. Down the corridor and turn right, there's a stairwell that will lead you up to the helipad. Go!"

Grabbing the bag, I left the observation room and ran down the empty corridor to a concrete stairwell—every movement caught on the security cameras positioned along the ceiling.

Reaching the exit to the first floor, I stopped.

The Admiral's still tracking me. If I go with the chopper, they'll follow; if I leave the bomb with the chopper pilot, Restivo's section chief will order him to turn around.

"Screw 'em, I'll do this myself." Pushing open the fire door, I exited the building, stepping out into daylight.

Keeping low, I made it across the parking lot, then ran down the middle of NW 2nd Avenue. The first northbound vehicle coming at me was a 2006 Volkswagen Beetle, driven by a tall, skinny man with a red beard, who screeched to a stop when I blocked his way.

"FBI!" I yelled, pointing to my clothes. "Out of the car!"

"What's the trouble?"

"A young boy was just kidnapped. I need your car and cell phone . . . mister?"

"Phillips, Dave Phillips. I have two young sons—take the car! Here's my cell phone. Hey, where's your shoes?"

"They fell off while I was chasing the suspect. Wait for me at HQ! Tell Agent Restivo I'm in pursuit."

Climbing into the car, I sped off—as a Sikorsky S-434 helicopter landed on the roof of the FBI building.

I took the ramp onto the Palmetto Expressway, dialing a memorized phone number.

"Hello?"

"Professor Patel? It's Kwan Wilson."

"Kwan? Where are you? You sound anxious."

"I need help. My father—he's involved in some kind of terrorist plot. I need to expose it, but I don't know how."

"Where are you?"

"North Miami."

"Can you get to my home?"

"Yeah. No. The car I'm in—there's not enough gas."

"There's a Tri-Rail station on Hollywood Boulevard. Do you have enough gas to make it there?"

"Yes!"

"Get to the Tri-Rail station, there will be a ticket waiting for you in the name of Rudy Patel, no ID required. Get off at the station in Delray Beach; I'll pick you up there."

"Great. And thank you. Thank you, thank you, thank you!"

I hung up; then I called the Tri-Rail for their schedule and directions to the Hollywood Boulevard Station.

Then I made one more call.

"Jesse, it's your old pal, Dave Phillips."

"Dave Phillips?"

"You know . . . from the Doors."

"Dave! Where are you, dude?"

"Disappeared. But I'm about to reappear, only I need your help."

I managed to park the car and sprint up the stairs to the Tri-Rail ticket window in time to catch the 4:30 northbound train.

At precisely 5:19, we stopped at the station in Delray Beach, the tracking device still embedded in my left butt cheek. I disembarked, searching for Professor Patel. He waved to me from his silver Mercedes-Benz sedan parked in the lot.

I waved back, then hurried down the platform steps to the lot, weaving my way around parked cars. "Professor, thank you."

He was standing by the driver's side door, his back against the open window—a gun pressed to his neck.

Jeff Elrod stepped out of the car, his 9mm Glock in his left hand, his right wrist in a cast. Within seconds we were joined by four more of his black ops assassins.

"Well, if it isn't my old pal, Kwan. We'll keep this simple—you do exactly as I say, or I put a bullet in your friend's brain."

A tear rolled down Professor Patel's cheek. "I'm sorry, Kwan. They have Anya."

"Drop the bag and put your hands behind your back, *Sharkman*."

One of Elrod's goons bound my wrists with three nylon wrist cuffs. Another took his superior's place, pressing his handgun to Anya's father's lower spine as Elrod opened the brown leather bag.

"What the hell is this?" He removed the object inside—a leather basketball with a brick duct-taped to one side.

I smiled as he shoved the barrel of his gun against the side of my neck. "Where is it?"

"I can't remember. Did I drop it in the ocean after I escaped from the *Malchut* or did it fall out of the bag while I was tanning on the nude beach?"

"Don't play me for a fool; you had it when you left FBI headquarters!" Elrod stepped back to the car, forced to holster his weapon to use his cell phone. "It's me. He's here, but he lost his luggage. We're on the way."

The black ops assassin nodded to his team. Professor Patel was shoved into the backseat of his Mercedes while I was led at gunpoint to a Ford Explorer where I was made to sit on my knees on the floor of the backseat.

We drove for only three minutes before we parked.

Dragged out of the car, I found myself at Seacrest High School.

We entered through the rear delivery door that accessed the cafeteria. My father was inside the kitchen, standing by the immense aluminum door of a walk-in refrigerator, a scowl on his weathered face.

"We don't have a lot of time, son, so I'll make this brief. The United States remains the most powerful country in the world because of our economy—an economy upheld by the energy sector and the military-industrial complex. It's a reality that dates back to the days of Eisenhower, and it's a reality that's going to continue whether you give us the SADM or not. Now let me share another reality with you."

My father opened the door of the walk-in refrigerator. Seated on the floor inside, their wrists and ankles bound, their mouths duct-taped, were Anya, Mrs. Solomon, and Principal Lockhart.

The Admiral pointed to a small explosive device mounted to the interior wall—a brick of C-4 attached to a cell phone. "You recognize this? It's essentially Dr. Gibbons's bomb without the enriched uranium. You have until seven o'clock—roughly ninety-six minutes—to retrieve the SADM and deliver it to Pier One at Port Everglades. If the SADM does not arrive by seven, then I'll detonate the nuke wherever it may be. Then, at precisely seven-oh-two, I'll place a second call—this one to the cell phone rigged inside this walk-in refrigerator and we'll add three more casualties to today's world-changing events."

"You expect me to just deliver a bomb that will kill hundreds of thousands of people?"

"Now see, you're thinking about this all wrong. What's done is done. You already delivered the bomb. Hundreds of thousands of people are going to die, regardless of whether the SADM detonates in Port Everglades or Miami. I'm simply giving you the option to save your friends."

"You think I trust you? Even if I deliver the bomb, you'll kill them anyway."

"I won't, and here's why. The school's security cameras recorded our group entering the principal's office. If the refrigerator bomb detonates, I'm implicated. If it doesn't, I simply make a call to one of my team, who removes the explosive and frees your friends. They won't talk, because if they do, I'll send out a hit squad to execute their families."

"You won't get away with this."

"How about you let me worry about that; you've got enough on your plate. All things considered, you really do want that SADM to be in Port Everglades when it detonates. See, there are three al Qaeda red herrings arriving by ship in about forty-five minutes who will be implicated in the event. If the SADM detonates anywhere else, then the FBI's security tapes will implicate *you* as the terrorist."

Sweat poured down my face, my muscles shaking in rage. I looked at Anya, who was deathly pale, her blue eyes filled with tears.

"I'll need a car."

"Take Professor Patel's; he won't be needing it. Oh, and if you try to double back after we leave, you should know I have men posted outside of the school. They see you, I make a call."

The Admiral slammed the refrigerator door, locking it from the outside. "Jeffrey, free Kwan's bonds, then give my son the professor's car keys. We'll take Patel with us . . . as added insurance."

Elrod produced a switchblade. He cut the nylon restraints, then spit on the car keys and slapped them into the palm of my hand. "Have a good ride, fish face."

I grabbed his left wrist, taking his knife. "I may need this. But don't worry, Jeff, I'll be bringing it back—to shove up your ass."

I sprinted past Professor Patel and out the backdoor to where the Mercedes was parked. Pressing the control switch, I unlocked the car and gunned the engine.

The dashboard clock read 5:38.

At precisely 5:19, the train I was on had stopped at the station in Delray Beach.

Nineteen minutes earlier, we had arrived at the station in Pompano Beach. Among those who boarded the train was a guy my age, with uncombed long dark brown hair and a thin, prominent nose set on a narrow face. He was lanky and thin, and draped over his shoulder was a vintage Doors backpack.

Jesse Gordon flopped down in the seat next to me. "You have fourteen minutes to convince me."

I handed him the leather carry-on, tugging open the zipper. "See for yourself."

He took a thirty-second look. "Okay, I'm convinced. Now what?"

"Did you bring the basketball?"

"And the brick."

"Empty the Doors bag so I can put the you-know-what inside. Did your dad agree to everything?"

"He said he'd meet us and listen to your plan."

"There's no time. Show him the you-know-what; then tell him it's essential I have something that's fast."

"I'll tell him; you sell him."

We stuffed the SADM into the Doors backpack, the basketball and brick into the brown leather bag. At 5:14 the train stopped at the station in Boca Raton where Jesse disembarked carrying a nuclear bomb, his father waiting for him in his BMW.

Five minutes later, I stepped off the train in Delray Beach.

* * *

It was 6:08 by the time I arrived at Marine One boat rentals in Deerfield Beach. Jesse and his father were on the pier, standing by a thirty-two-foot-long Sunsation Dominator powerboat, its stern equipped with dual 502 horsepower engines—exactly what the doctor ordered.

"Mr. Gordon, thank you."

"This isn't a rental; it belongs to my brother, Rick. Just use it to get that thing into deep water, then bring it back."

"I will, but first you need to help me with one last thing: there's a homing device embedded in my left butt cheek—I need you to cut it out."

"What?"

"It's how they keep tabs on you before they disappear you," Jesse explained. "Kwan, have you got a knife?"

I handed Jesse the switchblade. "Let's do this on board the boat."

We climbed down into the vessel's cockpit. Dropping my sweat pants, I laid on my stomach across one of the bucket seats, pointing to a tiny bump on my left buttocks. "Cut it out, but don't throw it out, we'll need it."

Jesse held the knife over my exposed flesh, his hand trembling. "I . . . I can't do it."

Jeff Gordon took the knife from his son. "This is insane. I'm a senior partner in a law firm, not a member of Homeland Security . . . and I'm definitely not a proctologist!" With that, he punctured my butt cheek with the tip of the knife, prying loose a tracking device no larger than a splinter.

"Jesse, hand me that plastic cup. Kwan, I'm putting the tracking device in the cup. Are you okay?"

I sat up. "Fine. Where's my backpack?"

"In the storage bin."

"This is important. I need you guys to take that tracking device down to Port Everglades in Patel's Benz. You have to leave it as close to Pier One as you can before seven o'clock."

Mr. Gordon looked at his watch. "It's already 6:14; with rush hour we may not make it."

"You have to!"

"I'll drive!" Jesse said, leaping off the boat to the dock.

Mr. Gordon turned to me. "You know what you have to do. Do it and get back home safe."

"Yes, sir." I watched him run after Jesse to Patel's Mercedes; then I freed the bow and stern lines before starting the powerboat's engines.

The twins rumbled to life.

I observed the No Wake Zone signs for about a minute before accelerating out of the marina and into the intracoastal. I followed the signs north that led me out of the maze of waterways to the Boca Inlet, gunning the boat's engines as I hit the Atlantic Ocean.

The dashboard clock read 6:23.

The bow raised high out of the water as I pushed my speed past seventy knots, heading southeast. Gibbons had told me the SADM would incinerate everything on land within a five-mile radius—two and a half miles from ground zero. Ground zero would now be at least a hundred feet underwater, severely limiting its range, but I wanted to be a good ten miles from land just to be safe.

Hitting a smooth patch of sea, I accelerated to eighty knots, the shoreline disappearing rapidly on my right. Checking my GPS, I realized I had already passed the entrance channel into Port Everglades.

It was 6:39.

The Sikorsky helicopter landed on the *Malchut*'s deck with a bone-jarring thud, nearly knocking loose Professor Patel's mercury fillings.

Admiral Wilson helped him from the backseat. "You okay?"

"A bit queasy."

"Let's get an update, maybe you'll feel a little better." My father and Jeff Elrod led the professor up to the bridge, where four crewmen were huddled around a sonar tech.

"Well? Where is he?"

"He stopped in Deerfield for about six minutes, presumably to get the package. He's back in the car, heading south on I-95 doing eighty miles an hour."

Admiral Wilson slapped Professor Patel on the back. "See that? You had nothing to worry about. Kwan will deliver the package and my men will release your daughter. She'll come out of this with nothing worse than a cold."

I was twelve miles from shore when I spotted the fishing trawler to the southeast in deeper water, less than a mile away.

I shut down the engines, my heart racing.

6:46 . . .

Stripping off my clothes, I secured the Doors backpack around my shoulders and jumped into the ocean, expelling the air from my lungs as I sank beneath the SADM's weight. Within seconds I was pumping water through my gills, my caudal feet churning the sea as I homed in on the trawler doing twenty knots.

By 6:50 p.m., the crew of the *Malchut* had joined the members of Black Widow standing along the portside rail of the fishing trawler, counting down the minutes until the anticipated mushroom cloud would be unleashed over Fort Lauderdale.

Moving beneath the keel, I located the outer wheel of the sealed diving bell. Grasping it with both hands, I inverted my body so my feet were pressed against the steel plates of the hull and forcibly wrenched the device open, snapping the interior lock.

Pushing the diving bell inward, I entered the ship, sealing my gills but maintaining my denticle skin.

The lab remained devastated from my last visit. Wrapping my body against the nearest steel bulkhead, I searched through a hundred vibrations, seeking clues to Professor Patel's whereabouts.

Instead, I found my father . . .

"Whiskey, Professor?"

"Douglas, you know I don't toast victory prematurely. Rumsfeld and Cheney made that mistake back in Iraq."

"You don't entrust a civilian to make military decisions. Had General Garner been left in charge, the outcome would have been far different. Bremer's decision to ostracize Saddam's army led to a decade of chaos."

"I am not a military leader—do you trust me?"

"War is not always waged on the battlefield, my friend. You have the instincts of a four-star general. The way you handled your daughter and my son—it was as if you saw the outcome three moves ahead of the game."

"Sun Tzu once said, 'Be extremely subtle, even to the point of formlessness . . . be extremely mysterious, even to the point of soundlessness. Thereby you can be the director of your opponent's fate.' Arranging Anya's internship at ANGEL served a dual purpose; it allowed me to keep tabs on Becker's work without being intrusive while contemplating how we could one day use the incredible mutations generated by her stem cell experiments. The day I met Kwan in the hospital, I saw a potential outcome. And here we are."

"You're the chess master. For me, that kid's been nothing but trouble since the day he was conceived."

"'Regard your soldiers as your children, and they will follow you into the deepest valleys.' Instead of looking at your son as a potential asset, you've ostracized him just as Bremer did with Saddam's Republican Guard."

"You don't get it. Kwan was an accident. I met his mother while I was stationed at the Chinhae naval base in South Korea. Back then, young Korean tail buzzed the base like bees to honey; every native girl out to find herself an American soldier. The difference between Mi Yung and the hundreds of other Asian sluts hanging around the base was that her father was a powerful businessman whose companies supplied the military. Mi Yung was gorgeous and knew how to flaunt her sexuality; she was probably sleeping with a dozen other sailors. When she found out she was pregnant, she named her highest-ranking partner as the baby's father—me! My superiors gave me a choice; either I marry her or receive a dishonorable discharge and face the wrath of the Korean government. See, it turns out Mi Yung was a lot younger than she looked in bed."

"And so you impregnated a minor and inflicted your wrath upon an innocent child."

"Could have been worse. I brought them to the States; I gave them a better life than they would have ever experienced in South

Korea. Anyway, that burden was relieved the morning the kid crashed the car and killed his mother. That day was the best day of my life, to be surpassed only by the moment that's about to take place right now. Are you ready to make a phone call that will change history?"

"As the Buddhists say, Douglas, it's your karma. You make the call."

The Admiral placed the call, beginning a thirty-second power surge that would ignite the SADM's blasting cap, setting off the C-4 charge and a nuclear chain reaction.

The deed done, my father and the man known as Amalek to his neocon cronies left the stateroom to watch the fireworks from up on deck—only to find a surprise waiting for them in the corridor: my Doors backpack.

"Kwan . . . you sonuva—"

I see your hair is burning, hills are filled with fire
If they say I never loved you, you know they are a liar
Driving down your freeways, midnight alleys roam
Cops in cars, the topless bars, never saw a woman so alone
So alone, so alone . . .

—The Doors, "L.A. Woman"

I *am fury.*
Naked in the cockpit of the speedboat, the cold wind pasting brine to my flesh, I watched the bow rise to greet the northern horizon as my fiberglass steed violated the sea doing eighty-five knots.

I am revenge.
Cold-blooded, my back faced a searing hot wind that blasted a hole in the sea, igniting a flame as brilliant as the sun—my enemies' ashes inhaled into the upper atmosphere.

I am destiny's offspring.
Conceived twice; birthed once. A dual existence condemned by my genes.

Orphaned by fate. Predator by design.

Alone.

Epilogue

Another Diver Devoured by "Virgin Mary"

KEY LARGO, FL (Associated Press). Two weeks ago, scuba divers had dubbed her the "Virgin Mary of the Deep," describing her as a black tiger shark with gray stripes, bearing an angelic face, fore-fins resembling human arms, and black animated eyes. Now they're just calling her the Devil.

She was first sighted by divers visiting Christ of the Abyss, a two-ton, eight-foot-high bronze statue of Jesus Christ that was submerged back in 1965 in twenty-five feet of water in Key Largo's protected Marine Sanctuary. The "Virgin" began appearing at dusk, perhaps attracted to the electrical field produced by the statue's metal surface. Word of the mysterious creature's presence created a surge of night dives in the area—and multiple fatalities.

The first victim was Lou Foster, a senior software developer at Studio-332. The shark-like creature targeted the silver-haired diver from a group of seventeen, repeatedly biting his neck until he was literally decapitated before horrified eyewitnesses. Two more attacks occurred over the last week—all bites to the neck.

Shark expert Dr. Sara Jernigan believes the creature's sensory system is ultrasensitive to the beating pulse of its victim's carotid pulse. "Obviously, we're dealing with an undiscovered species that has adapted to the taste of human blood."

Mary's latest victim was Ronnie Edward Rahn of Sheffield, Illinois. Mr. Rahn was scuba diving half a mile from the statue when the shark appeared suddenly from a clump of sea grass and bit the stunned diver in his stomach. Rahn was transported to a local hospital where he remains in intensive care.

Delray Beach, Florida

In the end, naval authorities attributed the twelve kiloton blast to the damaged nuclear reactor of the USS *Philadelphia*—a decommissioned Los Angeles attack sub that was returning from the Persian Gulf on a covert mission. According to my friend Jesse Gordon, "covert" is government speak for "we screwed up, but since we're in charge we don't have to explain ourselves."

Jesse and his father had arrived in Port Everglades at 6:56 p.m.

The Delray police arrived at Seacrest High School twenty minutes later where they freed a shivering Anya Patel, Principal Anthony Lockhart, and Rachel Solomon. The official story was that my father was delivering a sizeable ransom to the school, only my kidnappers panicked when I escaped (yes, I had been kidnapped from the Breakers Resort, not rushed to a drug rehab center as reported). The kidnappers locked up three eyewitnesses, then took the Admiral and Professor Patel to an undisclosed location where they killed them, incinerating their remains.

It was a gruesome tale, but as my friend Jesse Gordon says, "A lie remains the truth until it becomes conspiracy theory." Regardless, I've been warned not to bring light to the situation on *Oprah*.

Anya and her mother moved back to London. Professor Patel, being the kind and loving man that he was, had left his wife and daughter quite a large sum of money.

Admiral Wilson, being the career military man that he was, left his fortune to the Veterans of Foreign Wars. Yours truly received his sword and a box of medals, which my grandmother and I pawned to buy me a used car.

I never told Anya about her father. I would never want any human being to feel the kind of hurt I felt in those final moments aboard the *Malchut*.

Rachel informed me that the Amalek were the enemies of Moses and the Israelites. According to the Bible, King Saul was instructed to wipe out the nation of Amalek—every man, woman, and child—even the cattle. King Saul did his job, only he decided to spare the Amalek king, costing himself his own crown.

As for the Council of Amalek . . . they're still out there, no doubt seething over the trillion dollars I cost them by preventing yet another war in the Middle East.

I'm back in school, only my crown has lost its luster. Without the injections of human growth hormone, my muscles eventually returned to semi-normal size. I'm still cut and I can still play ball, I just can't dunk anymore—call it Asian man's disease. But my shark DNA remains with me, and when I'm in the water . . . or when I'm in that quiet place in my mind's eye, away from all the anger, I can still summon the predator within me—and I feel free.

I'm still not sure what my true purpose is yet, but as Rachel Solomon reminds me, God has a plan for each one of us. Sure, the unknown may be a bit scary, but we have two choices; we can either wallow in our own misery or be the cause of something far greater, creating happiness through the act of giving, sharing, loving, caring, and being generous to others.

For the record, I don't consider myself redeemed. You don't cleanse a tarnished soul by killing others, even if you feel they deserved it.

I guess in many ways, I'm still evolving.

— *Kwan Wilson*